D0933272

THE

QUIET QUARTER

For My Godson
and
great Buddy
with all my love
Christmas 2009

Joe

THE
QUIET QUARTER

Ten Years of Great Irish Writing

Edited by

MÁIRE NIC GEARAILT

NEW
ISLAND

THE QUIET QUARTER
First published 2009
by New Island
2 Brookside
Dundrum Road
Dublin 14

www.newisland.ie

Copyright © the authors, 2009

The authors have asserted their moral rights.

ISBN 978-1-84840-052-8

All rights reserved. The material in this publication is protected by copyright
law. Except as may be permitted by law, no part of the material may be
reproduced (including by storage in a retrieval system) or transmitted in any
form or by any means; adapted; rented or lent without the written
permission of the copyright owner.

British Library Cataloguing Data. A CIP catalogue record for this book is
available from the British Library.

New Island receives financial assistance from The Arts Council
(An Comhairle Ealaíon), Dublin, Ireland.

Book design by Inka Hagen

Printed in the UK by CPI Mackays, Chatham ME5 8TD

10 9 8 7 6 5 4 3 2 1

CONTENTS

PEOPLE

Fur, Feathers and Leaves

Travel and Place

LANGUAGE

HOME AND TIME

CHRISTMAS

ACKNOWLEDGMENTS

'Boat Dreaming' by Fred Johnston, from *Being Anywhere: New and Selected Poems* (Lagan Press, 2001) reproduced by kind permission of Lagan Press.

'Prayer' by Mark Roper was first published in *The Stinging Fly* (Summer 2002).

'Midwife' by Paddy Bushe, from *Digging Towards the Light* (Dedalus Press, 1994) reproduced by kind permission of Dedalus Press.

'Them's Your Mammy's Pills' by Leland Bardwell, from *Doestoevsky's Grave* (Dedalus Press, 1992). Reproduced by kind permission of Dedalus Press.

'Human Wishes' by Gerald Dawe, from *The Morning Train* (The Gallery Press, 1999). Reproduced by kind permission of Gallery Press.

Extract from 'Big Bang' by William Stafford, from *The Way it is: New & Selected Poems,* © 1998 by the Estate of William Stafford. Reprinted with the permission of Graywolf Press, Minneapolis, Minnesota, www.graywolfpress.org.

'Exposure' by Seamus Heaney from the collection *North* (Faber and Faber, 1975).

'Lunar Landing' by Vincent Woods from *Lives and Miracles* (Arlen House, 2006), reproduced by kind permission of Arlen House.

The publishers have made every effort to contact all copyright holders. If notified, the publishers will be pleased to rectify any errors or omissions at the earliest opportunity.

INTRODUCTION

The Quiet Quarter existed as a title long before the writing feature it now represents was thought of. In 1999 it was the name of a new series I was planning for RTÉ Radio 1, where I was a producer, but then RTÉ lyric fm was born and, as I was particularly fond of the title, I took it with me to Lyric and to Limerick. Eoin Brady was the first producer of *Lyric Notes*, the mid-morning programme I presented, and it was Eoin who developed the feature as we know it today – a welcome window for new writing. Eoin edited the first anthology of *The Quiet Quarter* in 2004, also published by New Island.

Lyric Notes and *The Quiet Quarter* ran for over ten years from May 1999 to September 2009. We saw the feature as a few minutes of quiet reflection in the morning, followed by music to suit the mood. Our guidelines to writers asked for a personal response to an experience, a person, an event. The response, the reaction, was what we called for rather than a report on the event itself. That personal element was fundamental to *The Quiet Quarter*. We wanted to present the listener with an excuse to step away from the daily grind, to stop and listen, to be moved, entertained, surprised and challenged at times, but always to be left with food for thought, a stimulus for the mind and soul.

The list of writers whose work has been broadcast over the last ten years runs into hundreds. Personal stories of love and loss, of people and places, of animals and nature, of Christmas memories: a story a day told on radio by its author. And how many different accents and voices we have heard, each adding to the personal quality of *The Quiet Quarter* and the authenticity of the experience recounted. All of these stories were written to be told, but they more than hold their own on the page. One writer didn't supply a script – that was John Moriarty. The microphone was turned on and John told his story. I've transcribed it for the collection. You can hear it in the original, in John's own voice, on the website www.rte.ie/lyricfm/quietquarter. Many more of the pieces in this collection are available as podcasts on that website too.

As presenter and producer of *Lyric Notes* I have found the commissioning of new writing an exciting and stimulating task. It's one I don't think I would ever have tired of. Opening an envelope or an email attachment and discovering a new, exciting voice was such a thrill and there are many such writers in this book, people for whom *The Quiet Quarter* was their first accepted work, and then there are many others who are well-known, well-established writers. I have laughed and cried with these writers over the years. I have developed friendships through telephone and email with people I have never met. I have shared an intimacy through our mutual passion for the spoken word and for that I give thanks.

Compiling this anthology has been a labour of love. My only regret is that it couldn't be twice the size, or even three times; that was the difficulty: trying to decide what to leave out. It wasn't an easy task.

My thanks to all the wonderful writers who contributed to *The Quiet Quarter* over the years.

Thanks also to everyone in Lyric who worked on *The Quiet Quarter*, producers Eoin Brady and Ethna Tinney, and the production co-ordinators who were responsible for much of the recording and editing: Kevin Brew, Jean Ní Bhaoill, Martina McGlynn, Michael O'Kane, Eoghan O Sullivan, Eoin O Kelly, Alan Ryan, Nicole Dunphy, Heather Gardner, Sarah Ní Riain and Síle Ní Dhubhghaill.

I do hope you enjoy this collection, and to all of you who tuned in regularly to *Lyric Notes* and *The Quiet Quarter*, *mo mhíle buíochas*, thank you for listening .

Máire Nic Gearailt

MUSIC AND DANCE

MUSIC AND SILENCE

FLYING WITH JOSÉ

Mick Hanly

In 1969, I went to London for the first time. I was twenty years old and had never been out of Ireland, or indeed on a plane, so I was excited about the trip. The true cause of my excitement, however, was the fact that I was going to see my first real concerts, one in the Albert Hall and the other in the London Palladium. At the time, Tom Paxton was popular enough to fill the Albert Hall and José Feliciano was playing several concerts in the Palladium. I knew all of Tom Paxton's songs from a double album called *Live At The Troubadour*, but I knew very little about José Feliciano, other than that he played guitar with a fire that I hadn't heard before and sang like a man possessed. Apart from the impressive contours of the Albert Hall, I remember little of the Paxton gig, but José's performance flicked a musical switch that nobody had flicked before. I had never been that close to such beauty, dexterity and passion, and ever since that moment, I've had a musical barometer that has served me well.

A young woman led José to the centre of the stage, and once he had settled himself on his stool, amid a sea of microphones, he took control of the Palladium like a confident pilot, taxiing a plane.

He wasn't long into his opening set when he growled, 'They wouldn't let me bring my dog,' and launched into a pull-no-punches song, called 'No Dogs Allowed'.

With that gripe off his chest, he spent the next hour running to the edge of the musical cliff and jumping with the compulsion of a fledgling chick. His voice soared and dived and when the rawness of his feelings overwhelmed him, he reached for his native Portuguese. English could no longer say it, and for those of us prepared to soar with him, it was an unbelievable journey. The gut strings rattled and hummed with authority and beauty. Then he did something, which for an aspiring guitarist like myself, dazzled the eye; while playing an instrumental version of a Beatles tune called 'And I Love Her', he detuned his bass string in mid-solo to reach a rich low D, which the tune required, and then retuned it to its natural E, without missing a beat.

I watched entranced, losing all sense of time and place, and the knowledge that José was in any way incapacitated. When he finished the last song of the first half, he laid his guitar aside and acknowledged the huge ovation. As the applause died, he sat back on his stool, awaiting the young lady's guiding hand. It was only then that I was reminded that our daredevil pilot was grounded. We had been flown to the sun and back a thousand times by the master, and now the master was being led to the wings.

A WINTER'S NIGHT, A GERSHWIN SONG

Michael Coady

He'd set out to locate and photograph a holy well but went astray on unmarked roads deep in lush greenery. Go on to meet a sign, he thought, until he found himself entering a small town where something vaguely tugged from his deep memory. He parked the car in the square and then in sudden rush recalled one winter's night a world ago.

Here's where he'd played at his first dance. The first of all his nights and times as a musician, the recollection fused with a particular song, remembered even to its key of E flat. He was going on seventeen, a learner on trombone, making a nervous debut with his uncle Peter's band. *Orchestra* rather: the musicians wore tuxedos and could read music scores. Two saxophones, trumpet, piano, bass and drums. And, on that night, tentative trombone as well. His initiation among elders, all of them now gone.

Standing in sunshine in that small town again, he remembered an archway and a tunnel-like entrance to a spacious dance hall and stage, with a supper room off to the side. Coloured lights and Christmas decorations. It was St Stephen's night. Tea, cooked ham, tomatoes, cream buns and cake and sherry trifle. Music and warm bodies weaving, touching, holding. Perfumed women, sleek-headed men. All subsumed within a winter past.

Here and now, an old-timer sitting in the sunshine on a window sill. Cross over to greet him and enquire.

'You must mean the Arch,' the man said. 'That was in my hair-oil days for sure. The Arch Ballroom. And cinema that was. Across the square behind you.'

A man is summoned from the bookie's. Hugger-mugger about keys. And then he's led to a bricked-in archway between shops. A door set into it is unlocked. Under that arch he steps again, as once before in time, into a long roofed-over passageway like a cave. And there, through swing doors at the end, the hall itself, now a community centre but essentially unchanged.

Lights flicker on in its windowless and haunted space of memory. Spacious; silent; eloquent. Sound of his own breathing. How mysteriously can chance resolve between intent and outcome. Setting out to find a well, unmarked summer roads return him to this space one winter's night long past.

Look towards the darkened stage.

There they are, who are no more. His mother, Dora, still with her good looks, sitting side-stage at the piano. The saxes up front, his uncle, Peter, standing at the single microphone to sing 'The Way You Look Tonight'. The brass behind, with bass and drums. That shy teenager seated at a music stand, in a badly fitting dress suit, jacket borrowed by his mother from one source, trousers from another. New white shirt and black bow-tie for his debut, from Bourke's Drapery, Main Street, Est. 1806.

'Put it down in the book until I settle after Christmas,' she said to Hughie Ryan. 'We have a dance to play for on St Stephen's night.'

The trumpet player beside him there. Joe Carroll, who would be friend and mentor to his coming out. Heart of kindness and innocent excitability. Sometimes, his embouchure might act up, or his hernia erupt if he overstretched on a high note. Tales of circus bands, brass bands, dance bands, pit orchestras.

Deep into that distant night, Joe will lead through the first chorus of 'Love Walked In', then take the trumpet from his lips, lean quickly towards him and above the music shout, 'Take it!' No time for nerves or backing off. With the next downbeat, he's thrust into the lead on slide trombone; breath and lips and pulse of Gershwin song:

> Love walked right in and drove the shadows away;
> Love walked right in and brought my sunniest day,
> One magic moment and my heart seemed to know
> That love said Hello!
> Though not a word was spoken…

One winter's night of going on seventeen. Upstream were all things still to come that would in time be gone. While Joe sat back, the trumpet in his lap, and smiled to hear and see a youngster coming on.

MY BROTHER

John MacKenna

There's a pencil of light from the gap where the hospital door is slightly ajar, just enough for me to write these lines for you, my brother. You're sleeping, your lungs are opened and closed and opened and closed by machinery. The shadow of my hand is falling across this page – just as the shadow of something darker, something a lot less certain is falling over your damaged body.

I want to comfort you. I want to be the reassuring one, as you have been so often to me. I want to come out from the shadow of the older brother and take charge of this situation. I want to tell you everything will be all right, but I know it won't. And if you could talk, you'd tell me that, too. You're the doctor, you're the one who'd know exactly what's happening and why.

You were the one who always found a way round things but you'd be the first to tell me there's no way round this.

In the car tonight, on the five-minute drive from your house to the hospital, I heard Elton John singing from the radio in the warm summer darkness:

Daniel, my brother, you are older than me,
Do you still feel the pain of the scars that won't heal?

Dearest brother, only brother, I love you.

I love you for all the days we shared and all the times we were apart. Your kindness was a soft voice down the telephone line, telling me things would work out fine, that there's no point in worrying. I wish I could say the same for you and know there was some truth in it. Instead, the night draws on and the moon retreats a degree or two and we share this room, as we once shared a room at home – you talking in one bed, me laughing in the other.

Now we're both silent but for the drive and draw of the machine pumping air into your wounded lungs and the soft sound of my pen crossing the pages of what's left of our life together.

I close my eyes and hear the echo of your words and the memory of my laughter and the song coming in on the late-night radio, its notes drifting across the empty car park, its tenderness hanging in the slow Carolina night:

Your eyes have died but you see more than I,
Daniel you're a star in the face of the sky.

THE HEALING SILENCE

Sharon Hogan

The room is ready. The curtains are drawn, a corner-lamp casts a soft glow over the low bedding. The cloths that will cover Gabriel when he lies down are folded on the lacquered table: a fuchsia swathe of Tibetan raw silk; a light, silk sari-cloth a friend brought from India; and also a warm, alpaca blanket imported from Uruguay – in case he's cold after today's chemotherapy. From the bookshelf, wisps of sweet Japanese incense waft around a single, stout candle. Light-flecks flutter across the carpet. At a volume so low you have to stand still to hear it, the delicate music of Arvo Pärt's 'Spiegel im Spiegel' seeps into the room. I wait.

The doorbell rings, I go downstairs to let him in. He's tired today – looks like he's been beaten up – apologises for not being able to climb the stairs more quickly. It frustrates him to have to stop at each landing to catch his breath. I say little as we make the now Himalayan journey to my treatment room, just smile and re-assure him that his tiredness is only natural after his session at the hospital.

I feel him begin to relax the moment we enter the room. I know that candles and incense and exotic cloths are really only set dressing, that the music filtering through the room is nothing more than ambience. But Gabriel has told me he finds the colours and textures and fragrances reassuring, and – though I normally work in silence – he has asked me to play the music of Arvo Pärt because, despite having been an avowed atheist for most of his life, now that death feels close for him, he says he senses something 'other' about Pärt's music. And so it plays quietly during Gabriel's treatments.

He takes off his shoes and jacket and slowly lowers his battered body onto the bedding. It hurts a little to watch him do this – he used to stand six-foot tall in his stockinged feet; now he's shrunken and stooped and every movement is full of effort. Despite this, he has told me he looks forward to these treatments; these sessions are, he says, the only time he is without pain. In what has become the opening ritual for his treatments, I name each of the fabrics as I cover him: the Indian silk, then the Tibetan, finally the alpaca from the mountains of Uruguay, as they slide over his weary body.

He closes his eyes. I place one hand on the crown of his head and the other on his chest. While there are other positions on the body that can be contacted during a treatment, I sense that what he needs today is a lack of busy-ness, a real stillness; so we more or less stay in this configuration for the best part of the hour. The only sounds in the room, and the only sense of movement, arise from Gabriel's breathing, my breathing and Pärt's delicate notes floating from the CD player.

This is a most extraordinary way to be with someone. In Silence. Gabriel does not sleep; I do not daydream. We are completely present with each other, present and quiet. Even the music feels more present in its silence than in its audible notes. We are intimate beyond friendship and loving beyond knowing a single thing about each other. Gabriel, Arvo Pärt and me – we are held in the healing Silence.

FOR THE RECORD

John O'Keefe

It is a truism that there is no greater hurt in life than to be unloved. This being so, in the world of musical instruments, the recorder must surely play the role of the most wounded of sisters. For those of you who thought that children's loathing of the recorder was simply youthful moaning, you might now wish to reconsider. What we all secretly knew, but were too scared to admit, has now been revealed. Children hate learning the recorder more than visits to Auntie May on a Sunday or family holidays in the mobile home in Courtown.

Research published in Britain has revealed that, in fact, recorders put children off music for life. Apparently, the repetition of 'Old MacDonald Had a Farm', on the bourgeois version of a tin whistle, does little to endear the little ones to this musical equivalent of hara-kiri. Not a wonderful legacy for an instrument of torture meant to encourage our love of music from an early age.

If we were all honest with ourselves, we would have to admit that that the unusual brown thing which was shoved into our faces as single-digit children looked and sounded awful. The sound was almost secondary to the look. What self-respecting thirteen-year-old boy would hang around the school gates hoping to see Mary from Loreto with a packet of Kola cubes in one hand and a recorder in the other? Not many I knew. And why were they always brown? When fashion experts announce that brown is this year's black, they should always include a caveat for recorders.

And there's another thing – I never seem to remember any of us having cases for our less-than-lovely batons. You could, therefore, never hide it – there it was like a plastic Toblerone sticking out of your school bag saying to the world, 'Look at him – he hasn't a note in his head and so plays me twice a week with 200 other ingrates!' The sound made by recorders is also worthy of mention. No matter how much you practised, no matter how much you listened to Ms Reilly, you always sounded like a wood pigeon with dysentery. Musically, this could discourage some children for life.

One of the remarks that leaps out from the Economic & Social Research Council's paper is: 'Children do not associate playing the recorder with their musical role models in the adult world.' *Quelle surprise*, I hear you roar, but this statement does go the heart of the problem.

There *is* no book entitled *Great Recordists of our Time*. Neither James Galway nor Robbie Williams have ever citied the recorder as one of their formative musical influences. Even my own music teacher, whom I met recently after many years, advised me that she dreaded our Friday recorder sessions more than childbirth. High praise indeed for an instrument whose only real value lay in attacking siblings from behind after two hours of beating out incomprehensible interpretations of 'Frère Jacques' and 'The Wheels on the Bus' – a sort of friendly fire of the musical world.

The truth about the recorder was, and is, that schools continue to encourage its use because it is hard wearing – as I found out when practising with it on my brother's head – and inexpensive. Here's a thought – although I have heard some fine music played on a paper and comb and even a dustbin lid over the years, it does not necessarily follow that durable and cheap means musically useful or melodious.

I know that there will be some of you who feel that the recorder should be made compulsory for the Leaving Certificate and have oral and aural components – that it should be awarded extra points and given the Freedom of Fingal. I beg to differ.

A full state funeral should be offered perhaps, where recorders from around the world might pay their last respects. This would then be followed by a simple but moving ceremony in the Phoenix Park when all recorders on the island would be cremated. Then, and only then, can we finally park this terrible part of our history and move on to a brighter, braver new world, where all musical instruments will be loved and cherished. All that is, except one.

WHEN THE WORLD HOLDS ITS BREATH

Paddy Bushe

There is a kind of silence when the world holds its breath that is terrifying and that seems to pound around your skull forever, even though it lasts only seconds, or less. The silence on the phone after, 'I was speaking to the doctor.' The silence after the screech of brakes behind you. The silence after a boat disappears behind a wave. During the eternity of this silence, you wonder if it will be broken by the world resuming its normal babbling or by it breaking into a wail. Whether you are experiencing an end or a new beginning. If it is a new beginning, the sound of the world's everyday humming rediscovering itself is as peaceful and regenerative as the deepest quietude and an exhilarating relief from the thunderous silence of the world holding its breath.

I remember one such silence vividly, after almost a quarter of a century. A group of us were walking along a fisherman's path by the bank of the Caragh River at Lickeen, near Glencar, County Kerry. It was a bright, boisterous spring day after a few days' storm and rain. I was carrying my infant son in my arms, and my daughter, then two-and-a-half, was walking ahead. It was when she stumbled and fell down the bank that I realised how flooded the river was, how strong the current, how foaming and rocky the channels the water was surging through. I was told afterwards that I laid my son carefully on the ground before jumping down. I have no memory of it; only of the tremendous gasp as the world held its breath over the following seconds. It was those seconds of teetering between life and death that led to this poem, whose title, I hope, will explain itself.

Midwife
for Ciairín

Daughter, that time you fell
From the high bank, in slow
Motion it seemed,
Your two-year-old body turning
Into the black and white
Suddenly loud Caragh River,
And your wide eyes pleaded for breath
Instead of that liquid burning:
That, indeed, was like a little death.

Daughter after my stretched hand
Had slipped – hair floating away –
And slipped again, then grasped, pulled
You, gasping, from the heaving water,
You cried, you were not hurt,
And you were swaddled up
In someone's coat, while the whole earth
Breathed again: o daughter,
That, indeed, was like another birth.

WHERE WE COME FROM

John Moriarty

I live alone and, sometimes, I'll hear myself singing one of the great songs like 'Caiseal Mumhan' or 'Slán le Máigh' or 'The Coolin' or 'Róisín Dubh' and you'd hear the great airs coming back to you off the walls of your own house. There are times when a great song is almost... like, you can almost pour yourself into the song and it holds your shape in the way a bowl would hold water. It keeps your shape for that day and, singing those songs, I some-times wonder where in God's name did they come from? I have a sense about them that they were never composed at all, that they came to people somehow and all they had to do was sing them. And I imagine some of them coming into the world like this.

There was a man visiting neighbours one night in an island off the west coast and he has only three fields to walk home in the night but he doesn't arrive home that night and he doesn't arrive home the next night and the night after that and it's all of nine nights later when he arrives home. His wife is cross with him and, the moment he comes in, she throws the tongs against the wall and she is mad with him because she thinks he has gone to some pattern, race or fair across the county bounds, you know, and he says, 'Mam, don't be blaming me this time because that isn't true.'

And he goes to the wall and he takes down his fiddle and he plays a tune and it is a wonderful, new tune that she has never heard before, that has never been heard before in that part of the world and she asks him to play it again and he plays it again for her and she is pacified now by the new marvellous air she has heard and she asks him to play it a third time and he says, 'Mam, how can I play an air that I heard in the other world in this world because that's where I was, Mam – that's where I was. I wasn't at pattern, race or fair beyond the county bounds. Where that music is played, that's where I was. We call it the other world.'

And there was one day in Connemara when there was a girl that I loved, she was walking in the door and Ted Millen saw her, a neighbour Ted, and Ted asked me, 'Where does she come from?'

I said, 'Ted, well now, if you ask her she'll tell you that she comes from Limerick, but God knows, Ted, when you get to know her that isn't the whole story at all.'

Of course, she comes from Limerick, but there's nature in her, and you know that day I put an imaginary fiddle in my hand and I played 'Caiseal Mumhan' for Ted and I said, 'Ted, would you listen to that air now?', playing it there in an imaginative way there on the side of the road. 'Ted, where that tune comes from, that's where she comes from, where "The Coolin" comes from, that's where she comes from, where "Róisín Dubh" comes from, that's where she comes from, where the great airs come from, that's where she comes from. That's where we all come from, Ted.'

So, some day, when you are bogged down in your life, just imagine that where the great airs of Ireland come from you too come from there. There's a part of you that comes from there. And not only do you come from there, there's a part of you that is that air. Don't listen to the people say that you are just transformed groceries, play or imagine one of those great tunes for yourself and say, 'Within me, deep within me, that's who I am. I come from the place where "The Coolin" comes from.'

SOUND MAN

Frank Corcoran

I'm a sound man. I have to be. I spend a lot of my waking time shaping musical time into a thing I call music, *ceol*, *Musik*, composing sound into vocal or orchestral or instrumental or, in recent years, what we grandly call electro-acoustic compositions. It's now a quarter of a century since I came to live and teach and write my music in Hamburg on the huge River Elbe. This Elbe flows up northwest to us from Dresden and, ultimately, the Czech Republic. It sings of Smetana's 'Moldau' and Antonín Dvořák's 'New World' down there; the Moldau meets it at Mělnik. Heinrich Schütz was active as Court Music Director in Dresden.

Mr Johann Sebastian Bach, if not on his bicycle, certainly with horse and trap (or carriage) would have often travelled the Elbe Road. It has already cut through Magdeburg, scene of the some of the worst slaughters in The Thirty Years War (which strangely produced great German Baroque lyric poetry and some of the best German folksongs and chorales). The Elbe almost touches Teplitz, in Czech 'Tiplice', where Beethoven on his summer holidays in 1822 bowed low before the buckled shoes of Goethe, Germany's greatest poet, and people talked for a century afterwards about the 'Meeting of the Giants'!

Hamburg's Elbe begins its epic meanderings up to disgorge into the North Sea actually on the Czech–Polish border in the Riesengebirge, or 'Giant Mountains', pumping out of a 1,600-metre high mountain the locals call Schneekoppe or 'The Snow-White Head'.

Thus Hamburg of the Hanseatic League is a city on a great waterway. I like it that way. It's good for a composer's musical flow, I suspect. Hamburg on the Elbe has seen many a composer, certainly. Bach as a still-young man had a shot at the well-advertised post of Director of Music at the City's Five Principal Churches. He had a wife and large family to feed, but the city's senators turned him down and gave the job to Telemann. However, Bach's second son, the great *Sturm und Drang* composer, Carl Philipp Emanuel Bach, did work in Hamburg until he left for Berlin in the 1770s.

Of course, when the subject of Hamburg and music ever comes up with proud Hamburgers, the great son of this city is without a doubt Johannes Brahms. The trouble is, they said no to him, too, when, in 1861, he applied for the big job as Conductor of the Philharmonic. He was twenty-eight years old and not yet internationally famous – the 'German Requiem', his big breakthrough, lay a couple of years ahead – but Brahms already had his admirers, also his female fanclub! One Hamburg lady recalled long after his death:

> Of medium height and delicately built, he had a high fine brow with flashing blue eyes, his fair hair combed back and falling down behind, an obstinate lower lip! An unconscious force emanated from the young Brahms as he stood apart in a jolly company, with hands clasped behind his back, greeting those who arrived with a curt nod!

Brahms conducted the Philharmonic a few times; in Hamburg Altona (which was still Danish at that time) he gave several chamber concerts and Lieder recitals with the great singer, Julius Stockhausen. Brahms travelled up (or down) the Elbe (depending on where you are standing, I suppose!) into Austria in December 1862, taking Vienna by storm. It didn't do him any good. The letter from the Hamburg City Cultural Office informed him that the post of Chief Conductor of the Philharmonic was being given not to him but to his singer-friend, Stockhausen. This was an insult; it was a lifelong injury to the identity and self-confidence of Hamburg's greatest composer, Brahms. His most intimate friends in Vienna reported that he never got over his fury, that rage and sadness, that regret that his native city wouldn't properly honour him. Hamburg on the Elbe. The city where I have to be a sound man.

PASSION FOR THE OPERA

Catherine Ryan

At a stage early in our opera education in the late 1950s, my parents decided to take us to the Royal Opera House at Covent Garden. This was quite an undertaking as we lived in Wimbledon and had no car. It was two hours before we reached the opera house. The front was a very imposing structure with tantalising glimpses of the magnificent red and gold staircase and shimmering chandeliers. The doors stood open, and I darted in the first time, proudly presenting my ticket. I revelled in the bejewelled and furred ladies and evening-clothed gentlemen, causing such an animated din. I was politely told the entrance to the amphitheatre was round the corner. What corner? Our door was ordinary with a mountain of drab steps before us. I always felt this shabby treatment of our poorer status was quite unjust.

Eventually, breathless, we staggered into the auditorium. We were at the top of the world almost able to touch the pale blue and gold ceiling. Below us lay the steep amphitheatre; oh the opulent red of those seats. If we leaned over the balcony, we could see below to the tiers of the circle and grand circle, decorated with cream cherubs resting against golden ornamentation. Shining in spotlights was the stage itself shrouded by richly decorated curtains. The dimming lights subdued the chatter. All eyes were on the orchestra pit below the stage and the figure sweeping through it to the conductor's podium. He bowed to us. We applauded. Then I was dazzled by music that gave my emotions new heights. They tingled inside me with yearnings I didn't know I had. Stories played out beneath me in a swirl of glittering action.

But tickets were not easily got. There was no simple telephone booking. We had to queue at the theatre before eight a.m. on a given day to get a ticket. That ticket gave the place number and time to turn up at the box office. For us, it meant leaving home around five in the morning if we wanted to see Callas. The fascinating thing about going into London at this time with my father was the eerie emptiness of trains and stations. Then, coming out of Covent Garden underground station, it was all bustle and shouting, Carts were being dragged all ways, boxes of fruit and vegetables thrust on them. This was the Covent Garden market in the tatty-looking glasshouse, the Vilar Floral Hall, right next to the opera house. While we stood in queues winding round the Opera House, the alien world of early traders played out before us. I never enjoyed those mornings more than when we went into the market café after eight and feasted on the largest breakfast possible. My father, who worked in the Strand nearby, patiently did this each season.

I loved the amphitheatre like a second home although some things were strange. There were only two toilets for all the ladies in the amphitheatre. I spent most of the interval queuing. My adult life took me far away from it for years. I returned just after it had been extensively renovated in 1999. My brother got us tickets in the amphitheatre for Rossini's *Otello* and, as usual, I headed for the side. My brother smiled and pushed me into the front entrance. The child in me was overwhelmed. I would happily have spent hours wandering up and down that magnificent staircase. But no. We were ushered to a new door at the side. I found myself looking up into a shimmering structure of glass and steel. It took me a minute to realise that this spectacular building was the Vilar Floral Hall. But what nearly made me cry was the steep escalator right up to the new amphitheatre bar which seemed to hang in the air. Had we really climbed that far each time? As I sailed serenely to the top, I noticed there was a new Ladies. I found one very excited woman inside washing her hands. She turned a radiant face to me and said, 'There are seventeen cubicles. I counted them!' I knew exactly where she was coming from.

BRAZILIAN CLASSICS AND A LOOSE GUITAR

Mary O'Malley

The piano which sits in the Aula Maxima – patient, sentient, grand – is one of the more elegant objects of human desire. It is sleek and dark and rich like a musical racehorse, and just as well bred, but stronger by far. It has rows of beautiful, dangerous teeth. Whenever you see one, don't you think of velvet and ballrooms and Irving Berlin, women in bare shoulders and men in black and nights coming slowly undone through a cigarette haze?

Forgive me, maybe it's something in the water, but who doesn't worship a grand piano? The answer, I have learned, is probably the pianist. Tonight it is absent, not needed. Tonight is the turn of the guitars, a bit less high class, more feminine and, let's face it, not as intimidating.

When the programme of Music for Galway tells us four Brazilian guitarists are in town, the cool and the hip and the young gather. There is a buzz in the Aula. This is a different crowd from the usual predictable mix. They are out for passion, if not rock and roll in a town awash with salsa and samba. Young Latin women are employed propelling newly loosed fifty-something Irishmen around dance floors in droves. Young Latin men with names like Cuba are doing the same in reverse. This crowd is hot to trot, or at the very least swoon. They expect to have their inner Latin lovers nourished.

The programme is flawlessly played, beautifully balanced, restraint in every note, in the 'Concierto Iberico', the 'Francisco Mignone Legend of the Outback' and the 'Bachianas of Villa Lobos'.

Not once does a loose guitar slide down a dark side alley, nor is there a hint of coquetry nor a flaring of skirts. This music has taken vows of purity and obedience and it is not breaking them tonight. The crowd applauds enthusiastically and hides its disappointment well, like polite children given the wrong toy by a distant aunt.

Over dinner, I asked the leader of the group if he played 'musica popular', which corresponds to trad here. He said, 'No, never. It is not the same discipline and I do one well, and stay within it.'

There was no hierarchy implied, it was as if a poet said, 'No, I do not write songs. I admire songwriters but that is not the same as poetry and I don't assume I can do both.'

'But,' he said in Portuguese, 'I am Brazileiro. If you give me a box of matches, of course I will play you Samba.' Maybe there's something in that for traditional and classical musicians alike.

The talk moved on to education and the setting up of over 100 youth orchestras in the shanty towns of Argentina. They were involved in the spread of a similar movement in the favelas of Brazil.

What struck me was how civilised these men were, how non-elitist. Twelve million to make a dog's dinner of the square and this city cannot boast a music school, much less an orchestra. And most children still can't afford music lessons.

The Brazilians understood something basic we have not grasped here: it is not only that all children deserve music, but the music, if it is to flourish, deserves all children. Galway, could you not release some of your well-preserved pianos and teach the kids to play?

A MUSIC ROOM IN VENICE

Marguerite MacCurtin

The music room of the church of the small hospital, or La Sala della Musica dell'Ospedaletto, is arguably the most elegant room in Venice. It is certainly the most unique because it is the last remaining example of the kind of music room which was once attached to the churches of the four main orphanages in Venice in the eighteenth century. Hidden away above a spiral stone stairway overlooking an enclosed courtyard, this oval-shaped room is an architectural gem of fresco paintings and *trompe l'oeil*. Its elaborate decorative scheme of cornices and capitals and marbled columns was meant to deceive the eye with notions of spatial grandeur and to startle the visitor with the drama of its classical beauty.

But it was the sudden rustle of the long, white curtains, swishing in the balmy stillness of a summer's day, that really startled me on my first visit there many years ago. I felt as if I was being watched or that there were other people in the music room and yet I knew that I was alone – then, suddenly, I saw them. A couple of girls standing behind a window, screened with a golden grill and framed by a sweep of red curtain high up on the curve of the wall. They were peering down with a look of deep concentration as if they were intent on listening to something. Their presence was so convincing that it took me a couple of seconds to realise that my spectators, too, were an illusion, a painted image in *trompe l'oeil*. Nevertheless, I stopped and followed their gaze.

Below them, I saw a large fresco painted against the backdrop of an imaginary theatrical set which depicted a concert rehearsal in full swing. On the stepped stage beneath a canopy supported by pairs of classical columns, a music master was conducting a group of girl singers and musicians of eighteenth-century Venice under the watchful eye of Apollo, the god of music. They were dressed in contemporary clothes of the time, in contemporary powdery shades of cream and green and gold and blue and pink and purple, with accents of contemporary jewellery and upswept hairstyles dressed with flowers and pearls. They were shown in a happy, lively, energetic mood, singing, playing music, reading a score, moving about, peeping playfully around columns, chatting. These casual actions, rhythms and gestures endowed them with a great air of spontaneity and life, all of which were taking place under the watchful eye of their music master. He was shown, also in contemporary dress, conducting the choir. In the foreground, a girl dressed in blue and white was holding the score of a famous aria from an opera called *Antigone* performed in Venice in 1773. '*Combatteremo insieme*' – Let us battle together – the first line, visible to the viewer, read. What aspiration could be more appropriate given the precarious situation that these orphan girls found themselves in. Abandoned and penniless, it was through their music that they eventually attained their professional, social and financial liberation. Their reputation for musical and vocal virtuosity made them a legend of their time. Music masters and composers flocked to Venice to teach them and to write for them. No visit for the discerning traveller was complete without having experienced the range, delicacy and finesse of their concert performances; although they were rarely allowed to perform publicly beyond the cloistered galleries of the churches and music rooms of the four orphanages which sheltered them.

And so I sat there transported back in time by the architectural illusion of this *trompe l'oeil* music room and the airy delicacy of the concert scene before me. I knew that, over the centuries, thousands of people had listened to generations of girl singers and musicians perform here. Perhaps it was the spirit of all that creative energy that had caused those white gauze curtains to rustle in the stillness of that languid summer's day. The kind of energy that crosses those mysterious divisions of time and space and manifests itself in the form of presences that needs to be acknowledged.

SILENCE

Judith Mok

Mother, you suddenly had to die. I cancelled my life and sat beside you until you became my child. Friends and flowers surrounded your bed that stood in father's study. Your bedroom was abandoned to the deathwatch. You had only a few weeks left to live, just before Christmas. Not that Christmas mattered a lot to us. It was December and winter and a bitterly cold wind blew against the windows. The first days, we would sometimes listen to it after we had finished talking over your life. But, then, it would remind us of other times and the sound of the wind elsewhere and what were we doing then and the talking would take over again.

I would travel with you to your youth and still you quoted Yeats, Heine, Goethe, Hugo with the same mad enthusiasm as then, when you first read them. Parties with Louis Armstrong playing the trumpet in the orchestra, ball gowns described in great detail, all specially made for you, British lords as dejected fiancées, the travelling you did and the languages you learned and later taught me, your mother who would climb on tables in restaurants dressed in her beautiful clothes and hats and proclaim socialism like a Dutch suffragette, your father who forbade you the only thing you really wanted: to stand on stage. Yet you loved him. The war that came down as a fatal hammer and crushed everything – your family, your home, your naïvity.

We hummed the folksongs you learned from your Russian friends who came to hide from the Nazis. Later, you sang them for me at bedtime. Now I did it for you, just as I made you listen to my newest recording of a Rachmaninov song. You listened with your eyes closed and whispered the words in your soft Russian, 'Never sing to me again.' I wouldn't. You had given me a first edition of Oscar Wilde's *Salome* for my first operatic performance at twenty-one. You had written solid and positive criticism in the programme during the show. You always did from then onwards. When I worked in Barcelona, you came to stay with me for a while. One evening, we sat a little bit lost in my tiny apartment and then, just for me, you quoted and translated Mandelstam, that great and persecuted Russian poet. All by heart. In your very last days, you wanted me to read your favourite authors to you, listen to Schubert and giggle about the huge amount of naughty things you had done. I sat and read Banville, Celan and Nescio. We talked about my father's, your husband's, books, but you read his poems yourself. We discussed some family life, you wanted Brahms for your funeral: All flesh is grass. We ran through more music, things I would sing in the future, composers. You grew silent. I washed you. After which you left me in the company of all.

LOVE AND THE GOLDEN AGE OF LUTHIERY

Dianna Robin Dennis

My love affair with the guitar started long before I fell in love with guitar players. I suppose it started before I knew anything about guitars – it started with the word 'harmony'.

My sister says I was around three when she said to me, 'You sing this and I am going to sing something different. It's called harmony.' If ever there was an epiphany, it was that moment.

She taught me cowboy songs, Burl Ives and Pete Seeger. When she went to college, she brought home Peter, Paul and Mary, the Kingston Trio, and Tom Lehrer.

Entering my pre-teen years, I borrowed that sister's old plywood Harmony and started teaching myself to play. 'Eve of Destruction', 'Long Black Veil', 'This Land is Your Land', 'Puff the Magic Dragon', 'Blowin' in the Wind': songs of the greats: Paxton, Anderson, Dylan, Lightfoot. And, of course, Collins, Baez and Mitchell.

Unfortunately, I destroyed my sister's little guitar with the wrong strings. Fortunately, she persuaded my godfather to give me a nylon stringed Yamaha classical. I've never looked back.

My first love in high school was a guitar player until he bored me with scales. It wasn't until I was at Sarah Lawrence and running the musical coffee house that I truly found love – not in his instruments, in his hands and his eyes as he played and sang his wonderful songs for me.

We found my grandfather's old guitar in our attic, and Richard introduced me to my first luthier. He also took me guitar shopping: we drove up and down the mideast coast highways and byways in his 1952 Packard. We must have visited every small guitar shop in New York, New Jersey, eastern Pennsylvania, and Connecticut, in search of *my* ultimate instrument.

Eventually, we wound up back in New York City – in a small shop on Bleeker Street recommended by a friend. A couple dozen beautiful guitars hung from the ceiling; there were stools over by the window. The owner, Matt Umanov, took the afternoon to show me all his wonderful instruments, even the special ones hidden in the back room.

He watched me play, disappeared, then returned with a Gurian – a beautiful, simply decorated, instrument, handmade by a friend of his in rural New Hampshire. The label read 'handmade on Earth, third planet from the sun'. Its sound filled the room and opened our eyes. But… Matt handed me another, then another. Then, at once, we noticed one last unplayed guitar – identical to the one in my hands.

'Should I play that one, too?' I asked, tentatively. Matt said, 'Certainly – they are handmade and there could be a difference.' One chord was all it took – I looked up at Richard, then over to the ever-patient Matt. Their bright smiles told me they heard it, too: magic – that guitar chose me. Today, that Gurian Model JM, my first luthier-built instrument, still radiates magic in my living room. Richard has remained my friend, though his career as a New York musician has been cut short by Parkinson's Disease.

You can still buy your guitar from Umanov's in New York's Greenwich Village, even though the Village itself has changed. Michael Gurian retired from building guitars around 1981, but respect for him has grown, and he is credited with initiating the current luthier revival. Many of today's fine builders owe their start to him.

Through adolescence and college, bass players and bars, my guitars have served me well. They hide the shy performer and open doors to meeting other musicians and music lovers. They've been beaten, neglected, found again – and they always seem to hold the harmonics of the universe.

Listening

fingers on strings
cut through my fog –
major, minor,
suspensions,
augmentations –
lift my spirit
then fling it
to my darkened past
where once
you played me.

I strummed those
smoke-filled rooms
'til gray poison
clogged
my voice.

now, my
stiffened joints
only allow
listening.

WILD BILL'S CLUB, MEMPHIS

Richard Stevens

Last night, I went to Wild Bill's Club somewhere in the suburbs of Memphis. Running a Saturday-night party. The crowd was middle aged to elderly, all black except for four whites who, like myself, I guessed were visitors, and an exotic looking English white man with long, grey hair and a guitar, known to most of the crowd. He played for a few numbers and was pretty good. The band was a good, old-fashioned Memphis band. The surroundings did not look as if an interior decorator had been employed to give atmosphere and image. Red walls, ceiling fans and plastic tablecloths on long tables, with dancing up front. It had a down-home atmosphere. The singer doubled on bass. He was a large but young man with lots of gold, including teeth, his hair shaved up the side and sticking up on top. A blues soul voice a bit like Bobby Bland. A good organ played by a small sparrow of a man, very dapper, hunched over the keyboard as if he wanted to be one with the machinery.

Sometimes the audience sang. The woman beside me was large and had a voice that would lift the roof. She could have sung at Madison Square Gardens without a mike and been heard at the back.

On the other side was a couple who were having a fierce domestic row. He looked scholarly and had natty two-tone dancing shoes made from patent leather like Bojangles. The row seemed to escalate and then sink to a bubbling simmer.

I was the object of great curiosity. There was a bar, so I bought a few drinks, but they gave me dinner and made me very welcome, a single elderly man. Half a dozen of the women had me up for a dance. When the rowing husband went for a dance with someone not his wife, she had me up for a dance and examined my hand to see if I sported a wedding ring. Her husband came back and she abused and shouted obscenities at him; he maintained a dignified silence. It must have been a regular event because she was dancing with him, hands roving all over him, a couple of minutes later.

I felt vaguely embarrassed at breaking into this local party, but I was not going to miss the music. This was the first blues of my visit that I had heard played for a local audience of listeners and dancers, not visitors or enthusiasts. This kind of music has been played in juke joints like this since the 1920s. I will be always grateful to the ex-prison officer with 'I love Jesus' on his cap for giving me directions and his friend, the taxi driver, who made sure I arrived.

PHILIP GLASS AND NO PROBLEM AT ALL

Ferdia Mac Anna

Last year Philip Glass played a concert in Dublin. I decided to go and see the composer who had been dubbed the 'new Beethoven'. Who could pass up a chance to be in the presence of genius?

So I phoned Ticketmaster. I got on to a chirpy Dublin sales guy who assured me that whatever I wanted would be no problem at all. 'Hi, I want to book two tickets for Philip Glass at Vicar Street,' I said.

'Who's he?' the sales guy asked.

'Philip Glass? He's playing Vicar Street next month, it's advertised in *The Times* …'

'Tickets? No problem at all,' the sales guy said cheerfully. 'I just want to know who he is.'

'Well, he's a modern composer. Some people call him the New Beethoven.'

'What's he done?'

'He composed the soundtrack for *Mishima*.'

'Never heard of it. What else?'

'He's recorded a symphony based on David Bowie's album *Low*.'

'Nope.'

I named everything I could think of by Philip Glass.

'Operas?'

'Sorry.'

'String Quartets with the Kronos Quartet?'

'Nah.'

'*Liquid Days*, collaborations on an album of songs with Suzanne Vega and your man David Byrne from Talking Heads?'

'No.'

Why was this happening? I felt like Philip Glass's unofficial publicist. All I wanted was a couple of tickets for a concert. Instead I found myself engaged in attempting to convert a stranger to the delights of a composer whose work even I had mixed feelings about. He may be the 'New Beethoven', but a CD of Philip Glass music has the power to clear a roomful of people in under a minute. Besides, I was paying for the call. I decided to forget about booking the tickets.

'Ah go on,' said No Problem at All. 'There must be something.'

I weakened. 'He did the music for *Koyaanisqatsi*,' I said.

'*Koyaanisqatsi*?' No Problem at All said. 'You mean *that* Philip Glass?'

'Yes, that Philip Glass,' I said.

There was a short pause. I could hear an intake of breath as No Problem at All braced himself for something.

'That guy,' he said, 'is effing brilliant.'

'Good,' I said. 'Now could I boo—'

'That man is so deep inside his own head.'

'Fine, now what abo—'

'That bloke,' No Problem at All said meaningfully, 'has really got his act together. Know what I mean?'

I said I did.

Finally, I managed to buy tickets and conclude our business.

Just before I rang off the ticket clerk said that he was glad he had been talking to me. He was definitely going to buy tickets for himself. 'You never know,' he chirped. 'I might even end up sitting next to you.'

'Thanks,' I said.

No problem at all.

THE REST IS SILENCE

Nóirín Ní Riain

In the amazing world of music, silence and sound are soulmates. One depends on the other. The rest is music. The rest is silence.

Yet, like a good human relationship, both remain other and enhance one another in the perfect balance and tension inevitable for the song or piece of music to spread its wings and fly. Silence is the sacred space out of which music weaves its way in and through our aural world. An interval of silence – appropriately called a 'rest' in music – a time of refreshing quiet.

Aldous Huxley, the British novelist, wrote: 'After silence that which comes nearest to expressing the inexpressible is music.'

The art of the rest/silence envelopes the inevitable trinity of actors in the drama of music: firstly, there's the composer; secondly, the performer/conductor; and finally, you, the sympathetic listener.

I use the word 'sympathetic' carefully. Its well-source is from the mellifluous ancient Greek language. *Patheia* means feelings or emotions and *sympatheia* puts a word on co-sharing, sharing these feelings with one another.

The composer is the midwife – the very source of the music – the god/goddess of the river of sound, just as Sionna is the source and goddess of this magical Shannon River beside us. The composer is reaching out for the perfect tune, finding the elusive equipoise between silence and resonance. And that resonance can offer incredible possibilities which, again, like silence, can mirror the measure of one's imagination.

It is this drive or inspired vision which spans time and timbre from, on the one hand, the precise measured silences of the Bachean *Brandenburg Concertos* to the innovative compositions by the late contemporary composer John Cage, such as *4'33*, on the other.

Bathed in silence again, the music remains invisible and still in the mind of the composer or on the silent page of manuscript waiting its moment to sing its song.

Then the performer is the one who strikes the bell of sound. But the heart of this sounding is yet another dance with silence – as the ancient Chinese proverb goes, 'the midnight when noon is born'. At that very point, the silence is broken and explodes on the universe of listeners like the Big Bang of Music.

William Stafford, the Kansas poet, captures that transformative life of the imagination. This poem, incidentally, he wrote on 10 August 1993, just eighteen days before he died.

A shudder goes through the universe, even
long after. Every star, clasping its
meaning as it looks back, races outward
where something quiet and far waits.
Within, too, ever receding, into its fractions,
that first brutal sound nestles closer
and closer toward the tiny dot of tomorrow.
And here we are in the middle, holding
it all together, not even shaking.

Hard to believe

LOVE, PASSION AND FAITH

BROKEN BOY

Brigid O'Connor

My little boy is broken.

He doesn't look broken but somewhere inside his wires are crossed and his output is scrambled.

A lot of people have tried to fix my little broken boy.

But it doesn't seem to matter, we go and see them, he does their little tests.

I will him on every single millisecond and inwardly cheer when he gets things right.

But somehow we always end up on the path home, hand in hand.

There are lots of new words for broken boys these days and lots of techniques to try and get these square pegs into round holes.

The experts examine and prod and try to help but all they see is a broken boy.

I too, see a little broken boy, but I have a gift.

I understand the broken speech, I share his thoughts and dreams.

I believe him when he tells me he used to live in an angel garden and wore angel wings while shelling peas in this enchanted garden.

We don't like the tutters, my little broken boy and me.

They're the enemy.

We meet them in shops and public places when the tantrums happen and things go wrong and spiral out of control.

They always 'tut' and never offer to help.

They judge, they tut and walk away.

I think they're a bit broken too.

My little boy has a broken grandmother too.

She too does her tests and we cheer inside when she gets things right.

Sometimes she gets her clothes on inside out and calls me by a different name.

That's OK. As long as it's someone she liked, it means she's happy with me.

She has a fancy name for her ailment, too, and pills and potions to help her through the fog of another day. Sometimes the pills help; sometimes they turn her into a cold shadow of herself.

Sometimes she just needs her hand held. Some human warmth to counter the icy grip the greedy illness has on her mind and body.

My little broken boy likes his hand held too.

When my older child was little, she couldn't sleep in a sun-filled room.

She asked me if I could turn off the sun.

I sometimes think of that now when I'm with my broken boy.

Or when I'm in a shadowy room with my disappearing mother.

I can't quite keep the blaring sun from both of them but I do my best to dim it a bit.

Maybe we all should.

LIKE ROSES

Tom Finnigan

That October in Rome in 1970, preparing for priesthood, I read St Augustine and blew smoke rings through the Trinity. My window opened onto the balconies of Via dei Cappellari. Mario Lanza serenaded from a transistor. Bras and blouses clung to suspended wires. And a smell of lamb, roasting in garlic, drifted over the roof tiles and curled around my desk.

The bells of San Andrea della Valle drowned the radios and chimed the Angelus. I was late for Evening Prayer.

Like all good Renaissance stairways, the three flights of marble descended in curves around a central pillar. Lifting my soutane, I flew – my shoes scarcely touching the shallow steps. I squeezed, red faced, into my pew in chapel and gripped a missal. Monsignor Brewer raised his ginger eyebrows to signal my hasty arrival, coughed and intoned in Latin, 'Angelus Domini…' Candles spluttered.

We sat facing each other like monks in choir: six lines of clerics, standing for the antiphons and sitting to recite the psalms. Above the altar, God the Father reached down to receive His dead Son, whilst the Holy Spirit in the form of a dove hovered above them. My friend Joe Moore nudged me.

'There's someone looking at you,' he whispered and nodded to the benches for visitors. I saw a girl watching me, black hair glancing from her shoulders.

My brother had told her to ask for me. 'He'll show you round,' he had said. We chatted about home. I showed her the chapel, told her about our martyrs. We ran our hands across the tomb of Bishop Bainbridge, feeling his ring, his mitre, the bridge of his cold nose. We walked the Cardinals' Corridor, admiring the portraits. I pointed out Thomas Wolsey and Newman. She smiled at the scarlet drapes and the red carpet. In the library, we whispered among the Greek Fathers. I opened a rare text. She bent to look and I caught her perfume – like roses. She turned to me and I was startled when her hair brushed my hand.

I gave her iced tea in the garden. We sat by the pond and poked at the goldfish. Her black hair danced. Swifts made pirouettes in the sky. She spoke in whispers, remarking on the smell of lamb cooking, the sound of dishes clattering. Light caught her eyes and lips. We walked to the Piazza Farnese. When the sun dipped, our shadows merged. We shook hands. My mouth was dry as I watched her taxi turn for the Corso.

The smell of wood burning in the pizzerias of Campo dei Fiori seeped through my window. Sinatra sang 'Strangers in the Night'. I flipped *Confessions* by St Augustine onto my bed and lit a cigarette. Lights glimmered below the dome of San Andrea. A breeze ruffled the curtain. I thought I smelled roses. A bell tolled the half hour and tobacco smoke floated, soft through the night, like the fall of a girl's hair on the back of your hand.

LETTERS IN THE ATTIC

Kate Thompson

I have only a vague memory of my maternal grandfather, who died some time in the 1960s. He was a painter and an art master at the Royal Academy in Edinburgh, and what was remarkable about him was that he had taught himself to paint with his left hand, the right having been severed in an accident involving a threshing machine when he was fifteen. My grandparents lived in Edinburgh, so I never had much of an opportunity to get to know them well. I have family photographs, of course, and memories of their beautiful Edwardian house with its cantilevered staircase and Adam fireplaces, and, to this day, the smell of linseed oil conjures up a memory of my grandfather's studio.

After my grandfather died, my grandmother, Winifred Jessie, continued to live in the house that had grown too big for her. When her short-term memory started to fail, my mother moved from Ireland back to Edinburgh to care for her, but once she began the inexorable descent into senility, she took up residency in an old-people's home. I visited occasionally and, because there was very little wrong with her long-term memory, she would talk at great length about events in her past. She had been a student at Newnham College, Cambridge – indeed, she was one of the university's first legitimate women graduates. She had lived through two world wars. She had hosted artistic salons on a weekly basis in her drawing room, and she had met numerous famous and fascinating people. However, because I was a self-absorbed teenager at that time, I only pretended to listen to her reminiscences while contemplating more pressing matters, such as boyfriends and fashion and becoming a famous actress.

My grandmother died in 1983, and I heard her voice properly for the first time just last year when I found her letters in the attic among some papers that had belonged to my mother. They were written in the aftermath of the First World War, between 1918 and 1920, and they were posted to her parents in Kent from various locations in Europe. The first letter was dated 10 November 1918. It was written from Rouen, where my grandmother was on active service with the British Expeditionary Force doing war work in the YMCA library, and it began:

> Dearest Mother and all,
>
> I arrived here finally last night. I was met at the station by 2 of the Educational Scheme people, so had no bother about conveyances. We little lot – 7 of us – live in a hotel, each have our own room and a small sitting-room. There are 3 men and 4 women. One man is an artist, with one arm, the other withered or something. He is very 'alive', and is always racing about somewhere – he has a perfect knowledge of the town, knows all the streets and buildings, shops and cafés. Everyone is awfully nice, and as long as my work turns out satisfactorily, I think I shall like the whole thing – so don't worry about me, Mummy darling.

'One man is an artist, with one arm, the other withered or something.'

My grandfather – Albert Charles Dodds! I felt my heart turn over. Here was a record in the first person of the very moment my grandparents had met! I felt as if my grandmother was talking to me across a distance in time of almost a century, telling me her story: and for the first time I was really listening…

LOVE AND ONIONS

Joe Kearney

My mother warned me never, ever to tell this story.

In the meantime, I have come to understand that love is not an emotion built on lavish extravaganza but is rather an accumulation of small things, an incremental treasure-trove of sincere honest gestures. When genuinely offered, such tokens will bring tears to both the eye of the giver and the recipient. So it was with Nancy and Michael.

Michael was a loving man but he hated two things with a passion: one was onions, the other Kilkenny hurlers. He hated the latter when his love for Nancy saw him transplanted from the rich soil of his beloved Cork into the barren clay of Kilkenny. His red and white flag was a confederacy of rebellion amongst the black and amber. He was a bantam of a man forced to shout his war cry above the hiss of cats, 'Cork-a-Doodle-Do… Cork-a-Doodle-Do.'

He hated onions because the pungency set him crying and caused his sinuses to react. Yet, he grew them because they were Nancy's favourite.

Each year, for the duration of the hurling championship, he would hang the tattered flag of his county allegiance high in the chestnut tree beside the road, a defiance to the passing neighbours.

And, each year, he grew onions as big and hard as sliotars and as sweet, to Nancy, in the depths of a wintry stew, as an out-of-season all-Ireland victory.

He nurtured, weeded, ripened and stored those golden alliums. He presented then to Nancy in her kitchen in plaited shanks as if they were Valentine bouquets of the rarest orchid. It seemed that the continuous loop of revolving seasons set its calendar and clock by Michael's onions.

During one season of perfect golden harvest, strangers arrived to the quiet townland of Cappahenry that was home to the couple. Pipe men came who were the contractors tasked with laying a conduit that would channel the fossilised breath of prehistoric natural gas from beneath the seabed at Kinsale. These men carved a scar diagonally across the landscape that would eventually stretch to the homes and industries of Dublin. Gas would flow under pressure beneath Cork and Kilkenny, ignoring both county boundaries and hurling rivalry.

For the duration of the pipe men's stay, Nancy and Michael would hear their laughter and music drifting across the evening fields and sometimes the breeze would waft with it the smell of cook-fires and an unmistakable aroma of frying steak. Within a few days, the pipe men were gone; their scar sutured neatly behind them.

The couple liked to take a stroll in the evening between perhaps *Kojak*, *Hawaii Five-O* or *Colombo* and the news. One such evening, when a fingernail sliver of harvest moon hung above their shoulders, they returned from their walk. Michael had arranged the onions on the lean-to-shed at the back of the house, lined up as if for some souvenir team photograph; in ripening ranks they faced southwards towards Cork, in the direction of the gas field, like needles on a broken compass.

'It must have been a bad year for the onions?' Nancy remarked to Michael.

'Rubbish, girl,' he boasted. 'That's one bumper crop. We'll be tired givin' 'em away they're so plentiful.'

But then he, too, noticed the cause of her concern, all that remained upon the roof were a scant few stalks... the onions were gone!

Truth slowly dawned on Michael. He remembered that the breezes blowing from the cook-fire contained upon their breath not just the smell of steak but steak... and onions. He rained down curses on the pipe men. He hoped his onions would cause them a plague of gas; that their internal pipework would suffer them pain and pressure no doctor could cure.

He located their point of intrusion beside the ash tree, on the ditch, saw the path they had beaten through the wither of late-season dock and nettle and glared northwards along their scarred line of departure.

Michael's flag no longer teases the passing cats. The chestnut tree is bare of rebel taunt. One of his last tasks was to spread a summer's harvest of onions along the windowsill, safely removed from predation but still coddled by the southern sun. 'These will last well into winter,' he promised Nancy and, true to his word, they did, but like all simple tokens of true love, they couldn't avoid bringing tears to her eyes.

My mother, Nancy, warned me never, ever to tell this story.

JOAN

Johnny Duhan

My mother once told me that her grandmother literally picked her grandfather from the gutters of Limerick as a drunken soldier and knocked him into such good shape that he ended up a sergeant major in the Irish army.

Joan, a young schoolteacher with luminous eyes and a stunning figure, whom I met at one of my first band's final gigs, did something similar for me. After going out together for several months, I was offered a job with a supergroup in London that was on the cusp of signing a deal with one of the major record companies for oodles of money. While we were waiting for the advance, I moved into a dingy attic in Chiswick and Joan moved in with me, after throwing up her teaching job and the pension that went with it. Our intention was to move to a proper flat when the advance came through, but, before that happened, I had a flaming row with the band leader over musical differences and left in a huff. Consequently, instead of moving to a pad on the Chelsea High Road, as Joan and I had dreamed of doing, we found ourselves relocating to the old bog road in County Galway, where Joan's parents ran a small farm.

I'd spent half my life dreaming with my eyes on the stars, so when we moved to the farm, I had a rude awakening: a donkey brayed in a far field, a cow lowed in a paddock, a pig grunted to its farrow, a cock crowed on a dung-heap. Out on the ploughed land among the scarecrows with my hands in the dirt, I hankered for the easy life on the open road. O, yes, a rude awakening brought me down to earth with a bang. But after this hard planting, I'll be laughing, reaping. While I was living and working on the farm, cut off from the mainstream of popular culture, I discovered my own voice as a songwriter. It was there too that my relationship with Joan deepened.

You always woke long after me, but once on a summer
morning soon after we married you woke at dawn
and asked me to go mushroom picking. We crept out of
the cottage, yawning and rubbing our eyes.
Outside there was birdsong in a pink coral sky and the misty
    fields
were grey with dewy spider webs. Sheep looked up from
their early grazing, a cow lowed near the dirt track,
a hare shot across a tussocky hillock. When we reached
the 'mushroom field' we filled a red basin to the brim
with a white froth of mushrooms. Back in the cottage we
left the vessel on the kitchen table beside the milk jug
and crept back to bed and warmed one another
with our limbs.

GRÁ TUISMITHEORA

Gabriel Fitzmaurice

Two little children in the sitting room at home watching a movie on television. Their father in the kitchen washing ware at the sink, a happy family scene.

Then screams from the sitting room. But are they screams of joy or distress? Worried, the father rushes to the sitting room only to find his darlings having high jinks on the sofa. Was his immediate reaction – worry – prudent or misplaced? Why is it that, in such a peaceful situation, his first reaction was to think the worst? Is he over-protective of his children? But wouldn't most parents do the same? Love comes with its own worries. And still we wouldn't have it changed.

Grá Tuismitheora

Cé chomh gar's atá glór caointe is glór gáire!
Mo pháistí ag féachaint ar *Dumbo* ar TV
Sa seomra suite taobh liom: i dtús báire
Ní aithním an bhfuilid ag gol nó ag gáirí.
Ag gairí nó ag gol sa seomra suite?
Téim isteach – táid ag déanamh spraoi
Ar an dtolg is oíche beagnach tite:

In ionad a bheith ag féachaint ar TV,
High jinks ar an dtolg – ní baol dóibh;
Mé ag tabhairt amach, iadsan ag sciotaíl:
Leanann a Ifreann féin grá an tuismitheora –
Agus iad ag gáirí, is eagal liom iad i mbaol.

A Parent's Love

How close the sound of laughter and of tears!
My children watching on TV
In the next room – are those wails or cheers?
At this remove their screaming worries me.
Do my children laugh or cry in the next room?
I check them out and this is what I see –
No light illuminates the falling gloom,
Instead of watching *Dumbo* on TV,
High jinks on the sofa – they're both well,
I tick them off, their giggles fill and burst:
A parent's love knows all it needs of hell –
I hear them play and strangely fear the worst.

STONES

Mary O'Donnell

Sometimes, my daughter and I lie in bed pretending to be stones. Yes, stones. The game has developed from a starting point where I was trying to get her to keep her feet still in the bed to something more involved. The idea is that we lie folded into one another and say nothing for a while. After a time, one of us might pass a comment, from the point of view of a smooth stone on a beach, for example. The beach stones are our favourite kind. Sometimes, she remarks on a seagull that has just passed overhead or the sound of a ship far out from the shore. All kinds of things happen on that imaginary beach among the stones. Sometimes, we are walked over by crabs, their claws clacking as they scurry sideways across our greyness; tiny insects move around us, beneath us, sometimes armies of ants file across us, on their way to some definite ant-ish goal.

What we like best is the incoming tide.

'Is it near? Is it getting near?' my daughter whispers in my ear, her whole body quite still.

'Not yet. Not yet. Yes, it's coming, I can hear it. The water is coming!' I whisper back.

Then we wait again.

'It's gone back,' I say forlornly. 'It was too soon.'

'There's a black-back gull up there,' she remarks with a sigh, as we wait for the tide. 'Ugh!' she shudders, almost forgetting that she is a stone. 'It just dropped something horrible on me! Yeuch!'

'Uh-uh…' I mutter. 'Look what's coming!'

'Oh no!' she hisses, alarmed.

We are always alarmed when people approach, because people, it is understood, can pick us up and throw us away from one another. Into the deep, up closer to the base of the cliff where we will never feel the tide running across our greyness.

'It's OK, they've gone,' she says with relief.

Finally, the tide washes in. It's as if we have waited all our lives for the salty water, the clear, bubbling, embracing silk of that first wave, and as it finally gushes over us, drenching us, we sigh with delight, restored by the scents and wetness of the ocean, from which we know everything has come.

After the tide has flooded over us, it inevitably retreats, but there is pleasure in that too. After the wetness, we look forward to dryness, to the wind shaping our curves, smoothing our roughness, keeping us primed in our stoniness, and to the sun, which we know will make us expand gently. Sometimes we make creaking sounds, as the sun warms our deep stone layers.

Recently, I realised that when we play Stones, we are unconsciously mimicking some of the things that have always affected people: the necessity to respond to change, for example, the dread of ugliness, of violence, the need for replenishment by a force outside the smallness of our own concerns; the pleasure taken in intuitively reading what is going on around us. And being stones and fairly permanent, we try to live forever in one moment, just enjoying it for what it is.

I NEVER SANG FOR MY FATHER

Ken Bruen

I've read so many accounts of the father–son relationship. Among the best are Blake Morrison and Tony Parsons. Years ago, I saw a movie on television starring Melvyn Douglas and Gene Hackman.

You want to talk harrowing! Phew-oh.

Gene Hackman, as the son, can never please his father. Boy does he try.

After, I sat with my head in my hands, said, 'Oh God.'

In my novels, fathers get a rough deal. They're usually

Violent

Cruel

Alcoholic

My dad was none of these.

In all my lost years, he never once turned away. I believed I could never impress him. He understood success in monetary terms. When my second book was displayed in Foyle's window, I must have walked Charing Cross Road a hundred times.

Rang my father. He asked, 'How much did they pay you?'

'It doesn't work like that.'

'Why?'

On receiving my Ph.D, I called him. He said, 'If you think you'll be called *Doctor* in this house, you can kiss my arse.'

After he died, beside his bed, I found copies of all my books. Interspersed through the well-thumbed pages, was every review I'd ever had.

One of my earliest memories is him sweeping all the furniture in the kitchen to the side. Then taking my mother's hand he danced her the length and breath of the room. I can still hear her laughing as she said, 'Ya big eejit.'

He said to me, 'Women will forgive a good dancer most anything.'

I'm still testing the validity of that.

It was a Monday morning my mother rang me. She said, 'Your father has fallen – he hit his forehead.'

I got up there straight away. He was in bed, sitting up. It tore my heart to see the cut above his eye. He asked, 'How's the writing?'

'There's talk of them filming one of the books.'

'Don't let them cod you.'

The doctor came, arranged for an ambulance. The way things are, the wait was lengthy. My mother brought him tea and he said, 'I hope you didn't put sugar in.'

'Do I ever?'

For the best part of forty years, he always said that.

I asked, 'Why?'

He gave a huge smile, said, 'Ary, it keeps her on her toes.'

Later, he asked me to get his wallet from his pants. I did. He used banks but didn't rely on them. Out came hundreds of pounds. He said, 'Mind that for me.'

'I will.'

The effortless trust was perhaps his best review. I went in the ambulance with him and he said, 'I'm fierce trouble to you.'

That was Monday. On Thursday he was in good spirits, said, 'They do lovely jelly with the dinner.'

'I hate jelly.'

'Ah, you only think that.'

He'd contradict the devil. The last thing he said, 'They're letting me home tomorrow.'

He died on Friday morning. With my mother, I counted out the bank notes. There was £630.

The reception after the funeral was at a Salthill hotel. I knew he'd like us to hear the waves roar. The manager asked if we'd any specifications for the meal. I said, 'No jelly.'

The bill came to… £628. I'll never forget the fierce pride in my mother's eyes as she said, 'Your Dad – he was a great man to price a job.'

THE DARK HOPE

Enda Wyley

The feather blows out of the flats, its strange colours flapping brightly. It's a magic feather. The children wish they could live in a different place. They know that if they catch this feather, they can make a wish on it and their dream will come true. So, they race down the steps and out into the bright day, the feather dancing above their heads, leading them on.

This is the beginning of a story I made up for children in Fatima Mansions as part of a creative writing workshop I ran for them late last November.

In the story, the children chase after the feather. It stops over a group of adults and children planting bulbs near the crèche, it moves on to the community centre where other children are making butterfly wings for a parade, painting their faces bright and singing newly learned songs.

The children in the story stop to watch all these activities and then run on after the feather as it passes a group of majorettes in their blue outfits, their hair scraped back into tight buns, rehearsing for a show. Then, as the feather moves out onto the training field, the children race after it to find a football team being coached for a league match.

The children never catch the feather. But, slowly, they realise that where they live isn't so bad after all, that their wish has, in fact, always been there around them. Maybe when the children walked home after the workshop, they thought about the magic feather and the different things it flew past in the story. Maybe they began to realise that the place they live in is not so different to that in the story.

In the places we least expect, hope can often raise its head and we are startled – as if we have pulled aside shutters in a dark room and felt light surprisingly fall like diamonds on a black winter floor. On Sean McDermott Street before Christmas, I remember how a priest blessed a new sculpture at the junction of Buckingham Street.

We remembered the dead – those who had succumbed to Aids in the decay of the surrounding streets and flats. I thought of one woman in particular, who in the last few weeks of her life only had one wish in mind – to get married and to be driven around Stephen's Green in a horse-drawn carriage. We all, at some point in our lives, have stood at a difficult junction, realising the bleakness of our situation but somehow have looked up to hope, like a brave man splattering blessings far out across the street with holy water – love's unexpected gifts.

And, suddenly, you are on a busy street corner, lost in thought, about to innocently step out into the wild sea of traffic and to lose your life – but a stranger's hand reaches from behind, pulls you so quickly back that you do not have time to think.

Love, the dark hope, not wanting to be thanked or noticed, moves on in the crowd and is nameless, faceless. The room fills with light again and you are, in a split second, saved.

HEATHCLIFF

Marian O'Neill

Wuthering Heights should come with a health warning. Packaged as an innocent-looking novel, described as a classic and blithely distributed to impressionable young women, well, it's just plain irresponsible and shouldn't be allowed. Censorship is an extreme word and so, censorship aside, there should still be some room for circumspection. I'd settle for a black-and-white banner proclaiming this book to be harmful to the reader and those around them. Or one that admits to the research that has proven that it can damage the heart.

What reality could ever equal that of the ripped-raw wilderness of the moors? What earthly passion could ever live up to the soul-sundering obsession that blasted Catherine and Heathcliff into a firmament of fervour before delivering them onto an uneasy eternity? How many quaking fifteen-year-old girls have asked themselves, 'Is this love?' Does love require brutality, violence, hatred, sadism, manipulation, betrayal, adultery and death? Does it reach its clawingly greedy arms through the sods of the grave, does it trail grasping tendrils through generations? Does it stoke the terror of waking nightmares, giving them breath to fitfully fuel the bright light of day?

Seemingly so. Seemingly, adult passion combines all of these traits and a true woman staggers to stand strong against the force, raving hair flowing, eyes flashing, fists clenched for the fight and heath-hardened body always skipping just out of reach.

One's Heathcliff demands all of this and so much more. He demands subservient loyalty, total devotion, exclusive attention and soul-fusing compatibility. Anything less and he will not be answerable for his actions. A heady composite of feral good looks, crazed animal passions and devilishly charismatic charm glossed smooth with a veneer of wealth and manners ensure that his demands are made to be met with. No fifteen-year-old could have the strength, or the will, to argue.

But the consequence of our acceptance is there for us to read. In that innocent-looking novel, described as a classic, our futures are mapped out in black and white. If Emily (oops, I mean, Catherine) had to pay with her life, and her soul, for this passion, what hope had we? Neatly folded into our school uniforms, obediently queuing for our bus, innocently worrying over Friday's chemistry test, what hope had we?

ANCORA IMPARO

Joe O'Donnell

There are two small plaques on the wall of my room. They are not really connected, but they'll serve as diving boards from which to launch an insight or two.

Let's take the first one: a small rectangle of dark bronze on which is reproduced in antique lettering the slogan – 'Ancora Imparo'. *Ancora Imparo* is Italian, and roughly translates as 'I am still learning'.

It was given to me, either with insight or irony, as a gift on a significant birthday. The story behind the phrase may well be apocryphal, but it goes like this: the words were scrawled by Michelangelo Buonarroti, sculptor, painter, architect and engineer, on the margin of a manuscript when he was a mere eighty-two years old. And – to me – it accurately pinpoints my day-to-day preoccupation. Less accommodating friends describe it as a magpie instinct and me as a 'snapper up of unconsidered trifles'.

That's from Shakespeare's *A Winter's Tale*. Act IV, Scene III, actually, and the phrase describes Autolycus, the Peddler. You see, there you are. Unconsidered trifles. Fruitful fodder for the table quiz perhaps, but hardly the stuff of that driven ambition that fueled the Celtic Tiger. But we stray from the mottoes on the wall.

Take the other one. It is a simple piece of parchment some

nine inches by five, framed in black and inscribed in *faux* Book of Kells style with the words: 'Fe sgáth a chéile sea mhairid na daoine'. Which roughly translates as: 'In the shadow of one another, live the people. We are dependent on one another'.

I'm not so sure about the sentiments expressed, not so sure whether I particularly subscribe to them or not. So why is it on my wall? Two reasons: the first is for the sheer beauty of the old Gaelic script, not that awful cumbersome and downright ugly Cló Rómhánach. This is the genuine article, complete with *séimhiú*s and *fada*s.

That's the first reason. The second is for the memories of the artist who created this miniature masterpiece. A man in his mid-seventies when he penned this, he was one of Dublin's characters: Captain H. Neville Roberts by name. He lived in an attic apartment on top of a furniture store on Grafton Street, a location I always envied. An elegant, white-haired gentleman with a military moustache as precise as his speech, he wrote poetry, drew and painted miniature masterpieces, issued inflammatory pamphlets on monetary reform and made a daily progress down Grafton Street to Bewley's Café for his customary hot milk and a cherry bun. I not only have the Irish motto on my wall, but tiny elegant scraperboard drawings of abstract landscapes, and an elegant coat of arms which he researched himself.

When he died in his late seventies, he had started to learn Russian. I haven't started yet, but *ancora imparo* – I am still learning.

METAMORPHOSIS

Maurice Cashell

When we first came to this area of France, the valley was covered with orchards. Reine des Reinettes, Golden Delicious, Jonagold, Granny Smith, Gala, they were all here. There were smaller trees between our garden and Monsieur Guerin's field, ornamental trees used for pollination only, yet producing thousands of tiny apples. The pollinators are still there, but the orchards have shrunk – globalisation, some say; others blame Brussels – and there are now four fine horses in the field behind the house.

One moonlit night before bedtime, we went rambling along the farm tracks while grown-ups watched the evening news. There was Áine, then four, Orlaith, exactly seven, and Daniel, almost nine. City kids, who jumped at every sound, were terrified of bats and couldn't understand why there were no streetlights. So, I started with the fairy apples. These apples, I announced, had magical properties when the moon was full, but terms and conditions applied. Everybody had to pluck their apple, shine it on their sleeves and take a small bite, eyes tight shut. Then, they had one wish.

'Really? You're not joking?' said Dan, doubtfully.

'Only works the once and on a moonlit night,' I responded.

'I'm afraid,' wailed Orlaith, flailing at a spider web.

'So was I when I was your age and I missed out on the wish,' said I. 'You don't get a second go.'

We moved gingerly along the row, picked our apples, took the bites and made the wishes. Áine wanted a pink bicycle, Daniel a new PlayStation. Orlaith wanted not to be afraid. By this time, the moon had risen above the line of chestnut trees down the road, and it needed little imagination to see oneself like Elliott and ET cycling through the air across the face of the moon. A magic night. Then we saw the glowworms. One was taken by Orlaith into the house 'to be shown to granny', and then transferred to a matchbox, 'just for the night'.

I suppressed the usual lecture about the environment and respect for God's creatures. As teeth were washed and pyjamas donned, I talked about metamorphosis, about how an animal or insect changes its shape or structure, becoming something else, often quite quickly. Tucking them into bed and warding off bedtime stories, I talked of biological process, cell growth and differentiation. I banged on about Goethe's 'Metamorphosis of Plants' and of homology and transformation until they were all fast asleep. Orlaith, hair and arms flung out on her pillow, slept with a beatific smile.

The first thing to catch her eye in the morning was the matchbox. Inside was a pearl pendant which looked – if you were an old and stuffy adult – remarkably like on old earring of Eileen's, but if you were an eight-year-old girl coming to grips with life's vicissitudes, sheer magic.

'It's metawhatchamacallit,' she shouted as she ran to our room. 'It's happened.'

That was last year. The 'glowworm' now resides on a chain around her neck.

This year, she's going to ride one of those horses.

And then, some day, she's going to be President of Ireland.

CELTIC SPIRITUALITY

Gabriel Rosenstock

Celtic Spirituality has gone through something of a boom in the past decade and there are many weird books and even weirder recordings cashing in on this thing… whatever it is. Everybody is adding their bit, historians, transpersonal psychologists, anthologists of every hue, folklorists, poets and translators. What's it all about? Seems to me that the essence of Celtic Spirituality is very simple really.

Example: in *Fiche Blian ag Fás, Twenty Years A-Growing*, the charming Blasket classic from Muiris Ó Súilleabháin, the author's grandfather is leaving his house. As it happens, he's going to another house, a wake-house. First thing he says when he walks out into the sunshine? 'Moladh go hard le Dia, nach breá an glór atá ag an lon dubh' – 'Praise be to God on high, isn't it a fine voice the blackbird has!' Simple as that. Praise. Without thinking. Mere praise. 'Rühmen ist', it's praise, stupid, as Rilke said, more or less. Praise as spontaneous response to all aspects of living, all phenomena. And this behaviour is found in the structure, idioms, proverbs, prayers and salutations of the Irish language. An Irish-speaking atheist would have an impossible task if he tried to exclude reference to God in his everyday conversation.

This intimate relationship with the divine and with nature is something found in the poetry and oratory of Native Americans as well. George Copway of the Ojibwe tribe said:

I was born in Nature's wide domain! The trees were all that sheltered my infant limbs, the blue heavens all that covered me. I am one of Nature's children. I have always admired her. She shall be my glory: her features, her robes, and the wreath about her brow, the seasons, her stately oaks, and the evergreen – her hair, ringlets over the earth – all contribute to my enduring love of her …

Well, our ancient Celtic druids would have loved all that … 'her stately oaks', yes, yes, we certainly share a lot with the poets and orators of the Native American tradition. It's time we found out exactly how much we have in common with them.

The loss of this wisdom has lead to the ravaging of the earth, even of the earth's sacred places.

Chief Luther Standing Bear says:

It was good for the skin to touch the earth, and the old people liked to remove their moccasins and walk with bare feet on the sacred earth… their tipis were built upon the earth and their altars were made of earth. The birds that flew in the air came to rest upon the earth and it was the final abiding place of all things that lived and grew. The soil was soothing, strengthening, cleansing and healing…

Beautiful words. Causing one to reflect, maybe: with each further destruction of the earth, we desecrate the graves of our ancestors and our own…

RED

Colette McAndrew

The first colour I was afraid of was red. Visiting my grandmother one summer and left to my own devices in her all-purpose grocery/bar, I came across a pile of picture-story classic comics and began to read my way through them. Eventually, I discovered *Jane Eyre*. Charlotte Brontë's description of the red room that Jane was banished to by her evil guardian terrified me in a way Frankenstein and Dracula with all their obvious terrors never could. Someone had died in the red room and poor Jane was left there on her own for hours. Nothing actually happened but, like me, Jane had an over-active imagination and Charlotte obviously knew red was the colour code for danger. It was years before I was comfortable standing on a red rug or even at ease sitting on red car seats.

Red is the most dramatic, eye-catching colour in the spectrum, the colour most women at one time put on their lips, cheeks and nails. Even now, the word 'rouge' retains a slightly naughty ring, as in the Moulin Rouge. It is the colour of sex. As in the scarlet woman with her scarlet letter *A* for adultery. In many cultures, it signifies the colour of the sins of the flesh, thus *Raise the Red Lantern* or 'above the door there burned a scarlet lamp', ' Oh, Ruby, don't take your love to town', and don't forget to wash all those sins away with a glass of red, red wine which, in moderation, is so good for us.

As well as sex, red celebrates love. The rose has many colours but still nothing makes a statement like a red rose, no one put it better than Robert Burns, 'My love is like a red, red rose.'

There seems to be so much power to shock in its shades from the princes of the church in their cardinal red and the bishop's crimson to the Japanese flag with its red circle on a white background, the rising sun. Many artists such as Van Gogh and Monet have captured this red splodge emerging from misty mornings. Picasso captured the pitiless Spanish sun in the bullring with blood on the sand in a few strokes.

But just as red is the first colour we may notice in a scene, it is also the first colour to disappear in darkness and underwater. Red is, of course, the colour of our lifeblood. Until recent years, no self-respecting Catholic household in this country was without a picture of the Sacred Heart exposed for all to see and usually under lit. The poppy which flourishes on the upturned earth, be it the fields around the Somme or a partially built housing estate, still catches the eye brilliantly.

IT'S ONLY A GAME

Declan Burke

As a kid, I never had any time for Celtic Football Club. This was despite being from Sligo, the original home of Celtic's founder, Brother Walfrid. Mainly, I couldn't be doing with all the sectarian nonsense. I loved football, was interested in politics and was fascinated by religion. But the collision of all three poisoned any possibility of reasonable discourse.

I went to London in the late 1980s, as so many others did, to work on the building sites. Coming from Sligo, London was something of a culture shock. The frantic pace of life, the multicultural interaction, the absence of anything approaching sentiment – all these I could handle. What was tough was the anonymity.

So, in London, I sold out. Bought a replica Celtic shirt, as a response to the anonymity. The irony of wearing the colours of a Scottish football team to identify myself as Irish only occurred in hindsight. And it didn't work. I came home, worn out by indifference.

The following year, I went abroad for the first time, flying into Turkey. The Celtic shirt came along with me. Say what you will about the sectarianism, Celtic's green-and-white hoops come second only to Brazil's canary yellow as a recognisable icon to anyone in the world who knows anything about football.

In Bodrum, a small fishing port on the southwest coast of

Turkey, we ran into a group of football fans, all wearing their colours. There was a Bournemouth supporter, a Wolves fan, and one wretched individual who'd grown up in Peterborough. There was also a Rangers fan, wearing the royal blue.

His friends wanted a photograph, Celtic and Rangers together. I had no problem with that. And perhaps that's where his animosity sprang from. He knew I didn't take the colours seriously. The shirt was only a cipher to me, devoid of any real meaning.

Anyway, the flash on the camera failed. We joked about how no camera could handle Celtic and Rangers together. He shook my hand leaving, but he didn't meet my eye.

The following year, I went to Coleraine, to spend three years there at university. The Celtic shirt came with me, even though – or perhaps because – Coleraine is a Protestant town. I played football for the Saturday team; on my debut, a centre-half, who looked a lot like a small island, kicked me in lower back and said, 'That'll do *you*, ya Fenian bastard.'

That did me just fine. I kept on playing football, but developed a Northern accent for the various shouts and calls required. I didn't take the abuse personally; by then I no longer considered myself Catholic, Fenian or Taig. The insults meant nothing to me.

I met a girl. She played trumpet in a marching band. One night she said, 'If my father knew I was talking to you, he'd break my knees.' She had nice knees, so we went our separate ways.

The political is always personal. I think of the Sikh who sweated beneath his snow-white turban on a Covent Garden building site; the Rangers fan in his blue on the southwest coast of Turkey; the girl playing trumpet in her Orange band.

I think of how maybe my generation of southern Irish have had it too easy. Playing fast and loose with symbols and ciphers, badges and logos, flirting with the legacy of green-and-white hooped hopes. How for us, all too often, it's only a game.

SKIING

Derbhile Dromey

Every year, a group of skiers descends on a corner of southern Germany seldom visited by Irish skiers. Our trip follows the traditional formula enjoyed by thousands of Irish skiers, thrills and spills on the slopes, frothy beer and yodelling. The only things that marks us out are our green vests, emblazoned with the words 'Blind Skier'.

Our trip is a far cry from the Twilight Warrior image put forward by television programmes featuring visually impaired skiers, further enhanced by an earnest voiceover designed to induce a warm, fuzzy feeling of admiration. In reality, we're more anti-heroes than superheroes.

The recipe for learning to ski is the same whether you can see or not. Start. Stop. Turn. Fall over. Rinse and Repeat. The only difference is that we ski to the accompaniment of roared commands, 'Left ... right ... hard left ... marvellous ... keep it running.' In my first year, I acquired the nickname Dangerous Derbhile, because I skied so slowly and so low to the ground. I found that the spectres my imagination creates are far more vivid than any barriers created by my eyes. But before long, skiing became a matter of course. This year, my fourth trip, I skied with the demons on steep, red slopes.

We have no choice but to get up close and personal with our guides; our relationship is a tactile one. The guides' friendly elbows steer us onto ski lifts, down slippery steps and into ski cafés. It's one of the perks of the trips, the chance to exchange affectionate gestures with well-muscled specimens.

Many of our guides are ex-army personnel, with the typical sighted person's horror at the idea of physical limitation. But seeing us sailing down the mountain helps them to realise that being visually impaired need not be a cage. For our part, the trip offers the greatest freedom we are ever likely to know. As we bomb down the slopes with the wind in our hair, niggles about rogue steps and elusive computer mice vanish.

Our trip may be life changing, but it is more than mere Chicken Soup for the Skiers' Soul. It's a far more potent brew. Its fiery afterglow lingers long in the minds – and the mouths – of all who experience it.

THE ISLAND

Nollaig Rowan

I lie in my bed, reluctant to move. From my window, I see a fuchsia bush dangling its purple-red earrings, hedgerows, a blue-grey house, several rooftops fading into the bulk that is Mount Gabriel on the mainland. Clouds hang low over the mount, shrouding its summit.

If I strain my neck, I can see a splash of blue, glinting in the morning sun. It attracts me, yet I'm hesitant to leave my warm bed.

I have promised myself a morning swim every day I am on this island. And so, I dress – swimsuit, shorts, T-shirt, flip-flops. It's all you need here in this sunny corner of Ireland. I haven't read a newspaper in weeks; no radio or television either, but they tell me it's raining around the country. Ah, the summer of 2007, the wet summer, people will say for years to come, and I won't be able to empathise.

I pull the door, leaving the key in the latch. I'll only be twenty minutes. My bike rests against the whitewashed wall of the old stone house. This bicycle has done other journeys – Ring of Kerry, Pyrenees mountains, lowlands of Belgium – but now, like myself, it sets its sights on shorter trips. Down the gravel path, under the fuchsia arch, descend the hill, swing left under the trees where the dew remains, up an incline to where you can see the inlet on your right, the ocean on your left. I turn left, drop my bike among the seashore grasses – maram and sea hollies. The beach is narrow, flanked by rocks. I am alone, apart from cattle grazing idly in a field above the rocks.

Shedding my clothes is the easy bit. A light breeze blows but it is not cold. There is a band of ochre-brown seaweed, wracks and kelps, at the water's edge. Some dislike this but I relish its soupy warmth like a bowl of minestrone. I wade in, ankles and calves now acclimatised to the wet, if not the cold.

I hesitate but I know that dilly-dallying at this stage is only fruitless procrastination. I'm down! 'I'm down!' I could shout if there was anyone to hear me. The water is icy and I feel my fingers stiffen so I keep them closed tight. I don't want to lose one to numbness so early in the swim. I jump and clap my hands like an excited child, before plunging again and searching for a rhythm. And then I find my stroke. One, two, breathe; three, four, breathe. And so on, and so on.

I'm tingling now, toe to head. Even my cheekbones feel as if they're bubbling, simmering under the skin. All extremities intact. No numbness today. I do several more widths, just for good measure, then splash my way out. My skin is mottled, pink, white and purple. But what matter! There's no one looking. Even the cows have turned their backs and are sleeping in the sun like lazy cats on a hearth rug. I stand and thaw before doing a sun dance mixture of t'ai chi and touch-your-toes. I dry and dress.

And then the journey in reverse. But no, I do not return to bed, although that would be tempting. There are other 'chores' of the holiday – coffee to be brewed; bread to be baked; book to be read; Slieve Mor to be climbed; a writer's notebook to be filled!

SAILING

Joan Ryan

There is no better feeling than stepping onto the deck of a boat, pulling in the fenders, catching the released sheets (ropes) flung by an obliging person on shore, and then push off... and I'm moving! The put-put of the engine brings me out through the narrow mouth of the marina. Within minutes, the exit seems to be reversing, nuzzling back into the skirts of Slieve Foy. The masts of the moored boats inside are knitting needles jutting up incongruously from behind the bulk of the receding breakwater.

Already the boat is bobbing, lunging; responding to the movement of the water under the hull. Stepping off land onto sea gives me the feeling of weightlessness. The laws of gravity left ashore, I am floating. Standing there on deck, I feel a surge of the freedom that comes when you are cut loose from a restriction that you didn't even notice, until it wasn't there any more. Land is left behind.

Moving out to sea brings exhilaration. Now the air currents catch my hair and whip my cheeks as I undo the ties that keep the sails tidy. Releasing them and hoisting each sail is when the boat seems to dialogue with me, 'Thank you for freeing me to ride the waves; to be my real self; to be all I can be.' Now the sails fill and the boat forges ahead, leaning on its side in a beat, levelling off in the reach and surfing over the surface in a run. It goes through the whole repertoire of possibility, and I, at the helm, am merely a facilitator, a guide, a willing witness.

The centreboard cuts through the water, slicing it as the craft is propelled forward. No engine. Only the hiss of the sea, the hum of the taut sails.

I am moving past landmarks; King John's Castle, a grey mass against the sky; a giant sculpture teetering on its sheer cliff-like podium. How it dominates the shoreline! Then past the harbour with its two arms lovingly protecting the small local fishing boats moored inside its embrace. Ahead, the port of Grenore; cranes and ships making it easy to spot. To port the Mountains of Mourne and to starboard the ancient line of tall trees that border the first fairway on Greenore golf course. Then, they are all left behind, or aft, as we say in the sea world!

It is a world of its own as, unlike the land world, to be static is not possible. On board, even when you think that the boat is stopped, there is the tiny trickle of a wake behind indicating the presence of a current, an imperceptible breeze, an ebb or a flow. The constant motion calls for poise and balance from the sailor. Yes, moving on sea, I am at one with the elements. Air and water. And fire? Oh it's there; deep in the belly!

CREAM CAKES

John Trolan

'Tell her to put it on the bill.' I knew as soon as I heard the words that this could be a remarkable solution to all of life's problems, though I couldn't quite believe it. Not until I held the messages in my arms and she had added up the total on a piece of wrapping paper on the counter. 'Me granny said would you put it on the bill?' And out I walked. It was as simple as that. The following morning, I didn't have to be asked. I was up before my granny, waiting to offer to run round to the shops. Haste, or if I have to be common about it, greed, had got me into trouble in the past, so I delayed until I saw how the bill was paid at the end of the week.

'Ask Kathleen how much do I owe her.' And that was that. No more questions asked.

Kathleen was a warm person, but there was something menacing about her. Her irritation hinted this if she had to get off the stool at the counter and walk for something you asked for. Though, as I learned, she was patient about other things. Her hair was always wrapped round spiky pink curlers and held up in a nylon scarf knotted at the top of her forehead. The smoke from a Rothmans, which hung permanently from the corner of her mouth, kept one eye closed. How the ash never seemed to fall from the cigarette is still a mystery. Sometimes, one of her daughters helped out in the shop and Kathleen would sit reading a magazine, resting an ample bosom on stout, folded arms. I'm not saying her breasts were large, but I overheard a rumour at the time that she had to get her brassière on prescription.

When the moment came, I didn't flinch. 'A batch loaf, half dozen eggs… and a cream doughnut.'

'Does she want the fresh cream or the imitation cream?' she asked, without removing the cigarette. The ash warped, but didn't fall off.

'The fresh cream,' I told her and I pointed at the cream-filled narrow doughnut with a line of jam running along the middle.

I had to scoff it down between one end of Maginn's Lane and the other. It took longer to clean off the grains of sugar that stuck stubbornly to half of my face. When the bill came at the end of the week, all that was said was, 'I'm sure that oul wan's robbin' me.' That's how I discovered that my granny was too proud to question it, but shite floats.

I tried a different cake six mornings a week until fresh-cream slices became my favourite. Two slabs of sweet, caramelised pastry wedged a dollop of cream with a spoonful of jam at its heart. I wasn't so complacent as to refuse the porridge waiting on me when I got back, but I took to eating it out the backyard where we kept a dog who wasn't fussy about things like that.

There's something paralysing about witnessing your own come-uppance, especially when it's quick and unexpected. I walked around the corner of Maginn's Lane one afternoon straight into my granny and I remember thinking, I'm glad it isn't the morning. I didn't worry, even when she said, 'Come on in to Kathleen's with me and carry a bale of briquettes out to the pram.' Inside, Kathleen leapt down from the stool and her arse started making buttons. Her eyes lit up and she snatched the cigarette out of her mouth.

'Howaya, Annie?'

'Not bad, Kathleen, terrible windy day, isn't it?'

'Yeah, it's blowin' people over out there. How are yeh keepin' anyway?'

'Well, the arthritis is still at me and I can't get rid of this weight I put on. I don't know if it's anthin' to do with the tablets the doctor has me on.'

'Tablets? Sure Jaysis, Annie! What about all those cream cakes you're eating?'

FALLING IN LOVE WITH ITALY

Pat Donlon

Having spent a large part of my life studying and living in Spain, I was always fiercely loyal to that country and indeed still feel it in my blood. Therefore, I was completely unprepared and taken aback to find myself falling helplessly and hopelessly in love with Italy – so much that I felt guilty as if I was being unfaithful to my first love.

There is something about Italy that is gentle yet exuberant, spontaneous and embracing at the same time. Looking back, it is hard to say when the great love affair really began, it just somehow crept up and captured me body and soul. The things which charmed me completely, infuriated my husband – the group of boys kicking a football in a medieval square with the ancient carved door of the church acting as goal. The almost impossible task of getting the bill at the end of a meal – for them, time is all you have on earth, so why not take and savour every moment of it. We both loved the large gatherings of families around the tables in the restaurants, in the squares with several generations strolling arm in arm for the *passagiato* – the evening ramble that is sacrosanct.

The public signs in English were a constant source of wonder – in Venice the tantalising possibility of the notice which read 'Beware of Falling Angels' and the one in Riomaggiore in the railway station for the lift which carries people up the several steep inclines that it takes to reach the top of the town which announces, 'If the wheather is bad the lift it does not go.' I spent the rest of that day muttering the children's rhyme, 'Whether the weather is good, or whether the weather is bad, we'll weather the weather, whatever the weather, whether we like it or not!' Restaurants, apart from providing wonderful food, gave great sustenance for those who love words: in one small town we were offered 'Rustic contortions of the Family' – which rather disappointingly turned out to be mixed vegetables. They also offered 'Fusillade of the Telephone' – but we declined. The most charming, if somewhat unappetising image came from the hilltop village of Corniglia – where the speciality of the house was 'Dormouses at the Grate'.

The language itself was like wine in the mouth – dull old railway platform is *binario*, and again had me chanting, 'Binario, binario', like a magic spell. Postcards and letters needing *Francobollo* conjured up pictures of a large family of Bollos, and not just Franco. And then there's that song. In 1880, a cable car, or funicular railway, was opened on the slopes of Vesuvius. For the occasion, Giuseppe Turco, a noted journalist of the day, and Luigi Danza turned out the lyrics and melody respectively. And 'Funiculì Funiculà' was born – one of the national anthems of Naples – and let me tell you once you start humming it, you'll need an exorcist to remove it from your brain.

So began my peregrinations around Italy – in love with the language, in love with the people, in love with life, but, as yet, savouring it all without allegiance to any one region or city and always with the possibility that this was just a temporary infatuation. And, then, about ten years ago, my travels led me to the Cinque Terre – five little villages which cling to the rock and mountainside of coastal Liguria – Monterosso, Vernazza, Corniglia, Manarola and Riomaggiore – again music to the ears: here there are no cars, no vespas, no traffic except for the sound of the railway horn in the distance and the chug of the ferry boat. Wonderful people, music, poetry, art, food and wine – what else could anyone ask for? The diagnosis was definite – it was a chronic case of utter, complete and total obsession – a love so intense that it almost hurts and for which there is no remedy, no antidote. Prescription: visit at regular intervals, and do not stop taking the remedy ever. Sorry Spain.

COMPASS

Eamon Morrissey

I have a little pocket compass that has been a great help to me on misty, unfamiliar hills, but nowadays whenever I take a plane journey, I try to remember to bring it with me. Now I know, in a modern, fly-by-wire, computerised Airbus, it is a bit ludicrous for me to be sitting there consulting my boy-scout-type compass, and indeed cabin crew do find it amusing. But the compass has a purpose. It is a remnant, a relic if you like, of the time when I sought to come to terms with an awful phobia, a fear of flying, which I developed. I sympathise with anybody who has a phobia of any kind. They are dreadful things. The world and your own reason can tell you that you are being silly, but exposed to the phobia, your mind and body fills with a terrible fear and panic, and to be free of my own phobia about flying was a wonderfully liberating event in my life. The pocket compass remains with me as a sort of talisman, but nowadays it has a more positive use, for it helps me to be aware of the experience of the journey itself.

For our ancestors, crossing the Atlantic in frail sailing ships was a massive and often dangerous journey. When steam arrived those uncomfortable, dangerous weeks at sea were replaced by just six days. Now we cross that vast ocean in six hours. But the extent of the journey is the same, the same great half circle, as we follow the curvature of the earth. Of course, in a jet, it is hard to get a sense of the extent of that journey. Today, we are inclined to measure travel in time rather than distance. The destination, the arrival time, is the important thing. The journey itself becomes a sort of non-place between two cities. Rather than being on a journey, we are 'in transit'. And that is a pity.

Now, I have no wish ever to be forced to travel in a leaky three-master across the Atlantic, although at the height of my fear of flying I would have preferred it. One time, we did return from America by ship and, although it was a good experience, for me once was enough. I am happy to get there, or back, in six hours, but to give me some sense of being on a journey, and not in a non-place, not 'in transit', is where my little compass comes in. It will not tell me exactly where I am at any given moment but it shows me the direction in which I am heading, and at the very least, that makes me aware that I am on a journey.

Now and again, I find myself thinking about my own journey through life, and I wonder for how much of that journey was I simply 'in transit', just getting from point A to point B, as quickly as possible. Although, at times, it can be scary, at least that journey of life does not fill me with fear and panic, and I am glad of that. But I begin to see, and regret, that there were parts of that life journey I embarked upon without even the guidance of a boy-scout compass.

HESTER

Celia de Fréine

Each summer as a child, I used to travel from Dublin to a seaside village in the North of Ireland, where I'd stay with my granny. One year a girl the same age as myself, Hester, appeared in a small cottage across the street. We became friends straight away.

Hester belonged to a strict religious sect who had to attend three prayer meetings on Sunday, a day on which her family were allowed do nothing else, not even cook a meal.

The swimming pool was out of bounds, as were the tennis courts and cinema, but because we were such good friends I was prepared to swim with Hester in the crab-infested sea, and play singles on the uneven pavement down by the gasometer.

My aunt was getting married this particular summer. Neighbours and friends came from all over, bearing gifts. One evening Hester's father arrived with some glassware. My aunt invited him into the parlour.

'How about a wee drop of sherry?' she asked.

I watched in horror as the amber liquid disappeared down his throat. What would Hester say? Her attitude, the following morning, surprised me – while members of the sect were forbidden to drink alcohol, it wasn't polite to refuse what was offered when visiting someone else's home.

The day of the wedding approached. I was to be a flower girl and had had a dress tailor-made. But my main worry was not about the ceremony itself, or the reception afterwards, but when would it end? Would I be back in time to catch the tide for my swim with Hester?

As soon as the hired car spewed me out at my granny's door, I was up the stairs and changed. Clutching my togs I shot over to Hester's. Her mother opened the door and brought me into the cottage. Inside everything was grey – the floor, the walls, the curtains. She explained that I could no longer play with Hester. Hester had been given special permission by her church to play with me until now, only because no one from her own religion lived nearby. This was about to change. A young girl, one of their own, had moved in around the corner. Hester would have to play with her from now on.

I made my way down to the sea. Some local women who swam every day were already in the water. They beckoned me to join them. I should have been thrilled at being accepted into their company, but my mind was on Hester, on how her family could end our friendship, and on how we could do nothing about it. Bending the rules, imbibing the odd glass of sherry was one thing, but to defy openly their religious leaders would be out of the question.

I never saw her again. When I went back the following year the grey cottage had been sold. I often think of our friendship, and of the girl I was that summer. The feelings of disappointment and disbelief I experienced then go a small way towards understanding the terror and bewilderment I see, in news reports today, on the faces of children, here and abroad, who are victims of religious or ethnic hostility.

REJECTION LETTERS

Stephen Buck

At least you know what's happened when the whole script is returned. You can see it sitting there on the floor in the hall, a useless package in a useless brown envelope, its useless stupid failed self. You should have taken Truman Capote's advice: don't send a stamped-addressed envelope with your script; it will only make it easier for a reader to reject. But a little brown or white envelope is different. The contents of that envelope could change everything, they could 'validate' your whole life, convince you that you have a deep talent, or so you believed until some sort of proper view of the world, and your place in it, set in. It was Africa that did it, although if I had been a little brighter, if I had a little more sense, I wouldn't have needed to go to Ghana to get some sort of realisation of my place in the scheme of things.

All the newspapers and magazines and television and novels and films, all the paraphernalia I live my life through, seemed like so much fluff when, sometimes in Ghana, the most important thing to do in a day was to get to the post office before it closed but after the sun had gone down so as only to be baked by the humidity rather than be burned as well. On the way to the post office the children playing football in the dust and parading in their jaded school uniforms in the yard of the Methodist church seemed a million miles away from rejection letters.

And then I came back. I had written a play about the friendship between Scott Fitzgerald and the sports and short story writer Ring Lardner. It had been rejected years before because, as the reader said, the relationship between Scott and Zelda was too sketchy and not sufficiently developed. At the time I wanted to write back and say, of course it isn't because the play isn't about Zelda but thankfully I didn't. Writing crossly to people who reject your work would surely lead to some sort of mental illness. The play lay dead in a drawer for five years and then, one day, when I had no ideas for anything new to write, I sent it again. There was the familiar drama of opening the envelope, scanning the last paragraph of the letter, looking for the word 'unfortunately'. But the play was accepted this time.

And the best part of your mind pretends that it doesn't care if your writing is accepted or rejected (that brutal word), that it's the work that counts, especially the 'doing' of the work, everything else is just hullabaloo. Of course you would continue to write plays if you knew they were never to be produced, oh, yes, there is some sort of psychological need to do it. And you are so steeped in your petty personal success and failures when really you are living this almost obscenely comfortable, smug, privileged and honoured life. And another part of your mind walks you down to the pub where you can lead the conversation around to your success and revel in it like a toddler in a sandpit screaming 'look at me'.

PEOPLE

ACTION MAN

Cyril Kelly

There are few buildings that harbour as many echoes and ghosts as an empty school. Pause in a corridor of an evening, watch late autumn light slanting through the windows. Motes, like memories, twinkle in the beams. Memories, like motes, swirl up and subside. Apparitions from the past flit and prowl between light and shade. The occasional draught rattles some door with a hollow, spectral sound.

Atmosphere and incident clog the empty classrooms nearby. The corridor is more conducive to clarity. Its long converging lines and concrete walls pare image and sound back to bare essentials.

A snatch of 'Oró sé do bheatha bhaile' swells and fades. There's a distant, staccato chant of multiplication tables. Sleeves rolled up, Stainless Steve swerves into his scholarship class. As the din dies, he slowly shuts the door. Bachelor Pat sees that the coast is clear, sidles into sultry Miss Clinton's class for the morning break.

The wall on one side of the corridor is covered with a chronology of Communion photographs. Choirs of angelic faces, year on year. Those toothless grins are like omens; they mark the end of the 'age of innocence', the start of the 'age of reason'.

When those little lads arrived at eight years of age to begin the senior cycle in primary, they usually remained anonymous around the school for months. But there was one who was known by almost everybody on his very first day. From the beginning, that lad answered not to his name, Tony, only to his nickname, Action Man.

Without ever courting or revelling in it, Action Man was the centre of attention. There was something about the kid, some guileless vulnerability. It added a twinge of sadness to the hilarious things he did and managed to wring hilarity from his rare moments of sadness.

Among his classmates in the Communion photograph, Action Man is wearing a beige suit and a wide, gap-toothed, jaw-jutting grin. In the corresponding Confirmation photograph, taken five years later, he is missing. The word 'missing' is but a euphemism, as if he might have been 'on the mitch'. Unfortunately, nothing as convenient as that. By the time Confirmation came around, Action Man was ... well, gone.

In third class he got meningitis. The condition deteriorated rapidly. Within a very short time, he was on life support. His distraught mother asked me to go in to the hospital, sit at his bedside, 'For God's sake, talk to him' She had heard about some child who was in a coma and who had responded to a familiar voice.

My initial efforts were abysmal. I was overwhelmed by the task. Totally distracted by the hoarse, rhythmic breaths of the respirator, by the pallor of the child's skin. I struggled through self-conscious efforts at conversation. Unsure whether to use nickname or Christian name, at times it was Action Man, then again, with various pleading, joking, summoning inflections, it was ... Tony? Tony!

As day followed day, I fought my awkwardness. Galvanised by the desperation of fading hope, I went in equipped with a roll call of friend's names, anecdotes to relate. Even tried a few faltering lines of 'Oró sé do bheatha bhaile'. But still Action Man lay motionless on the bed. The sheet remained starched and stretched beneath his hands. Sometimes, staring at his face, I imagined the euphoria if I could only spot the flicker of an eyelid, a twitch from those mauve lips.

I can't recall how often I sat by that bedside. Can't even recall how long it took before his mother, almost berserk, agreed to have the respirator switched off. I do, however, remember the bewilderment and grief I felt at the time. That vacant desk in the classroom challenged me every day.

All these years later, I still have Tony's memorial card. From time to time, I come across it. There he is, on his Holy Communion day. There is Action Man, smiling out at me, still only seven years old.

THE MENTOR

Thomas F. Walsh

When I was a small boy in the west of Ireland, the one thing I wanted to be was a county footballer. Under the whispering thatched roof of the house where I grew up, fretful dreams took shape in the tumbling darkness before sleep. Togged out in the maroon and white of my native county, I soared high in the cauldron of Croke Park and fetched a ball from the clouds. Familiar faces gathered round me and slapped my back for scoring the winning point for Galway in the dying seconds of an All-Ireland final.

In the field beside the house, I kicked the old leather football around between the haystacks in the summer twilight and my father leaned over the limestone wall and shook his head. He had played football in the time when men were giants, when life and limb were risked in every game. Somewhere in the hidden boxes of the press beside his bed, I had found an old, tarnished medal: 'Corrib Shamrocks – West Board Champions, 1927'. Old men of the village told legends of his strength, tales of rowing boats across the Corrib in the mist and conquering the cream of Connemara. As I fingered the old medal reverently, my night-time dreams stretched into day and would not leave me be.

But every dream needs to be nurtured, and, like Telemachus, son of Odysseus who set out to find his father after the Trojan War, I was lucky enough to find my mentor. My mentor, though, did not take the form of the goddess Athena. My mentor was the local butcher. Every Saturday, I cycled the two miles into the sleepy town of Headford and bought the Sunday roast. I waited and watched him serve the women in headscarves. I watched him saw the fresh carcass that hung from hooks on the tiled wall and chop the bones on the block. I heard him enquire after the well-being of relative and friend, but I always waited for the shop to clear. Then, he would tell me how we would play, how we would win, how I should train, how good I was. When he talked about football his small, blue eyes lit up, his voice rose, the chopping on the wooden block quickened, the bones were flung into the bin with added force, the world around him changed. I suppose that's what happens when you love something enough. The world around you changes.

Sunday would come and at least a dozen of us would pack into the butcher's station wagon to be driven to the match. No amount of meat ever filled it so much as the human cargo of juveniles. Faces pressed against the glass, we lurched and swayed around the bends and hills of white roads in north Galway, to places like Milltown and Mylough, Caherlistrane and Carntrilla. We togged out under the bushes and struggled with jerseys that were big enough for bedclothes and when the match was over, we returned to hear him talk over his shoulder and tell us how it didn't matter that we lost. We were still going to train. And the next day, we would win. We were good enough.

When I grew up and went to college in Dublin and played football for other teams, I would call in to see my old mentor when I came back, and we would talk about old times and he would tell me how good I was when I was small. He sawed the carcasses a little slower, he chopped the board with a little less vigour, but when the talk turned to football, his eyes took on that old familiar sparkle and his voice still rose in that old tiled space beside the quiet street.

Over the course of the next year or two, I was lucky enough to pull on the beloved maroon and white county jersey a few times. And each time I did, I thought of the outsize jerseys that we struggled to put on in the back of the butcher's van. His words of encouragement stayed with me always. They brought out the best in me. I even won a medal or two and, like my father long ago, I stashed them away in a box somewhere.

Soon, time, 'the subtle thief of youth' stole away those football years and dreams faded into responsibilities. In the midst of some family crisis of my own, I heard of his passing and I was sad that I was not there. The next time I visited my home town, the butcher's shop was closed. People were buying their meat in the supermarket at the top of the town. 'The old order changeth, yielding place to new,' as the poet said, 'lest one good custom should corrupt the world.' When I returned to my own home, I took out the medals and saw his eyes sparkle in the old silver. I thought of him up there lining up with the team of Telemachus and Athena and Odysseus, in his just and rightful place.

Everybody needs a mentor, even the gods of old.

LITTLE MAN

Conor O'Callaghan

Last week it was 'actually'. Last week everything was 'actually' this and 'actually' that. This week it is 'ridiculous', said with a big twinkle in his eye and pronounced as if it were a perfect rhyme for 'Nicholas'. He thinks it is ridiculous that he should be expected to eat all his Weetabix. He thinks the lollipop lady on our way to school is ridiculous. He thinks staying in school until three o'clock and not half-past twelve as it was before Christmas is ridiculous. He thinks the noise his father makes when he sings along with the radio is ridiculous. Just last night, I heard him chatting in the bed as late as half-past nine; when I went up and asked him what the matter was, he said he thought going to sleep was ridiculous.

Our son is four. He seems to have it in his head that four is when you come of age. He has already taken to beginning sentences with phrases like – 'When I was a small boy' or 'Now that I'm big'. He seems to have it in his head that four is the age of consent – the time of life when you get the key to the door. He thinks he should be allowed to come out playing snooker with me and his uncle on Tuesday nights. He really believes that he could manage the car – if only his parents would let him. The odd evening when he and his sister are feeling giddy, he stands in the hall in his pyjamas and my jacket and boots and calls back to us in the kitchen, 'I'm away out for a pint of Guinness.'

Since turning four, he has become philosophical. He has begun to ask awkward questions, although about nothing so trivial as the birds and the bees. Umpteen times now, we have found ourselves sitting there nodding at each other, as if to say, 'It's your turn to answer the unanswerable.' He wants to know what it means to be old, he wants to know why dolls don't die, he wonders why the sky is blue. His mother goes for the truth. Once, I stepped into the kitchen to find that she had arranged soggy pears and kiwis into a DIY solar system. He was sitting on the sideline with binoculars and a stethoscope, looking as if he regretted asking where the sun goes at night. Later, I told him that two men go up every night and carry the sun down in a net hung between their separate helicopters. I told him that they keep the sun in a big shed, in a small coastal village three miles from where we live, and that they clean it once a week. He prefers my stories, but I think he believes his mother.

Since starting school, he has become conscious of his appearance in a way that he never was before. It used to be that the morning after we gave them a bath, he would wake up with his hair standing on end, looking as if he had been struck by lightning in his dreams – and it didn't bother him in the slightest. Then, one of the other boys at school said something about his hair to his best friend Desmond, and then Desmond said it back to him. Now, he insists on wearing a baseball cap while eating his breakfast. Time and again, I am struck by how strange the day-to-day life of a four-year-old is. When he was teething – a couple of years ago – he used to soothe his aching gums by chewing a Volkswagen Beetle. Nowadays, he takes a Wagon Wheel for his break and he alternates between an alien (with alien babies) and a penguin for company. He keeps the shaft of plastic golf club beside his bed and calls it a 'gun'. He drifts off every night to the sound of my grandmother's music box, unwinding through 'The Isle of Capri'. And he thinks you don't die until you're ninety-nine.

In his teens, years from now, he will spend his summers sleeping in until two in the afternoon and shaving twice a day. He will beg for money from us and accuse us of never loving him – all in the same breath. So, for the time being, I'm inclined just to enjoy him being my little man. And I have begun to realise – that four is probably as good as it gets.

DEATH OF A POPE

Michael Harding

I watched the Pope die on television. Before my very eyes, every night on satellite TV he was there, behind the curtain.

And I wasn't alone. A medieval pilgrimage of young people from all over Europe was moving towards Rome to be close to the dying priest.

It was a pageant worthy of Fellini. A great warrior death. And, yet, sitting by the fire in Leitrim, I felt I belonged to Rome, and I felt myself part of this deathwatch. Reality television at its most powerful perhaps.

I sat on the sofa with the cat, and flicked from one channel to another until I was emotionally exhausted. It was a long wait. There was no end to the personal sorrow of young people who cried on the screen and said it was like their father was dying.

And between hobnob biscuits and cups of tea, in this global village, I, too, felt moved on my sofa. I, too, felt a sense of sonship. Felt the uneasy presence of my father's ghost.

Day after day, I watched the window for any movement in the curtains. Any significant change in the light. And each night, after the toil of another day, I put my feet up on the cushions and tuned into the black tied anchormen and women of CNN and BBC.

Commentators lunged from one banal moment to the next with great groans of eloquence. It was a death that typified the man, they said. He had a lesson to teach us, they said.

This was a man in control, declared some Vatican consultant on Sky News at four in the morning, on the day Karol finally slipped into a coma. I nodded at cliché after cliché. And I drank a few tears of whiskey from a Waterford crystal goblet, as a mark of respect.

And by the end of the week, I began to wonder what was happening. For here was a man who had been dismissed as unenlightened, conservative, insensitive, and generally autocratic and patriarchal.

Yet, to my surprise, his television death seemed to be moving half of Europe to a reappraisal of the Christian tradition.

What was it about him? That he was not frightened or helpless in the face of death? That he was not lost in a fog of confusion as he moved towards his last breath in a public ritual? Who was this Polish peasant, Karol Wojtyla, that he should be so important for the world?

In the month of April, in the year 2005, I began to feel uneasy on my little sofa in a quiet corner of Leitrim.

His simple coffin took my breath away.

WAITING

Martina King

The railway station was bleak. A solitary engine revved sporadically as though about to depart, but stayed put like the rest of us. We were all in abeyance, standing about, resting on grimy benches – waiting. An icy wind kept us company. Hopping from one foot to the other, we briskly rubbed our hands together, but there was no escaping that chill. It slunk along the train tracks at one end and swung in from the bus depot at the other, slapping into startled faces with the intensity of a wet rag.

My son was disappointed. It wasn't the arctic ambience, it was that the engine had no smiling face like the ones in his favourite storybook.

'Mam, would you mind giving a read to that, and tell me have I the right day?'

He startled me. I hadn't noticed the elderly man approach, but there was a honesty about the blue-grey eyes that looked me straight in the face, and I took the folded page from his outstretched hand without a second thought.

'Dear Dada …', it began.

It was a difficult letter to comprehend, most words were misspelled and the sentences constructed in a childish manner. She had no job. Patrick was two years old last week, and there was no minding him, he was into everything. It was a terror on account of the place being so small. Himself had work beyond in Bethnal Green, she didn't see much of him now, but he gave her a few pounds the odd time. She'd like to come home, maybe she'd manage it in November, around the twenty-sixth, but she didn't know. Wouldn't it be grand, she and the baby and dada together, and Patsy only down the road? There was a park nearby. She couldn't go there a lot since they were on the ninth floor and the lifts didn't work more often than not. But it had a bit of a stream along the edge and blackberry bushes beside the path, and when she went there she thought of Mama, Lord rest her, making the blackberry jam. The page was signed, 'Your loving daughter, Bernie.'

'Is it today, Mam? Have I the right date?'

'Yes, today's the twenty-sixth. But wasn't there anything else since the letter? A phone call maybe?'

'Divil a call I ever get.'

I handed back the yellowing paper. It smelled of turf fires as did his heavy black coat. 'She mightn't arrive today,' I said.

'She mightn't 'tis true, but sure wouldn't it be a fright if she came all the way and there wasn't a sinner to meet her?'

'How long have you been here?'

'Since the morn. You wouldn't know what train she might be on.'

He must have left before dawn; his were the soft tones of West Clare.

The sound of an approaching train interrupted us. A voice boomed from the PA system that it was the four-thirty from Dublin, and with rumble and hiss the great orange machine slid to a halt. My son was delighted; it mightn't sport a happy face, but this train was long and noisy and very impressive. He dragged me forward to join the crowd milling about gate number one.

'I'm frozen!' My daughter complained. 'There was no heat on

that train. And I'm starving, what's for dinner? I haven't been home for weeks; I can't wait to meet my friends. Mum, Let's go! What are you doing?'

I was looking back, trying to find him. There he was, scanning the remaining stragglers alighting from the train.

He was the last to leave the platform. I watched him return to a shabby bench, and sit there, erect and dignified – waiting.

NANA MULCAHY'S GERANIUMS

Mae Leonard

Nana Mulcahy, who lived across the road from us in Limerick, was, well … different. Always in black, she wore a capable black apron over her black dress, thick, black stockings and laced up ankle boots. Her faded sandy-coloured hair was pulled back into a tight periwinkle twist at the nape of her neck. She'd wind herself into a big, black, woollen shawl that covered her from head to foot and she'd flick the fringed corner over her shoulder – then off she'd go about her business like a black mummy on wheels.

And snuff. Nana Mulcahy was partial to snuff. She would tip a pinch of the brown powder from a little round silver box onto the back of her hand and sniff. Then there followed a few seconds of shut-eyed breath-holding until the explosion. Sometimes, I thought that her head would drop off as she was seized by a paroxysm of sneezes.

She kept hens in the backyard and, by day, she allowed them to run free on the derelict patch of ground behind her house called The Abbey. She sat on a stool outside her back door talking to and caring for her flock better than any shepherd. Well, she did have a little help from the rooster. A magnificent specimen with auburn feathers and a high, black curved tail that was sheened with brilliant green. That handsome rooster hated me and I was terrified of him.

He bit me twice and that was enough for me to give him a wide berth.

The black shawl, the snuff and the hens were all part of what she was, but Nana Mulcahy's greatest achievement was her geraniums. People talked about them in awed tones and they came from far and wide to see them. Every window ledge of her house was laden down with pots and each one was cared for like a precious child. And just like her hens, she talked to her plants and they rewarded her by blossoming into colours that put butterflies to shame. The flowers were a conglomeration of velvety mauve, pink, red, purple and white. Glorious, they were. Nobody could grow geraniums like Nana Mulcahy.

When there was a hint of soft, summer rain on the wind, and Limerick gets plenty of it, Nana Mulcahy knew before everybody else. Or at the whisper of winter sunshine, those geraniums were all put outside on the path in front of her house only to be taken back inside again before a shadow could fall on them. Other gardeners sometimes dared to ask her for cuttings, or the secret fertiliser she used, but Nana Mulcahy feigned deafness and ignored such requests. Nobody, but nobody, was given as much as the tiniest slip of her geraniums. However, once upon a time, because she liked my mam, she grew a cutting for her and it stood on our front window … for a while. It seemed to be doing all right but gradually brown spots began to develop on the leaves. My mam had been entrusted with a precious baby and it was dying. And it did die. That was the end of my mother's venture into the world of gardening.

I was reminded of Nana Mulcahy recently when I was given a geranium just like one of hers. I looked at it and thought of my mother's efforts to keep her one alive. So I consulted an expert only to be told that my plant is not a geranium. It's a pelargonium. The main difference being that the geraniums come from Europe and pelargoniums come from South Africa and they must be treated accordingly. And fertiliser? Chicken manure is best, I was told. Isn't it amazing that Nana Mulcahy somehow got it right without ever having to consult an expert?

WRITER-IN-RESIDENCE

Carlo Gébler

Because I am a writer in my real life outside the prison gate, I obviously believe in literature. Therefore, it isn't exactly hard work spending one day a week in HM Prison, Maghaberry as writer-in-residence, trying to help prisoners to write.

I also believe it's good for me. I need to be in the world. If I wasn't working in the jail, I hope I'd be working for the Samaritans one evening a week.

Because I'm in the jail regularly, I have also occasionally been able to do something I felt proud of. One episode stands out. It didn't involve literature.

Crossing the circle one day, I noticed a prisoner on a chair on the other side of the grille. He was obviously new because he was sobbing and shaking.

The officer let me through the grille and locked it behind. I touched the prisoner on the shoulder and he looked up. I asked what the matter was. He explained he'd gone to court that morning with his wife. He'd expected a huge fine. Instead, he'd got a custodial sentence. His wife had collapsed and he had been brought to jail. He had never been to jail before. He was terrified. He feared assault or rape.

I asked him why he was sitting at the grille. He said he was hoping the MO would come. He wanted something to put him to sleep.

I told him frankly there was little likelihood of him being assaulted. I couldn't pretend these sorts of things didn't happen. But, I pointed out to him, which was true, all the assaults I'd heard of during all the years I'd been working in the jail had been by prisoners on other prisoners they knew. I'd not heard of new prisoners being attacked.

'I could be wrong,' I added, 'but I've never heard of it.'

He asked me what I did. I told him. We started talking. I didn't ask why he was there. I guessed he'd killed someone when he was driving. I talked instead about what to do. I told him not to accept cigarettes, not to accept favours and to talk only when spoken to and otherwise to keep quiet. If he was harassed, he was to go the officers and tell them. He would either be locked in his cell or moved.

This was not earth-shattering advice. Nonetheless, after about twenty minutes, he stopped crying and said, 'You're the first person not connected to the courts or the police or the prison that's spoken to me today.'

'Why don't we walk up to your cell?' I said.

He shook his head. He was determined to wait for the MO. But he was going to be all right now, he assured me. 'Really,' he said. He was emphatic.

We shook hands. I went up on the wing. I never saw him again.

I tell this story not because I did something special or remarkable. I didn't. I did what anyone would have done. I just stopped and talked for a while. It made a difference to the prisoner – I really believe that – but anyone could have made that difference. I just happened to be the person who happened to walk by.

The real point of the story is that it pinpoints what it is we who teach in the jail are really there to do. Of course, we are there to teach. But over and above this, we have a more important duty. We are there to be human. As long as that is how we are, then there always is a chance that sometimes we can do right.

THE LAKE OF BRIGHTNESS

Brian Leyden

You were our first caller, to our first house, that first summer in Dromahair. We'd bought a gamekeeper's cottage a meadow field away from the Bonet River that flows into Lough Gill – from the Irish, meaning the lake of brightness.

Welcoming, gallant and eager, the boat trip was your idea; the weather being fabulous, with Gulf Stream warm seas, dolphins and giant sunfish off the west coast. While, inland, the dogs drank like fish and the fish sweated like dogs.

We sloughed off work and slapped on sun lotion, thinking of this gloriously unreal spell as Gatsby's Lawn: a charmed dreamtime to play house, to enjoy, to live with our eyes closed to sorrow. Not recognising another parallel with Gatsby: that something preyed on you, a 'foul dust' floating in the wake of your readiness to join us in living for the moment.

For the boat trip, we packed the cool-box with salads, soft cheese and hardboiled eggs, bread, salami, wine and delectable summer strawberries. You brought the can of petrol for the outboard.

You had this mongrel, black, fibreglass boat designed along the lines of an Aran Island currach. It was capable of taking a half-ton load and steady as a barge with cargo. But it felt plastic and bouncy without ballast and the engine stalled, unwilling to be press-ganged into pleasure cruising.

Nevertheless, you plucked the cord, the propeller spun and we took to the open water with not enough life jackets to go around if we came to grief.

Heat haze made the countryside blue as the inside of a mussel shell cleft open where Cairn's Hill rose before us, crowned with two ancient stone mounds said to be the burial sites of Omra and Romra: a Celtic Castor and Pollux and the co-rulers of a mythical city submerged under the waters of Lough Gill. A submarine world sunk in such impenetrable depths the lake had a reputation for never giving up all of its capsized, storm-lost or drowned.

We passed the famous Lake Isle of Innisfree that you said was only 'a clump of bushes'. Arriving instead on Church Island, we rolled out the rug in a sunlit pasture full of clover and the smell of bluebell pollen. Then you stripped off for a dip, letting out yelps of scalded delight plunging into the lap of the serenely inviting lake.

You were a determined and a competitive swimmer. But when your head surfaced suddenly, I noticed your neck ringed by ripples like portents, now in hindsight, of the noose you would fashion with such careful ingenuity when the black wave of depression took you under.

In the backwash of your suicide, our grief was terrible, thinking back on that lovely summer and the boat trip; the blissful weather, the enchanted setting, our risk taking happiness in a strange craft suspended on a glassy membrane of bright water over a dark and cruel kingdom of citizens lost to the deep forever.

GRAN'S ANGELS

Carmel Maginn

'There's an angel at my table!' My grandmother had so quiet a way of saying that at any family celebration that required her daughters and their progeny to gather around her, that it left an afterglow in the fall of her words. Their 'homecoming' was like the flocking of migrating birds obeying the silent command of the unseen … their presence evident in the clutter of baby's prams in the front garden and the huddle of secret smokers in the backyard.

At six years old, in the way of a child that gives her heart unquestioningly to those she adores, I believed that my grandmother's words applied specifically to me… that I was her 'angel' the chosen one, the greatly loved. And after her seeded words took root in my imagination, I'd stand in her bedroom examining my shoulders for any bump or bristle that would signal the first sprouting of my wings, and force myself up on tippy-toes convinced that I could fly, that only a grain of disbelief was holding me down. Many years later, when not a single feather had sprouted and my beloved Gran was long gone, I found myself grounded in sorrow having buried a stillborn daughter. I took refuge from my grief by exploring the hidden corners of my grandmother's life hoping that, somehow, it might bring her closer to me. Instead, it brought me to a profound realisation: that her reference to 'an angel' referred not to me, but to any one of three much-loved children who had taken flight from this world long before their time: an infant of nine months; a boy of seven who died alone in a Dublin lane after being knocked down by a bike; a girl of seventeen, familiar from a cracked photo in Gran's prayer book.

In all the years of our closeness, she never spoke of her losses or sorrows, but there was so much more between us now... and so much more to my understanding that in acknowledging her 'lost' children at the family table and their 'living' presence in her life, she was gifting her surviving children with a confirmation of their family history... remembrances that, in defiance of the passage of time, would strengthen family bonds across the generations.

So now I call my own 'angel' to the table. Their 'absent' sister has long been a presence in my children's lives, and their great-grandmother's story has led them to realise that the kind of courage capable of sprouting new hope and new life out of the shoulders of sorrow and bewilderment that defined her, is part of their inheritance that will sustain them when the winds of adversity blow. And should that courage wane, I know they'll find comfort in the loving presence of something or someone, just a heartbeat beyond the borders of their visible sight.

NO PAUPER'S GRAVE

Patsy Quinn

Margaret cried a lot and this was very annoying, especially at night. Sleep was very difficult.

In those days, a visit from the doctor had to be paid for so, unless things were pretty serious, we didn't send for one.

This was where the older neighbours came to the rescue and all sorts of recipes were tried.

I remember the baby seemed to have stomach pains.

Gripe water could be bought over the counter and this was tried.

Another remedy was a teaspoon full of whiskey but nothing worked.

Eventually, the doctor was called. Even the nurse was called.

Their best efforts came to nothing and Margaret kept crying. Sleep would only come for short periods and, when it happened, it happened more from exhaustion than from relief from pain.

It was early on a dark morning. I wakened in the big double bed that my brother and I shared. It was time to get up, dress and go down to the big jarbox in the scullery, to scrub our ears and get ready for school.

As soon as I came downstairs that morning, I knew something was wrong.

My father wasn't at work, the house was very quiet, my mother, who would normally be chivvying us along to get us to the table for the porridge and out to school, was quietly crying. Her eyes were very red.

My sister, who regularly took charge, told us that our three-month-old baby sister was dead.

She told us very, very quietly, in a whisper even, we would be staying at home that day.

Later that morning, my mother took me down the street and I realised she was about the business of arranging the funeral. It was necessary work even for a heartbroken mother.

Friends and neighbours stopped us along the way with phrases like, 'Sorry for your troubles, Brigid' and 'Sure she's a wee angel in heaven' and, still again, 'God love her, all her wee troubles are over'.

There was weeping and sobbing at every stop.

Brendan Gallagher, the grocer, came round the counter very quickly, he put his arm around my mother and asked what was wrong.

When he heard, he took us upstairs to the place where he lived above the shop and settled my mother in a comfortable chair. Mrs Gallagher made the tea.

I remember the cakes were really good.

'Now, Mrs Quinn,' said Brendan, 'how can I help you?'

'Brendan,' sobbed my mother, 'I have no money to bury my child.'

'Mrs Quinn,' the grocer replied, 'you have no need to worry about that at all. The government have just announced a new scheme of grants to help with funeral expenses. Just go and see Gerry McArdle and he'll make all the arrangements.'

The kindly man then took out a pad and with my mother's help he made out a list of groceries that would be sent to our house right away. There would be no question of payment.

The events of those twenty minutes in the home of the grocer Brendan Gallagher meant that we left in a better frame of mind than when we arrived.

Even at my young age, just ten years of living, I knew that my mother's step was firmed on the hard path of Hill Street and her head held higher.

A BOY AND HIS DOG

Brendan Harding

It was the flash of yellow wings which slapped my attention as I stepped from the air-conditioned jeep and out into the furnace of the African day. Above me, in the single shade-tree by the cross-roads, the weaver birds' nests hung like straw baubles from the bare branches. The owners squabbled fiercely as they clamoured from branch to branch, occasionally darting from cover to paint the sky's blueness with a streak of golden light.

On the journey, which had taken me far into the bush, the brownness of the countryside had parched my sight, leaving it thirsty for colour. Hills stooped in conical mounds, their far-off silhouettes hugged the landscape in a progression of dried-out ochres. The ground itself was a single-coloured palette of red earth as far as the eye could see, dotted with stunted brushwood and vicious thorns that waited to snag and tear at any unprotected flesh. But, here, in the tiny settlement of Kavuti – a sparse gathering of bedraggled mud and thatch huts – the flamboyantly colourful richness of the weaver birds' plumage brought a timely and welcome visual respite.

As I watched the weaver birds, I was vaguely aware of people craning from makeshift doorways to see the 'Mzungu'; the white-man who had come into their midst. But one pair of eyes above all others dragged my attention earthwards. There, a young boy of maybe six or seven, leaned on the angle of a broken and long dead tree, his bare-boned dog at his side, posing for a photograph that waited to be captured. I waved, but there was no response. I could only imagine what he made of this whiter-than-white man who had added a new colour to his familiar world.

'*Jina lako nani?*' I asked in basic Swahili. What's your name? But his face remained blank. He looked towards the dog that lay panting in a single stripe of shade, as if the animal could provide some answer to his questions. I held my camera up and made the universal sign for taking a picture, but still the canvas of his face came back empty. Stealing photographs of people without permission can be invasive and even rude, so I photographed the dog instead, who graciously turned my way, as if nodding *his* permission.

On the digital display of my camera back, I held the image of the tawny-coloured dog outstretched for the boy's inspection. He stepped, suspiciously as first from behind the sanctuary of his tree, leaning forward inch by inch to view the image I held in my white hands. At first, he wasn't sure. He moved closer. But with his slow realisation of the magic I had just performed, there came a smile that was brighter than the equatorial sun. Again, he moved closer. His eyes danced quickly from the small image to the dozing animal, and back again to the image, before his wide lips parted and a shout of laughter came from deep within. Quickly, he covered his mouth with dusty hands, attempting to stifle his joy. His dark smiling eyes drank in the picture. He pointed to the dog and then to the camera; look, he seemed to say, there you are, sleeping in the box. His face formed a question mark that screamed, HOW?

Then, he looked around him, and searched for someone to share his special moment, but there were no one.

Who would believe him? And so, with a shrug of resignation, he slapped his hands together and another great burst of laughter exploded from his small frame, launching the weaver birds in a screaming, whirling splash of yellow from their nests, high in the tree above the crossroads at Kavuti.

THE AGOIN PEOPLE

Rowan Hand

We found Seabeach Village on the southwestern shore of Nigeria quite by chance.

Father Eddie didn't think we'd be interested but we followed him in down the rough track road that took us through the sand dunes. High coconut palms lined our way to left and right and the foliage touched and entwined in the canopy high above.

'These are the Agoin People,' says Father Eddie as we navigate our way through the rough terrain, 'the people of the greetings. You will like them.'

The great ball of the golden sun has already started to climb up from the meniscus of the land and ocean to the east. The trees sway to the tune of the wind and the beach with the white Atlantic rollers over the high dunes to the right is alive with fiddler crabs in the first moments of their new day, and lined with a dozen or so dugout canoes awaiting the toils of the fishermen in another day in the life of the people of the greetings.

My cameraman, Paul, will later say that these are his national geographic moments and, with his great skill, he will weave into the tapestry of these visual delights, the tones and the drones, the singing and the other sounds of this great Africa.

It's not yet six in the morning but the people of Seabeach Village have gathered in the palm-leaf chapel for mass.

The women are magnificently clad in their national costume, babies on their backs, and topped off with headdresses in silk and satin, in all the colours of the rainbow.

Father Eddie Hartnett, an SMA Father from Cork, is joined on the white linen-covered wooden altar by Father Tom Curran, a visiting colleague, a man of Africa and of Wexford.

Vestments are verdant and shimmering in the candlelight, the gold braiding picks up the yellow warmth and glow of the flame.

The priests and the people pray their mass together. The language, Yoruba, has all the intonations and musicality that you might expect of Africa.

I am in a wonderful place that might well be in another time and space an ante-room to the infinite, a waiting place for those about to enter heaven.

By seven, the mass is ended and we walk into the heart of the village that cannot have changed a lot since the Stone Age.

We pass children in their uniforms of light blue and dark blue walking along towards the school block just above the high-tide mark. Each child trails behind a giant palm frond, maybe seven feet long. You see they have their school floors and their school yard to sweep and the leaves of the coconut tree will act as their broom.

The child that Father Eddie takes in his arms has some dreadful illness. The little girl's face is a mass of broken sores and we who are not of the strong believing of the Fathers stand back in the same measure as Eddie closes in and takes the child in his arms.

Immediately, our car becomes a make-do ambulance and mother and child, Paul and I, with Eddie at the wheel head off for town and the doctor.

'He is a Muslim man and a good man and he will look after my little friend,' Eddie tells us and reassures the mother.

It will cost a thousand naira, and I discover that the priest of Seabeach Village is the National Health Service as well.

Sarah will get better but it will take a week of coming back to the doctor for daily treatment. Mother and baby will have to travel over the waters of the lagoon by dugout canoe. It is the way and the rhythm and the life of Africa.

Father Eddie, priest of both soul and body, is there for everybody.

Last week, I heard from Eddie that little Sarah was well again and happily playing away with her friends among the sand dunes.

It doesn't get much better than that.

THE TEAM SHIRT

Carmel Dennison

'And here's a shirt you might like. Everyone's buying them at the airport.' My sister slings over the green and white Ireland T-shirt. I'm delighted, and more so when I see number 10 on the back. Ronan O'Gara. This is the best present ever.

Since the start of the Six Nations, my sister has been slightly ir-ritated during our weekly phone calls. 'Rugby. No interest,' she says curtly.

I find it difficult to explain my interest. I don't know the rules, struggle to understand technical points or referees' decisions. No one in our family played or was a serious supporter. Still, the game has a powerful hold on my imagination.

'It just takes my breath away,' I say. 'The drive forward, team re-grouping… not a second lost, the constant search for opportunity, the pace, the pressure.'

I love the TV commentaries: 'repositioning will now be crucial', 'that was a gritty performance', 'the clock ticks away', 'the fresh-faced O'Gara'. Yes, that's it … the O'Gara influence. I hold my breath as the manic pace slows to a standstill. Hush. O'Gara positions the ball on the ground … the iconic upward tilt of the head as he focuses on the goalposts … concentration … step back and swing sideways … action.

Pure theatre.

Always a loner, for the first time in my life I see clearly the impact of team synergy. Talents and individual energies poured into the team pot to re-emerge as amazing strength and skill. I hear that O'Driscoll is a tough captain who demands 100 per cent commitment from his team during practice. Who dares to drop the ball? I suppose those who play team sports understand this strict discipline, but as one who's always resisted orders from others, for me this is something new. And who can question O'Driscoll's commitment on the field? His own performance is often spectacular.

Last week, I completed a form to do with claiming my state pension. The clock ticks away. Here, in the UK, much is made of the baby boomer (post-war generation) sometimes called 'the headstrong generation', always causing trouble, contesting everything government says and does. I'm delighted to be part of that group: wilful, non-conforming, constantly questioning. We have much to challenge and achieve. I heard someone say that politicians loathe the grey brigade, but acknowledge that, as they are the only group that can be relied upon to vote, they have to be contended with.

Some years ago my local MP told me to toughen up. This was in response to my complaint of unfair treatment when involved in community action. When I heard a few weeks ago that Peter Stringer was criticised in the press for a previous performance, I was outraged. His ducking and diving on the field mesmerises me, I see him take on men double his size. He's another of my inspirations and, clearly, like other team players, he has learned to take the flack as well as the adulation. That toughness of character is to be admired as much as the spirit of team play.

And wearing the shirt? I wore it last Saturday during the Ireland–Scotland game as I watched on TV. I'm eyeing it now wondering how I am going to get away with wearing it on the non-sporting days of 2008 … as wear it I will!

THE POSTMAN

Margaret Lee

My sister was in her twenties before she realised that the postman's job is to deliver letters, not post them. Our postman in the parish of Granagh-Ballingarry did both. When we wanted something posted, rather than cycle three miles to the nearest post office, we simply placed an envelope on the window so that it could be seen from the road. This was the our postman's signal to call for what-ever items needed posting – varying from letters to the food parcels that were sent to us in our boarding school.

Our postman was a man of many and varied functions. Ned Dollery who lived in Rathkeale checked into the Post Office in Ballingarry every morning at half seven. He sorted the post with the duo of postmistresses and then set off on his rounds – cycling up Noonan's Hill, turning left at the Tinker's Cross – this was pre the era of political correctness and, to my knowledge, the place has not been renamed. He pedalled across the ancient territory of Knockfierna – hill of truth or hill of the fairies – take your pick. He swung a right at Chawke's Cross and came on through Killatill.

When he came to the crossroads where we lived, he took a rest at the local shop. He sat on the long stool and dispensed news and views. He told us of the Travellers' wedding, how the whole town celebrated and that there was drink for all in the local pubs – how the party spilled (in every sense of the word) onto the streets – it all sounded so exotic and colourful in the Ireland of the 1950s. He was an expert on the films being screened in the Central Cinema and we had the benefit of his reviews. On the strength of his recommendation, my mother and aunt hired the local hackney driver and brought us to see *The Great Caruso*. It was my first time hearing of Mario Lanzo. Ned advised against *The Quiet Man*. He thought that the scene where John Wayne dragged Maureen O'Hara across the fields lacked credibility. Medical advice was within his range – following an epidemic of flu, he told us that the nuns in the local convent took a tonic of stout and mild after their dinner so as to hasten their recovery. Having regaled us with his stories, he continued his journey through Ballyealen, back to Ballingarry and on to Rathkeale. The round trip was at least eighteen miles.

When we were in boarding school, we were allowed to write home once each week. He knew our individual handwriting and would announce the name of the letter writer as he delivered it. If, for any reason, there was more than one letter in the same week, he waited while the letter was opened – in case there was a crisis or some bit of interesting news.

In the 1960s, I spent some time on the west coast of America. I sat up late one night watching *The Quiet Man* on TV. I remembered Ned's assessment and agreed with it. But by now the winds of change were blowing through the Irish postal system. Vans were replacing bicycles. Ned was assigned to a different area – to Ballyanlin, where my uncle lived. As he delivered my American-post-marked Christmas card, he asked my bewildered uncle, 'What's Maggie Lee doing writing to you?' I was still in California when he died in 1974 and, regretfully, I missed his funeral. If he had a bird's-eye view from heaven, I believe that he could identify the writing of every mass card on his coffin.

Rathkeale is now bypassed. Most boarding schools have closed and regulating correspondence between children and their parents would be classified as systemic emotional abuse. My sister now knows that the job of the postman is confined to deliveries – and, anyway, she now uses email.

KATE'S MOTHER

Rita Ann Higgins

Kate's mother had a psychiatric illness, but it was easier all round not to mention anything that sounded remotely like mental. The euphemisms generally used were, 'Mammy isn't well', or 'Mammy is poorly' or 'Mammy isn't herself this weather'.

Mammy wasn't herself for a long time as far as Kate was concerned. Kate was a carer. She got a carer's allowance, it was her job to care. It was her job to cope. After all, wasn't she being paid to do so? She had her own family as well, Sean and the four children. But looking after her mother took most of her time and energy.

About five years ago, her mother started to go funny in the head. She was getting directives from the FBI and Rome. Kate used to tell her to give up that nonsense. At first, it was a hoot hearing about what the voices had said to her that morning or how she had to meet the president of the High Court in the afternoon. Still, Kate was getting tired. Sean and the children were missing her, only half being there. Kate was his wife and their mother. In bed, she was too exhausted to respond to his sexual advances. With the children she was contrary, she tended to fly off the handle for the least little thing. She was there but she wasn't with them.

Over the years, the voices from the mother began wearing Kate down, they were getting louder. Kate was quietly and calmly having her own personal breakdown. The family wouldn't entertain this at all. No carer of ours is going to crack up, no way José. Kate was a carer, she always cared for other people, even when the government didn't give her a derisory sum to do so. And once a carer… It was ridiculous Kate having a breakdown; it wasn't just ridiculous, they weren't having it. No carer of ours is having a breakdown. There'll be no breakdown on our watch, baby. Only, it was always her watch.

Sean told her in no uncertain terms that he'd put up with her neglect for long enough while she was waiting hand and foot on her mother. He told her to stop her carry on, bursting into tears at the breakfast table and spreading despair and gloom all over the house with the fears she was collecting. She was afraid what the postman might bring. She was afraid of the Angelus on the TV, she was afraid of the wind in the trees. She was afraid.

Sean was losing patience with the coper. 'For crying out loud,' he'd say, 'what's wrong with you? You can't even go out the back for a bucket of coal. Last year I saw you hauling a bag of it over the back fence.'

Kate no longer knew what cope meant. It was only a word that was used a lot in the house. It seemed to her to be a very heavy word. A word loaded with stones and it was resting on her shoulders. When she stood up, cope made her stoop. When she tried to walk, she stumbled with cope. When Kate's mother slipped in the hall and broke her hip, Kate ran clean out of cope.

THE BEDOUINS AND SECURITY

Manchán Magan

I approached the Bedouin tent from behind, making sure to cough loudly as I did, having read that not to do so might be construed as an attack, or at least bad manners.

A Bedouin's tent is open to the desert on all sides. The sense of privacy is created through an intricate system of good manners followed by all.

I coughed again, and called out, '*As salaam alaikum*', but there was no reply. I made my way around the tent in a wide circle repeating the greeting until, eventually, an elder appeared, dressed in a pristine white *galabeya*, replying, '*Alaikum salaam*', and signalling for me to sit by the fire, which was burning high, despite the intense heat of the Arabian desert. He handed me a tiny engraved glass of tea.

He had no idea who I was, or what I was doing there, but immediately he had invited me into his home and offered tea. And this was only the beginning; as a guest, I was entitled to three full days' lodgings and the best of food from him with no questions asked. It was the law of the desert – the only way to be sure of survival for nomads making their way through the harsh desert environment. He had to know that any camp he came across would offer food, security and shelter.

Ar scáth a chéile a mhaireann na daoine.

It set me thinking about the whole notion of security. The reason the rest of us gave up nomadic life and settled down to farm was for security. We wanted to be in control of our food supply – to be able to produce it, as and when it was needed. For this, we gave up freedom in the Garden of Eden and took on the burden of taming nature – chopping trees, clearing rocks, damming rivers, draining marshes, ploughing, tilling, weeding, fertilising, spraying, laying hedges, killing predators, building barns; the endless day-to-day work involved in maintaining the totalitarian regime that is farming; the Sisyphean task of holding back nature.

Was it a price worth paying? It seems so. We are definitely the winners – the nomads have almost been wiped out. But who knows what'll happen now – in a world of dwindling resources, where the land is turning to desert and the water table in drying up.

Yet, it's not the issue of settled versus nomad that most comes to mind here; rather, the idea of creating security through being dependent on others.

Ar scáth a chéile a mhaireann na daoine.

Despite their lack of food security, the Bedouin can travel through the most hostile environment on earth, without adequate provisions, because they know for certain that they can rely unquestionably on every other human being they meet. And it's not because they're some peace-loving band of idealists – in times of war, they can be the most vicious, ferocious warriors; but, nonetheless, they understand the simple concept that no one is secure unless everyone is.

THE LION-SLAYER OF TSAVO

Martin Ryan

The 16th of September 2007. Mile 131 on the iron snake coiling inland from the east African port of Mombasa. I'm sitting on the single-track railway bridge over the River Tsavo. The land is sleepy in the torpor of equatorial afternoon heat. It's the dry season, and the river, some four metres across, is shallow as it splashes through the harsh bush country of eastern Kenya. This is one of several side excursions I've made over the past few years on a search for the origins of an Irishman known as John Henry Patterson. There is nothing here on the River Tsavo in any way connected to the puzzle of Patterson's birth and childhood. But that doesn't matter. I knew this before coming.

I'm admitting to myself that what I began as some standard documentary research into Patterson's early life has turned into something else. What was a tedious and frustrating trawl of old files and registers has become an adventure, rich in unexpected finds. I see these finds as pieces for a collage, a memorial to an unusual man.

And, as a bonus, where I have followed Patterson has given me riches like this day in the Kenyan bush. An immensity of solitude, with the strongest sounds an occasional rustling through the fronds of the date palms that shade the sandy river banks, and, from the road bridge some distance upstream, the faint rumble of truck traffic toiling upcountry towards Nairobi.

It was in the wilderness of Tsavo in 1898 that Patterson made his name. He was working as a bridge builder on the railway when two man-eating lions began terrorising the workers. Over a period of months, they killed 28 labourers. Ferocious and cunning, they came to be thought of as devils in animal form.

It was Patterson who ended their reign of blood. He was a recklessly courageous hunter – his favourite toast in life was, 'Here's to trouble'. But the public man was not the inner person.

Sitting by the Tsavo River last September, I eased from my shoulder bag a photo taken by Patterson in March 1898. It shows a crude wattle hut roofed with palm. This was where he spent his first solitary night in Tsavo. He lay on a canvas camp bed, from which, through the holes in the decomposing roof, he drank in the cold brilliance of the night sky. He was a 32-year-old ex-army NCO, starting on a pioneering enterprise. Yet in his diary at the time, he wrote: 'Feel very miserable and lonely and wish Francie were with me.' He had left his Belfast-born wife Frances in England – she was expecting their second child. The loss of their first, a baby girl, in India while Patterson was serving there, had devastated the couple. Equatorial Africa was no place for Frances to endure the ordeal of a second pregnancy.

One month after Patterson's arrival in Africa, he had news from Frances. She had given birth to a son – but the infant had died within days. Patterson was on a two-year contract with the railway. All he could do was write a letter home.

I looked, again, at the photo of that wattle and palm hut and thought of the dejection of the man who had lain there under the high, cold sky at the start of his east African sojourn.

1950S UGANDA – PETER

Nuala Rothery

I was told that the first thing I had to do was to hire a houseboy. This thought had never crossed my mind, as I had had every intention of doing my own housework. After all, the bungalow Sean and I were about to move into consisted of a concrete box containing a living room, one bedroom, a small bathroom, smaller kitchen, and a veranda. It didn't seem to me that I would need any-one to work for me – but I was assured that I had to have a house-boy. It would simply never do for a memsahib to be seen to be doing the menial work of cleaning her own house, however small. Also, if I did so, I would be doing an African, who really needed it, out of a job. Reluctantly, I agreed.

We moved into our brand-new bungalow and, within an hour or so, several applicants arrived at my door. I chose Peter. He came armed with references which pronounced him to be honest, reliable and hardworking. I think he was about forty, and I was a young, newly married woman of twenty-two, who hadn't previously been farther from Ireland than London. My knowledge of the world in general, and Africa in particular, was small to non-existent.

Peter soon began to educate me. He lived in a little hut at the bottom of our garden, and arrived for work promptly every morn-ing. He had a wrinkled face, and very flat, bare feet. He was dressed in worn khaki shorts and a T-shirt. He informed me at once that since he would be waiting at table, especially when we had guests, he would need a white kanzu, with a broad green belt, and also a red fez. Helpfully, he also told me where I could buy these things. So, to the African Clothing Shop we went, and a very happy Peter emerged some time later, fully dressed for domestic service.

My education did not stop there. The common language among all the different tribes in Uganda was Swahili – which was also used by Indians and Europeans when talking to (or more likely ordering) Africans. Peter took it upon himself to teach me Swahili, although he could speak perfectly good English.

I had bought a Swahili–English dictionary, which became my constant companion. I would painstakingly look up the words I needed as I struggled to communicate my instructions to Peter. He would correct me if I made a mistake, or fill in the missing word if I couldn't find it in the dictionary. If I tried to ask for something in English he would shake his head and point to 'the book, Memsahib, the book' (in Swahili, of course). Thanks to him, I became fluent in a very short time.

Peter taught me a great deal. He told me about his life in the small village he had come from, where his wife and family still lived. One day, he proudly showed me the first few tight white curls on his otherwise black head. Proudly he told me, 'I will soon be *mzea*, Memsahib, an old man.' I was surprised at his pleasure in this and asked him to explain. He said that, as a *mzea*, he would be honoured in his village. His advice would be sought, and he would be listened to with great respect.

I was impressed. That old age would be considered something to look forward to came strangely to one who had been brought up to believe that if you were young, the world was your oyster, and old age meant slippers and a cardigan by the fire while you waited for death.

There was an assumption at the time that Europeans were superior, and that we were doing Africans a favour by giving them the benefit of our considerable knowledge. That we had things to learn from them was a very strange idea indeed, and not one commonly held – but I, for one, learned a lot from Peter.

EASTERN ENCOUNTERS – PEMA

Aisling Maguire

On returning from my trek to Gorepani, I spent a week in Pokhara, a Nepali town built on a lake and once favoured by hippies whose trace remains in the shops selling tie-dyed T-shirts to a soundtrack of Led Zeppelin and The Doors. Having exhausted these possibilities, I hired a bike to visit the old town. When I dismounted, a skinny, black dog approached and followed me into a park beside a temple. A young woman, one of a group selling jewellery, asked if the dog was mine. I laughed and said, 'No, but he thinks he is.'

She replied, 'In Nepal, the dogs belong to everyone.'

Struck by her good English, I went over to speak to her. I discovered that she was Tibetan and lived in a refugee camp. Her name was Pema and she was accompanied by her little sister and their aunts. She had learned English in school but her education had been cut short as her father had TB and, being the eldest, at eighteen, she had to take on his business to support the family of six children. I bought several gifts from her, including a prayer wheel and bells bearing the sacred mantra 'Om Mani Padme Hung'.

The next day she brought me to meet her parents. The camp had been built with donations from various organisations, the school provided by the Swiss Red Cross, the community hall by the Dutch and the communal toilets by Americans. Pema's home comprised two concrete buildings in a small garden, one a kitchen, the other with two rooms used for living and sleeping. Her father, a frail, dignified man, told me that he had been a shepherd before fleeing Tibet in 1959. He presented me with a white scarf, symbol of respect, and a string of lapis lazuli, for safe travels. Her mother made a flask of butter tea and encouraged me to drink several cups. Tibetan shepherds drink up to forty cups a day to protect themselves from the cold. Pema showed me the woollen goods she makes in winter for sale when the tourist season comes around again.

Ten years later, I remain in contact with Pema. Her father died two years after I met him and she continues to support her family, ensuring that all her siblings get a full education. They reward her by earning good marks in their exams. At every *puja* – religious festival – Pema prays for Westerners who help her people financially but whose souls are suffering.

THE RIDDLE OF THE PLASTIC BUCKETS

Ian Fox

At first I could not work them out at all. I would find them stacked in piles in front of small shops, usually with two or three neighbouring outlets stocking them, too. They were cheap, saffron-coloured plastic buckets, the kind you would find in any kitchen or garden shed. But they were packed full of things, and often then wrapped in cellophane, again it would sometimes be a matching saffron.

The contents were really quite bizarre: a packet of tea, a toothbrush, a torch, a tin of sardines, a jar of fruit, a bar of soap, a cough bottle, a can of cola, a roll of toilet paper, an umbrella and so on. I could not work it out. So I asked a Thai friend and all was revealed: 'monk bucket' he said with a smile and, seeing my continued puzzlement, explained that these were gifts you would bring to a monk when you visited the Buddhist temple. And sure enough there was a large temple, or *wat*, just down the street.

There are over 25,000 *wats* in Thailand, inhabited by some 200,000 monks. Although the word *wat* is usually translated as 'temple', perhaps 'monastery' would be more accurate. It is a walled compound with a number of buildings for different functions: the church itself, a library, rooms for meditation, living quarters for the monks and even a crematorium. Often a school will be attached, though education is now governed by the state.

Being a Thai Buddhist monk is quite a tough business. The rules, there are 227 of them, would make the edicts of St Benedict or St Francis seem like a doddle. First comes celibacy. Indeed, it goes even further and a monk must not touch, or be touched by, a woman. Even more to the point, a monk and a woman cannot touch the same object at the one time, so if a lady wants to present an offering in the temple, the monk will place a cloth on the floor in front of him, she will put her alms or gift on it and he will pull it back towards him, thus avoiding any kind of contact. A particular problem arises when a bus is driven by a female driver. The monk has to give his ticket to some man on the bus who in turn passes it on to the driver, to ensure the rules aren't broken.

Another key tenet is a vow of poverty. 'So,' you might say, 'what's new? Christian monasteries observe the same rule.' However, the Buddhists take it literally. If you get up early in the morning, sunrise is usually around 6:30 in these parts, and walk around the town, you'll find the saffron-robed monks, with their shaven heads and eyebrows, walking slowly along, over one shoulder is a large cotton bag and in their hands a metal bowl, covered by a lid. People will approach a monk with offerings: it might be cooked food, rice, fruit. He will also get gifts of tinned vegetables, a bottle of milk, small sums of money and the like, which are dropped into the shoulder bag.

When he has gathered enough for that day's two meals – breakfast and lunch – he heads back into his *wat*. He can share his spoils with his brother monks or consume it himself, depending on the day's pickings. The important thing is to finish eating for the day by noon. So lunch is around eleven o'clock, with temple gongs sounding the warning. No more food is allowed throughout the rest of the day. Monks retire to their cells after praying and meditating, by around nine o'clock. Then the begging for the next day's food starts again around dawn. The Thai people take generous care of their monks and one does not hear of any going hungry.

While there are many great formal Buddhist ceremonies, and a number of big festivals during the year, including one where you throw water over everybody else (at least it is hot and you soon dry out), they do not have the usual regular daily or weekly services in the temples, you can just drop in any time of the day and there will be a monk along soon to chant to you. In one rather far-sighted temple in the northern city of Chang Mai, there was a table and benches in the courtyard with a sign in English inviting you to come and talk to a monk, the nearest thing to proselytising I have come across, but with 90 per cent of Thais already Buddhists, there's not much room for expansion.

I was strolling around our local temple recently and was amused to see a couple of monks busy on their mobiles – now where do *they* fit in with those vows of poverty?

MAUREEN POTTER

Patrick Dawson

'We're rebuilding the whole backstage area of the Gaiety Theatre,' announced my architect pal. He gave me a brief description of the project and I was keen to see how the work was going. The next time I was in Grafton Street, I ventured tentatively up Tangier Lane, ignored the builder's warning signs and peered through the hoarding at the back of the theatre. It was gone! The entire stage, backstage, flies and dressing-room section of the theatre was demolished from top to way below street level. Nothing but a great hole remained. It was as if all the years of music, the laughter, the drama and the backstage life had been swept away in an instant.

I wondered what quip she'd have made about it if she were still around. The 'she' I'm talking about is the late Maureen Potter.

It isn't often that you'd work with someone who entertained the infamous Adolf Hitler. Maureen Potter had done just that in 1938 when a child singer with the Jack Hilton Band.

By the time I came to work with her in two summer shows and six pantomimes in the Gaiety Theatre, she was the star whose name above the title kept that fine old venue open during the 1970s and 1980s.

I had performed in some satirical revues with that other great female star, Rosaleen Linehan. Rosaleen spoke very highly of

Maureen as something of a comedy mentor to her and more or less suggested I do a couple of shows at the Gaiety to watch and learn from the 'master'.

So it was that, in the summer of 1977, I found myself rehearsing comedy sketches with Maureen and others for her *Gaels of Laughter* Gaiety variety show. It was produced by Fred O'Donovan and directed (in that anyone 'directed' Maureen) by Ursula Doyle, widow of the late Jimmy O'Dea. A few months later, I was involved in my first Gaiety Christmas pantomime.

Having had no experience of variety performing, there was much to learn. This was a different world than that of 'straight' theatre. The script was not sacrosanct. Sketches were often rehearsed from the memory of the older performers. Some of these sketches, such as the 'Echo' sketch and 'Doctor Fare Thee Well', had the feel of antiquity about them. There was an element of the oral tradition about the older variety people. Nevertheless, if they were adapted to the times and well performed, the traditional sketches went down well with the audiences. The dialogue was improvised in rehearsal. A direction might be, 'You run on left, tell Maureen that you've lost your money, you do some dialogue together and then you run off right.' The rest was up to you. In performance. too, the opportunity to inject a comic line or action could be take advantage of without reference to anyone else.

In each show, Maureen Potter had a solo act which no one saw rehearsed till near the end of the rehearsal period. Vernon Hayden, the veteran 'straight' man with whom I shared a dressing room, told me that Maureen was never fully confident that her solo act would work. It was said that Fred O'Donovan, being aware of this, instructed the Billy Barry children to laugh at the act during its first rehearsal so that Maureen's nervousness about the material might be allayed.

It was not till the first public performance that anyone could be certain as to how the material would go down with the 'real' audience. Maureen never took it for granted. It takes courage to put your name over the title of a show, invite the public to hand over their hard-earned money to see you and then go on stage and make them laugh for two hours. Maureen, however nervous she might have been, never lacked that courage.

THE WATKINS MAN

Tom Sigafoos

Although we didn't perform Duck-and-Cover exercises in the Ashland public schools in the 1950s, we still knew that the Cold War was rumbling along. Yellow-and-black signs in the lower corridors of the school buildings designated the areas near the toilets as bomb shelters. Stencilled cardboard boxes in the halls stored the crackers and American cheese that we were supposed to eat while missiles and bombers blasted Cleveland, Akron and Toledo into rubble.

My mother looked down her nose at the whole idea of civil defence – it was just another excuse for self-important, small-town men to boss other people around. But we had our own Duck-and-Cover drill when the Watkins Man came to our house.

The Watkins Corporation employed salesmen who peddled soap, scouring pads and other cleaning products door to door. They were the last representatives of an American tradition of itinerant pedlars who had walked from farmhouse to farmhouse in the old days, selling needles, lace and other odds and ends that were known as 'household notions'. The actor William H. Macy recently appeared in a made-for-TV movie about a handicapped man who sold Watkins products in Seattle. Bill Macy was endearing. But the Watkins man in Ashland was a smelly old coot who wouldn't take no for an answer. There was something sinister about his persistence. He'd push himself halfway into any door that a house-wife would open, conjuring up disturbing possibilities of rape and murder.

My mother, who was friendly and polite, had no weapons in her arsenal to deal with the Watkins Man. And on a sunny summer afternoon in 1957, she burst into the living room where my sister and I were whiling away the time with a jigsaw puzzle. 'Tom! Susie! Come here!'

My nine-year-old sister began to cry. Mom shushed her and herded us into the corner of the living room, away from the win-dows. We crouched on the floor. After a few seconds, there were heavy footfalls on the front steps. The doorbell rang.

Susie started to cry again, and Mom put a hand over her mouth. She whispered, 'It's the Watkins Man!'

The doorbell rang and rang. I desperately wanted to peek through the window to see him, but I knew I'd catch his eye – people always noticed when I looked at them – and then he'd never leave. We huddled motionless for what seemed like an eternity, the silence punctuated by Susie's quiet snuffles and the jarring, brassy alarm of the doorbell.

When the ringing stopped, I started to get up, but my mother held me back. 'He's probably still out there!' My knees hurt and I had to pee. I could hear the cars in the street. The silence seemed to accumulate, and, eventually, I could hear our next-door-neighbour's kitchen radio.

My mother finally risked a look and announced, 'He's gone!' We stood up and stretched like civilians emerging from a bomb shelter. I looked out the window and watched for a long time while a shabby man in a duffel coat limped down the street.

VALDIMAR

Louis Brennan

Valdimar has had many lives. It may be easier to do so in Iceland, land of the highest life expectancy. It may be the fish or the work ethic; but that is for another day.

His first career, as radio officer on a whaling ship, took him round the world, moving freely between the magnetic poles, hunting in the days before conservation and public opinion brought some regulation to the unequal contest. Then, he married Ingiberg and he moved closer to home to fish cod. He was fortunate to survive when the fleet was caught in a relentless gale, trawlers being ever vulnerable in unpredictable storms, when mountain waves toss boats to and fro like a practice football. A two-day battering left his, the mother ship, the only survivor, as six boats went down in one of Iceland's worst disasters.

Valdimar left the sea and built a small import business in leather goods, an enterprise kindled by some light smuggling in his trawler days. He had an affinity for things leather; like Shakespeare, his father had been a glover. But he went bankrupt in the 1970s when the first oil crisis hit the Icelandic economy.

Now in his early fifties, he was fortunate to gain employment in a public utility where he worked with good humour and shrewdness. He welcomed the steady if reduced income, enjoying the reassurance of a permanent day job. In time, and beyond any legal obligation, he repaid any debts outstanding from his bankruptcy.

He swam everyday, even in winter when the hot pools are circled by thin ice that crunches under the tentative step. Reaching the normal retirement age of seventy, he drew his pension and was off again. Valdimar, quintessential Icelander, vanquished but never a victim, would revive the craft of saddle-making for the Icelandic horse.

The Icelandic horse is a low, broad-backed animal with enormous stamina. It is still in use in the countryside; it is commonplace to see lone figures move across the skyline like ghost riders in a B movie. The breed is the survival of the fittest. In famine times, which were frequent, there was little winter feed for people, let alone horses. Today, the horse is bigger due to year-round nutrition. Some say it is related to the Connemara pony.

Valdimar restored a local industry. He worked alongside his Fás-style apprentices to revive a forgotten craft, to produce a wider saddle for a special horse. Not content to supply his Icelandic clients, he haunted trade fairs in Minneapolis and Cologne to pursue the many riders in the US and Germany who treasure the breed.

He succeeded, juggling limited capital, to build a steady business; He achieved a lifetime ambition at seventy-five, sustained by a love of horses, knowledge of leather and quite irrational optimism. He sold out, recovered his capital and repaired to hospital for overdue maintenance.

I caught up with him after he had had surgery; he was, of course, out of bed when I called. A kind gentleman in a white coat sighed, 'Ah yes, Valdimar', and took me to him in a coffee shop on a lower floor. Valdimar introduced me to my guide: Tryggvi, his surgeon.

In Iceland, democracy knows no bounds.

THE ORIENT EXPRESS

Ita Daly

The Orient Express was well past its glory days when I travelled on it, from Paris to Istanbul in 1971. By then, millionaires and film stars were travelling on aeroplanes and the Orient Express had become just another shabby train, trundling across Europe. But for me and my friend, Valerie, it still spelled romance – a train which would take us across Europe, breach the Iron Curtain and deposit us on the doorstep of Asia. We left Paris in the afternoon, ate a fine French dinner in the dining car as we passed through Dijon and woke up with a hangover in Italy. As the day passed, people came and went from our carriage and by the time we arrived at the Yugoslav border, the French and English and American passengers had been replaced by older men and women – dark-skinned, badly dressed, flashing metal teeth every time they smiled.

We listened, wondering if what they were speaking was Serbo-Croat or Bulgarian or even Turkish. Around them, bulging cheap suitcases, and bags and packages of all shapes and sizes. I recognised them immediately, migrant workers, returning home on holiday. I was reminded of the Irishmen and women that I had sat beside on the boat from Holyhead to Dublin. Though they came from very different cultures, their experiences had put a common stamp on all of them.

As light began to fade outside and our hangovers began to lift, we suddenly felt hungry. A man opposite, reaching into a bag produced a sausage, as if he could read our thoughts. We decided it was time to head for the dining car, only we couldn't find it. We walked the length of the train but somewhere between Dijon and Yugoslavia, the dining car had disappeared. Perhaps our fellow passengers knew something about this mystery; maybe someone would come round with a trolley at some stage before we all settled down for the night.

Back in the carriage, we tried to make ourselves understood, through a mixture of sign language and any odd word of any European language that we had between us.

Eventually one woman knew what we were talking about. 'Ah – *essen*,' she said, smiling broadly, metal teeth glinting. Then she shook her head. The others, understanding now, joined in and soon we knew that there was no food for sale on that train in any shape of form.

What followed was the best meal of our lives, an intercontinental feast of bread, pies, cheese, sausage, pickles, yoghurts, plum brandy, wine. We were urged to eat and drink, to enjoy. And in the morning, we were offered coffee from someone's flask.

We had decided to break our journey at Belgrade and soon we were saying goodbye to our new friends. We didn't know any of their names, we couldn't speak their languages, we would never meet any of them again. They must have seen us as privileged young women and yet they had shared their food and drink with us without reservation.

Any time I buy a copy of the *Big Issue* nowadays and am rewarded by a metal smile, I am reminded of that communion of strangers.

FUR, FEATHERS AND LEAVES

THE ULTIMATE COMPLIMENT

Barbara Scully

I love cats. And I have four of them. The youngest is Pasqua, who, although neutered, is very male and not in touch with his emotions at all. He does not like to be touched or stroked. He might sit on a chair in your vicinity but never on your knee. He is very independent in a 'don't mess with me' kind of way.

He had a dodgy start in life, however. When he was just about a year old, he arrived home in a terrible state altogether. He had been hit by a car and his mouth was all torn. The vet said that if Pasqua had been a dog it would be all over, but cats are very resilient and so Pasqua's mouth and jaw was rebuilt. After four days at the vet, he was released home to us. In order to assure his peace and total quiet, I installed Pasqua in the spare room, with water and his litter tray. Like all good patients, he slept and slept. I visited with him regularly and, sometimes, just sat and read while he slept. Within a few days, he was improving no end, and, as soon as I entered the room, would come over to me and head butt me and curl around my legs. He seemed to be saying thanks for making him feel better. The personality change was quite amazing.

Within two weeks, Pasqua was more or less fully recovered. His masculine beauty was forever changed with his new crooked mouth. But it gave him a quirky charm. His personality reverted to normal but there was a kind of secret knowing between us, as I had seen his softer side.

Unbelievable as it sounds, within six months poor Pasqua was in the wars again. I don't know if it was the same car or if Pasqua, had actually taken to playing 'chicken' on the road, but this time it was his leg. Down again to the vet, stitches and x-rays and twenty-four-hour observation and home he came to 'sick bay' in the spare room. Our previous pattern was re-established and, sure enough, in his vulnerable state and in the privacy of the spare room, Pasqua became a complete cuddle puss!

Once recovered, however, his personality resumed its normal mode. And now he sported a gimpy leg, to go with his crooked mouth.

Within six months of his second accident, I was taken to hospital for some 'keyhole surgery'. Everyone said, 'Keyhole – a walk in the park.' Without going into gory details, it was not quite the walk in the park I had in mind and I came home a very sick girl in a lot of pain. I couldn't sleep for longer than about forty minutes at a time and so both day and night I took up residence on the sofa in the lounge and radiated very deeply unhappy vibes.

Within hours of my arriving home, Pasqua came to keep me company. He sat beside me on the sofa and did not sleep. He kept watch. If I got up to move around to ease the discomfort, he came too. I remember one particular morning, when I was feeling particularly bad, going into the garden at sunrise. Pasqua was at my feet. For a full week, he only left my side to eat and to toilet. He took his responsibilities very seriously.

When I began to get better, things returned to normal and Pasqua reverted to his 'don't mess with me' machismo. But now, in the evening, he sleeps under my bed and, when I retire, he jumps up and takes up watch on my side of the bed. There have been nights when I have woken to find him perched on my thigh just looking at me – enough to freak out a cat phobic big time. But, to me, it is the ultimate compliment.

SHAGGIE

Enda Coyle-Greene

My father, who loved dogs greatly, had been dead ten months and it had rained all that Sunday in the bleak second week of February. I was away for most of it at an arts festival and missed all the excitement.

Despite the rain, she, wrapped up and welly-booted, had been playing outside with her friends. There was a little gang of them that day, sturdy, outdoors children who never felt the cold or noticed what the weather was doing. As it got darker, they began to play Tip the Can, a game with a convoluted set of rules. She was hiding behind the gatepost of next-door's garden when the dog trotted up and just stood there staring at her, immediately giving away her hiding place to the other children. She shooed him off, annoyed at being 'out'. But it was no good. He had found us.

As was usual when she was playing outside, the front door had been left open and, when my husband went out to call her in for the evening, he passed the also open door into the sitting room. There, stretched out before the fire my husband had lit earlier, was a bronze-coloured dog with creamy-white markings. The dog stretched and sighed with pleasure. My husband wondered how Sasha could be in two places at once, when he had just left her in the kitchen. He went in and marched the interloper out.

Three hours later, the dog was still there, lying across the front-door mat. My husband capitulated and invited him in. 'He ate three tins of cat food,' my daughter told me later, when after a spot of car trouble that had necessitated a tow, I eventually arrived home, cold, wet, hungry and exhausted. In the sitting room, I relaxed into a chair, and the dog, really only a very large puppy, flopped down in front of me and laid his big, square head across my feet. He had huge paws. I felt my heart crack open.

During the weeks that followed, I put notices in the shop windows around the town and in the Parish Bulletin. I told the child that she shouldn't get too attached to him, that, after all, we already had a dog, and that out there somewhere, some other little child was looking everywhere for him. She decided she would name him Shaggie.

At the end of the month, I thought it wise to take him to the vet to get his shots. I didn't want poor Sasha catching anything from him. She, far from being jealous, as I had feared, was realising that dogs are pack animals and was enjoying her new role as leader of hers. I asked the receptionist for a receipt for my money, saying that I would look for a refund off whoever came to claim Shaggie.

The receptionist asked when we'd got him and told me they'd had a report of a car up at the harbour that had slowed down only long enough for a dog to be thrown out. This had happened on the afternoon he'd moved in with us.

It all fitted. He had been a puppy for Christmas, not for life, who, once out of the cutest, ball-of-fur phase, had proceeded to wreck a house that was not used to animals. He was really getting into the swing of it in ours.

'But the harbour's the other end of the town,' I said. 'Why on earth did he choose us?' My daughter didn't even have to think. 'Granddad sent him,' she said.

THE BULLY

Kevin McDermott

After a summer spent pestering Dad, he finally relented and brought me to the cats and dogs home where we, *I*, fell in love with Prince, a young Alsatian. That big, hairy lúdramán liked to jump up and lick you senseless. But to my seven-year-old way of thinking, Prince was the most ferocious guard dog that ever walked the earth and, with him at my side, I was going to teach our neighbourhood bully a lesson he'd never forget.

I spent all of five minutes in the back garden, training Prince. And then I went in search of my quarry.

'Right, J. J.,' I said, 'you think I'm afraid of you. But I'm not.'

And before he had time to react, I threw out my arm, clicked my fingers and cried, 'Get him, Prince.'

Sensing my excitement, the most ferocious guard dog that ever walked the earth jumped up and knocked me over. In a flash, J. J. was raining blows on me, while Prince danced around, barking and wagging his tail.

Next day, my pal, Michael, came to comfort me. He was one of the nicest fellows I knew. He was a Protestant – 'a perfect little gentleman,' my mother said. And he had no mother. Well, I know he had a mother, but she wasn't there and where she was, or where she might have been, I didn't know. But not having a mother lent

Michael a certain fascination, as did his collection of comics. *The Hornet* and *The Hotspur* were his favourites, and he brought them over to cheer me up. And then, wonder of wonders, he invited me to his house to see his new electric train set.

You see, no one was ever invited to Michael's house. Mum said I could go, but not to stay too long and I wasn't to touch or break anything. On the way, we ran into my nemesis. He taunted me till the tears came.

'Don't mind him,' Michael said.

And then J. J. called out, 'Where's your mother, Prodser?'

With the greatest deliberation Michael handed me the comics, and then he flew at the Bully with more force than I could have imagined. He was not an orthodox fighter – Michael, my Protestant, motherless friend, my perfect little gentleman – but his arms whirled like the sails of a windmill. And if he didn't exactly give the Bully a hiding, he gave him a fright.

'I was only messing,' J. J. gasped. 'Can't you take a joke? I'm sorry. All right?'

That 'Sorry' was the sweetest word I'd ever heard. Life was looking up. I was going to play in my best friend's house; our local Bully had lost his power over me and I had a dog that might yet turn out to be the fiercest dog in all of Ireland.

DOING NOTHING WITH BLUE-BIRDS

Clare Lynch

Here it is so easy to get nothing done.

'Here' is Nada monastery, Crestone, Colorado, where I'm taking two months out of my year to experience a desert retreat.

Here's what I'm doing with my time.

I'm sitting outside my hermitage sipping coffee in the Adirondack chair watching a hopping bird with a red skull cap move across the sandy terrain towards my hermitage. It's like he's on a pogo stick. (Later research pins him down as being a Towhee.)

The bird feeder isn't wobbling at all this morning. It's calm.

A gentle breeze blows my hair dry.

It's 9.35 a.m. Colorado sky muted bluey-grey-white like a Constable painting.

A plane rumbling somewhere in the sky's vast stomach.

Mr Bluebird perches on the log pile. Mrs Bluebird is probably hard at work in the nest under the eaves.

Cleaning and sweeping hearth and floor.
And fixing on their shelves again.
Her white and blue and speckled store.

Oh now, there she is.

She has suddenly appeared on the bird feeder. She's such a dainty little thing, and more brown than blue, like she's wearing a smock for her housework. She makes the feeder wobble on its upright. It could be because she's craning her neck to get a good look at what I'm up to. She's never quite made up her mind about me. I hope she realises that I've been her water sponsor for the past six weeks and if it weren't for me, that birdbath would have been miserably empty outside my hermitage window.

To advance our relationship, I start talking to her, telling her how gorgeous she looks today. She leans her head to one side as if shyly taking on the veracity of this statement. I am sure Mr Bluebird does not shower her with compliments much nowadays, although I have seen him flying home from work with the occasional insect takeaway, fair play to him.

I enquire cautiously after her family.

'Are all her young ones raised and on their way to independence? Little Boy Bluebird, how's he doing?'

I must confess, I was a little worried recently about Little Boy Bluebird. He was flying right into the hermitage window on a continuous basis and I thought he'd never pull through the training phase. I was fearing a bit about brain damage. I voice this concern to her and she twists her head around with a jerk as if to imply that it wasn't her side he took after.

'Does she have plans for more family?' I ask.

I imply that it can't be that easy for her to be a homemaker with Mr Bluebird being the gadabout that he is, forever slacking off on the woodpile. Flitting to every pinyon in the land to rest his weary butt while she maintains the nest. She leans her head to the other side and I believe the truth of this matter has hit home to her and she's glad somebody understands. Even a foreigner who speaks funny.

To further strengthen the blossoming friendship between us, and to show her that I am somewhat like a bird myself in the talents I possess, I start to hum an Adiemus track. She's fascinated. Transfixed. The head now going like crazy.

She's wildly impressed, I can tell. I build on this by launching into 'Come Back Paddy Reilly to Ballyjamesduff', just to share a little bit of my Irish culture with her but I've hardly got to the 'bridge of Finea' bit before she's flown off in aural disgust.

What have I done wrong?

Or sung wrong?

Oh well. Can't win 'em all.

Maybe I would have fared better if I'd started with 'There'll be bluebirds over the white cliffs of Dover'.

I'll try that tomorrow.

DEEP ECOLOGY AND THE OAK TREE

Dick Warner

I have become interested in the ideas of an eccentric Norwegian thinker called Arne Naess. He called his philosophy 'Deep Ecology'. Some of the ideas are rather complicated and I don't fully understand them, but I'd like to give you a feel for how Deep Ecology works.

Imagine you are walking in a wood. It's an old wood of native oaks. You come to a little clearing in the wood and you sit down on a mossy rock for a rest. You are looking idly at a large oak tree on the other side of the clearing. What, you wonder, can I say with any authority about that tree? Well... I can say that it is a separate living organism, just as I am. And I can say, rather more obviously, that I can see the tree but it can't see me.

Deep Ecology would question both of these statements.

Let's take the simpler one first. Undoubtedly, you can see the tree, but are you quite sure the tree can't see you? In order to be able to see, you have to be sensitive to light. And there are few living things more light sensitive than oak trees. When that oak breaks dormancy at the end of winter all the processes – the initial rising of the sap from the roots to the top-most twigs, the final bursting of the buds and unfolding of the leaves – all those processes are controlled by day length. So that tree is not only deeply sensitive to light, it can also measure the amount of it in a day with more precision than you can without instruments.

For trees, life in a forest is a battle for light. They grow away from the shade, reaching for the sun. Oh, yes, that oak tree can see you, probably better than you can see it and it can also see your shadow. It may not understand what it sees, but then I, too, see many things that I don't understand.

Now let's go to that other assumption. You are a single living organism and so, separately, is the oak tree. Not really. The more we get to understand nature, the more we realise that the real organism is the forest. The forest is an incredibly complicated system that works through networks of fungal mycelia stretching like nerves through the leaf mould, by complex hierarchies of insects, birds and mammals, by a finely balanced rhythm of birth and death. It's a machine designed to serve the true monarchs of creation – bacteria. The oak tree is only one cell in that organism. And, of course, while the oak may live for centuries, the forest is potentially immortal. A strong point in its favour, in evolutionary terms.

And take you, that body and soul sitting on a damp, mossy rock. Are you sure you are an individual organism? Maybe you are just a colony of little organisms, of bacteria and funguses and individual cells, all with their jobs to do. Maybe you are just an ants' nest or a beehive. Or are you a forest?

It's interesting stuff, this Deep Ecology.

FOOD FROM THE WILD

Gerry Galvin

On restaurant menus these days, salad is often described mundanely as mixed leaves, indicating the use of different lettuces, sometimes with the addition of edible herbs which are usually cultivated in commercial greenhouses or, in some cases, actually gathered from the wild. Foraging for wild foods has ceased to be viewed as a dangerous eccentricity, and it is a measure of serious cooking to feature *cuisine sauvage*, as the French call it. I have been a promoter of wild food since the 1970s, when Hedli MacNeice, the then doyenne of Kinsale restaurateurs, introduced me to sea beet, also called sea spinach, which she collected on a patch of waste ground adjoining the sea near the Old Head of Kinsale. Sea beet thrives throughout the summer around the Irish coast, close to beaches, on sea walls and on paths. It is a firmer and stronger plant than its various cultivated relatives, but its taste is much the same as garden spinach, and it is, of course, full of valuable iron and minerals.

It was in West Cork also that I first found fennel, fronds of it waving in the sea breeze, protected by a roadside wall near Timoleague. There is no more aggressive herb, growing profusely in exotic plumes of hair-like leaves. Its scent is strongly of aniseed, which is much prized in fish cookery.

I have been using wild herbs for years. Ubiquitous stinging nettles are old friends and, like constant friends, sometimes unfairly maligned – a case of familiarity breeding contempt! Nettles were a subsistence food during the Famine in the 1840s. Nettle soup spiced with nutmeg, using potatoes as a thickener, is tempting on any menu. A free-range egg on a base of nettle purée, baked with a scattering of grated cheese, is a healthy and attractive-looking dish. All you need for harvesting nettles are gloves, a pair of scissors and a bucket. According to a nineteenth-century family herbal guide, nettles 'taken inwardly in moderate quantity' were capable of exciting the system and acting as an aphrodisiac. For really assiduous lovers, a few oysters added to a bowl of nettle soup should work wonders for the libido. A note of caution: nettles cooked after the end of May are excessively laxative. And therein's the sting!

You can make soups with watercress, always mindful that the cooking kills off the liver-fluke larvae which can be transmitted from sheep and cattle to humans. The simple, effective rule is always to cook wild watercress before you eat it.

Walking through many damp woodlands, anytime from the end of March into May, one is almost certain to become aware of a pervasive smell of garlic. The source is ramsons, or wild garlic, which grows with aromatic abandon in Ireland. The leaves are bright green and the beautiful flowers, with delicate snow-white petals, are a startling contrast to the dark green of the woods. They are a wonderful food source as soups or blended into sauces. They give a distinctive tang to salads, and you can make delicious garlic butter by mixing chopped leaves with softened butter. I wrote a Haiku once, which went like this:

In the wood a soup
Anticipating springtime
Damp, garlicky green.

TREES

Kevin Connolly

What is it about trees that entrances us? That delights us? That grieves us when they are damaged or callously removed? That pacifies us? That stirs within us a docile acceptance of their existence?

Is it their sentient, innocent wisdom? Is it their stubborn tranquillity, sustained in spite of our efforts to create a maelstrom of activity about them? Is it even their inhumanity or the peace that creaks from them in which the universe can be contemplated in awe and astonishment?

Once, trees covered 60 per cent of the world's land surface. Now it is closer to 6 per cent. Mankind has been almost exclusively responsible for this denudation of the planet. We have razed, and continue to raze, huge tracts of forest. However, we would not be the society we are today without having done so. Most of our European forests were already decimated by the end of the seventeenth century and it is a symptom of civilisation everywhere that we alter our landscapes in the pursuit of progress. Witness the wholesale demolition of avenues of trees across the country in the interests of road alignment.

However, this does not need to be one-way traffic. Richard Jefferies, the English naturalist, believed that each one of us should be responsible for the planting of at least one deciduous tree in each of our lifetimes. There is a sense of selfless yet overwhelmingly satisfying retribution in the planting of new trees. It is a timeless, unconditional gesture – a gift to the future and to those who will occupy it. To this end, wherever I go, I collect seeds, cuttings, saplings and plant them wherever I find the space to do so. A small field in County Sligo is now a small wood with chestnut (horse, red and Spanish), alder, ash, oak, beech, birch and the ubiquitous, but no less worthy for that, sycamore.

For the past fifteen years or so, I have grown trees there. Those years have witnessed the gradual evolution of a new and exciting world within the field; the emergence of a rich and varied ecosystem. Birds, other animals, insects and plants thrive and shelter under the trees' leafy foliage. In this field, a quiet world has emerged beneath the lengthening boughs where the luminous vortices of colour converge and dance with the daylight to create hushed secret places. Amongst these shadows glides a universe, the north and south of it; the east and west of it; the latitude and longitude and length and breadth of it; the infinite boundless beauty of it; the four winds and the sacred space of it; the knowing and unknowing and the succulent promise of it; the silence and the deep, primeval hum and unfathomable mystery of it.

Here, too, is the space to allow my often-occluded sense of wonder the opportunity to simply 'be' and to marvel. Amongst trees, regardless of season, we learn to leave the world's shrill voices behind us and to allow ourselves to be subdued by the whispering limbs around us. The poet Edward Thomas wrote: 'I like trees for the cool evening voices of their many leaves… for their still shade and their rippling or calm shimmering or dimly glowing light, for the quicksilver drip of dawn, for their solemnity and for their dancing.'

BEECH TREE

Kate Dempsey

We had a huge beech tree in our garden when I was growing up. It shaded part of the house and left a golden carpet of leaves and beechnuts every autumn. The trunk was so wide it would take four of us to circle it, arms outstretched. The first branch started too far up to be climbable, so we left the tree alone. It grew on a slope so steep few plants could take hold other than a spread of primroses and a few clumps of nettles.

One day, my parents had taken my sister to the doctor. She spent a lot of time in hospital as she had a small hole in her heart. I was left as usual with our neighbours, the McCues. I spent the morning sulking in the garden. It was windy, but nothing out of the ordinary for late autumn. Mrs McCue gave me a biscuit-tin lid to make a miniature garden. I was engrossed in digging up some moss when suddenly there was a terrible groaning sound. Like a giant with indigestion, like a dragon with a headache, like someone ripping my world apart.

I ran as fast as I could to where the McCues were watching. Something was happening in my garden, close to where I had been playing. The beech tree was moving, leaning very slowly down the slope. As we watched, it hesitated.

'Do something,' I yelled. 'Why don't you do anything?' I started running back to the tree. I don't know what I thought I could do. Mr McCue grabbed me and held me tight.

'I can't stop it,' he said. 'I'm not superman.'

We watched as the tree shifted again, toppling slowly then faster until it crashed to the ground in a cloud of leaves, scattering birds and breaking wood.

An eerie silence followed. The wood pigeons were quiet. Even the thrushes stopped singing. I could hear my heart beating fast inside me. I was too shocked to cry. I stared at the garden. The whole landscape was different, the same but different. It reminded me of when we took down the sitting room curtains and the whole room had changed. It was to do with the light. The skyline was opened up. The huge beech tree lay slumped down the slope, its branches in the field, its roots in the open air. You weren't supposed to see a tree's roots. It was like seeing your neighbour's underwear on the washing line. I averted my eyes. When I found my miniature garden, it had been crushed like a used tissue beneath a broken branch.

My father hired a chainsaw, a large, screechy version of the electric carving knife we used on Sundays. We cleared out the field and tidied up the roots. The smaller branches were cut up and piled by the outhouse. We had firewood to see us through several winters. The rest of the tree was too large to saw. We had a bonfire party, setting a fire where the tree trunk split in two. It burned for days, smouldered for weeks. We had more bonfire parties, baking potatoes in the embers and scorching sausages on twigs. My sister and I came in every night covered in soot and ashes. We discovered beechnuts explode on the fire like Chinese crackers and crisp packets burn with coloured flames. We discovered when things are falling, you can't always catch them and nothing, even a beech tree four people wide, is forever.

THE OAK

John Feehan

Beside a waterfall near the head of one of the few glens in Slieve Bloom that remains free of conifers, there lives an oak tree not much older than I am. Its roots are anchored deep in the ancient rock that forms the mountain's heart so that it can lean with confidence over the stream before raising its arms again to the sky. I take the time at least once a year to visit this glen, for the beauty of the place in general certainly, but mainly to be with this tree which touches me in a way few others have done.

It is not a textbook tree; it lacks the symmetry of the mountain oaks of pictures, yet part of its beauty, its very magic, resides in the uniqueness of its form, which is so utterly tuned to the place it lives in. It has moulded itself to, and itself been moulded by, the unique exigencies of this particular place, which are repeated nowhere else: its roots and branches propped and anchored and extended just so to withstand the winds and rain that sweep up the valley in winter, and the frost that can lie for days against its shadowed shoulders. It looks to where the sun rises and feels it setting at its back. The community of mosses, liverworts, ferns and lichens in which it is clad have their own geography, an ecosystem state quite like no other. The oak and I will be together for an hour at a time maybe, not quite in silence for there is never silence here beside the stream; there is always the song of wren and chiff-chaff, and sometimes, even in winter, the heart-stopping, seldom-heard warbling of the stream's dipper on its daily patrol, checking all is well at its waterfall.

It is enough to be in the presence of this oak; I don't need to hug it or chant mantras before it. I am embraced by it so deeply the feeling is beyond, indeed before, words: from the long dawn when the human mind first unfolded to self-awareness in a time and place where great trees governed the world and the new human spirit wondered and stood in awe before their majesty. Inner peace is returning to the place within us that wonder springs from.

I think every tree, every tree especially that has made its own way in the world, has this presence which is the very heartbeat of the spirit of place. But this is my tree, the tree I bonded with decades ago. If we still believed in tree spirits I would worship its daimon at the altar of my household gods. Sitting here with the oak, I understand the awakening which came to the early hermit saints of Ireland who took themselves off to the woods to find God and did, indeed, find Him but not in a way their books had promised, for He (and maybe it was not a He after all) spoke through the presence of the trees and the natural diversity of life which revolved about them and in them. I understand why Colmcille sat for such long periods under his favourite yew, why so many of these holy ones had their special trees.

I know a year will come when I no longer make my annual visit because I will be gone. There is a great reassurance in knowing the oak in the glen will live on beyond me, perhaps for several lives of men, and that although it has welcomed me for so long, it doesn't need me. In a world without trees, we are in danger of forgetting where we came from. Children who have never experienced trees still see them in their dreams.

IRISH GIANTS AT RISK

Thomas Pakenham

Henry Grattan, the eighteenth-century Irish statesman, has always been a hero of mine. When his agent told him that the safety of one of his houses at his estate in County Wicklow was threatened by a magnificent beech tree, Grattan refused to cut the tree down. 'I know that tree,' he is supposed to have said. 'It means no harm to anyone.'

Of course, trees can be dangerous and have to be removed. New suburbs have to be built, new roads carved out of the forest. But people are often indifferent to the price of this kind of progress. Or they do care, but it's too late. A great tree is taken for granted until the moment it is cut down, or blows down. Then we feel a pang of bereavement. But why had we never looked more closely at this giant on our doorstep? Perhaps that beech had been there for 200 years and knew the village many generations before it became a suburb. Or perhaps that oak was planted to mark some famous, or infamous, event. But nobody bothered to pass on the details of the oak's pedigree and now it's gone to the knackers. Our failure to appreciate this part of our heritage makes a mockery of our supposed new respect for the environment. Why do we not use our eyes?

Consider the raw facts about trees. The giants of our native (and naturalised) species are the biggest living things on this island, heavier than any land animal, taller than most buildings, older than many ancient monuments. If a big tree were not a living organism, it would still be a remarkable object. A big oak or beech can weigh thirty tons, cover 2,000 square yards and include ten miles of twigs and branches. Each year, the tree pumps several tons of water 100 feet into the air, produces 100,000 leaves and covers half an acre of trunk, branches and roots with a new pelt of bark.

Yet the tree is alive and uniquely individual. There is no mass production; every tree, sexually conceived (as opposed to cloned), builds itself to a different design – as we see at first glance. No wonder that writers have so often admired, and stood in awe of, great trees. Turgenev, the Russian novelist, said that the sight of a pine forest filled him with a sense of his own nothingness. He said that after a walk in a forest, he returned thankfully to his own world, where he 'dared believe in his own power and importance'. Herman Hesse, the German poet, found trees the most 'penetrating preachers'. As he put it: 'I revere them when they live in tribes and families, in forests and groves. And even more I revere them when they stand alone. They are like lonely persons. Not like hermits who have stolen away out of some weakness but like great, solitary men, like Beethoven and Nietzsche.' Emerson said that in a wood, 'Man casts off his years as a snake his slough.' Restored to childhood in the silent temple of nature, he felt that, 'Nothing can befall me in life – no disgrace, no calamity, which nature cannot repair.'

Of course, a few writers have found the silence of trees not only awe-inspiring, but also frustrating. John Stewart Collis admitted as much. 'Their silence, their indifference to us, is almost exasperating. We would speak to them, we would ask their message – for they seem to hold some weighty truth, some special secret.'

But for most people the opposite is true. We welcome the silence of trees. It is friendly and companionable. Trees make such excellent listeners. And, I assume, this was the great attraction to the numerous statesmen who have admired trees, from Henry Grattan onwards. After the hurly-burly of politics, it must be such a comfort to find an audience that doesn't answer back.

By the way, Grattan did decide to do something about the great beech tree that was overhanging his house in Wicklow. He told his agent to knock down the house that was threatening the tree.

TRAVEL AND PLACE

SOUL JOURNEYS

PJ Curtis

If you have ever headed off – suitcase in hand or rucksack on back – to a sea port or airport – chances are you fall into one of the three categories of tourist, traveller or pilgrim.

As tourist, one invariably seeks the physical pleasures of a short holiday break, typically in a well-known sunspot destination.

The traveller is a 'seeker' – determined to experience and explore a world beyond the known horizon… while the pilgrim seeks a sacred site that will nourish the soul and uplift the spirit.

This is usually a specific place – be it Medjugorje, Mecca or Memphis.

I have to confess I fall into all three categories, though I'd like to think – for most of my journeying – I've been mainly a traveller, sometimes a pilgrim.

These days, I try to ensure that all my journeying – to both near and far – is undertaken with an intent of purpose, heightened awareness and with the hope that my travels will unfold for me experiences that are both transformative and soulful.

The American poet-author Phil Cousineau in his marvellous book *The Art of Pilgrimage* writes:

Each Pilgrimage can be a powerful metaphor for any journey taken with the purpose of finding what matters to the traveller.

That's the key to what I call 'soulful travel' – finding what *really* matters on your journey – which of course can be found through visiting sacred sites, shrines or temples, art galleries or even a sporting or music destination – be it Angkor Wat, The Louvre, The Olympics or Graceland.

What I long for most on any journey I have taken is that moment of 'arrival'. This can happen any time along the way, when the traveller experiences an often fleeting moment of illumination; a quiet, inner knowledge; the truth of the moment or space towards which one has journeyed.

I have experienced many such 'soul-moving' moments on my travels. In Bangkok, standing quietly in front of a huge reclining Buddha; in Chartres Cathedral, bathed in the Otherworld light filtering from the great stained-glass window; watching a full moon rise over an ancient Zuni Indian site in the Arizona Desert; seated inside a portal tomb in the Burren and, recently, while contemplating the frozen architectural poetry and ethereal beauty of one of the many Palaces of the Alhambra in Granada.

These precious moments are true gems gifted to the traveller and cannot be pre-planned, pre-booked and are not listed on any of the official tourist brochures.

I believe that – like flowers waiting to bloom in the sun – these moments offer insights which blossom in the illumination of a soul in direct touch with the energy and sacredness of the space it has been seeking.

These are the magical moments along our way that can transform even the most tedious, difficult or aimless of journeys or pilgrimages.

For, in some mysterious way, it is the soul that sets out on its journeys and we are but vehicles in which it travels to heal and renew itself and to drink from the sacred wells of the world.

As the Author Martin Palmer wrote:

> True Pilgrimage changes lives ... whether we go half way around the world or out in our own backyard.

So, as I prepare for yet another journey, I ready myself as best I can and remind myself to pack that most time-honoured and essential item of clothing – the cloak of the traveller-pilgrim.

In the meantime, if you are planning a journey, may I wish you a traditional farewell.

May the Stars light your way
and may you find the internal road.
Forward!

JOURNEY TO JERUSALEM

Chuck Kruger

As I passed through Jerusalem's Jaffa Gate and entered the Old City for my first time, I found the walls so charged with beauty and history that I walked through the souks as if in a dream. I'd no interest in buying anything, so overawed was I by the sensation that here, despite twenty centuries of suffering, was a city of soul.

Suddenly, I awoke standing before the Church of the Holy Sepulchre. Guides pressed themselves upon me. Street urchins tried to sell me postcards. Vendors ran past carrying trays of steaming drinks and falafels. But all I could see were the quiet tan and light brown blocks out of which the church, or churches (for it's really a conglomerate), had been constructed over thousands of years. Soon, I was wandering up and down wide stone staircases; into candlelit, four-foot-high burial chambers; alongside fourth-century frescoes; into tiny, incense-filled caves lined with the holiest of icons and relics. I found myself in Joseph of Arimathea's tomb; I was standing feet from where Jesus had been crucified on Golgotha, now a Greek Orthodox Chapel; I was deep below ground level seeing spotlighted where the rend to the veil of the temple had descended unto the foundations.

Later, I wound through streets whose names I already knew, like Via Dolorosa and El-Wad Road. I heard the muezzin announcing one of the daily calls to Muslim prayer. Jewish lettering on shops gave way to Arabic. At one point, I slowed down to examine some columns that were roughly twenty feet below street level. And then, with those columns in view, I dropped down by modern stairs another twenty feet, from where I could view at once large chunks of architecture from the time of the crusades, and from Roman days, and from the twentieth century BC.

The next day, I revisited Jerusalem with an international group of storytellers. Over lunch, I sat opposite Benjamin, our guide, and asked, 'Have you any Arab friends?'

'Yes,' Benjamin assured me.

'Good friends?' I continued.

'As good as friends can be.'

'And have you ever been inside their homes, or they inside yours?' I asked.

He hesitated. 'No.' He looked down and added quietly, 'He would be a traitor were he ever in my home, or I in his. He could be shot, knifed.'

After lunch, after a stint against the Western Wall, which non-Jews call the Wailing Wall, we boarded our bus, sped up hill and down dale, around Jerusalem, out of Jerusalem, around the hilltop Hebrew University of Jerusalem, finally coming to a halt at the architecturally joyous Mormon University. Nearby, we saw the Mount of Olives; across the valley Jerusalem itself, the Old City centred in the low sun, the golden Dome of the Rock resplendent, the walls of the Old City casting shadow on the ancient cemeteries and ruins below. And as we looked out the gracefully arched windows of the auditorium, a rich organ filled the hall with a Bach toccata. I wished everyone could hear it together – in each other's homes.

WALKING TO NYALAM

Dermot Somers

Not a single star fell in the Himalayan sky across the Tibetan plateau. No flight-lights flickered, no satellites drifted among the points, like stars quitting their stations.

I was lost in the dark and walking uphill on my own. Somewhere below, our lorry was stuck in a snowdrift. I had slipped down the same slopes, by daylight, years before, running towards the Tibetan border with Nepal. The roads had been wiped out that time. Avalanche, rockfall, floods … I was dubiously legal then; arguing every stage of the journey with armed Chinese soldiers.

Military occupation alters a landscape. There are secret nodes within reality, weaknesses in the surface of things, where contradictions coincide – you take a false step and break into a different world. The blind man's bluff of the refugee. It can be casual as an unanswered challenge, a cliff-edge in the dark, an encounter with a Chinese patrol … In a country haunted by internal space and the denial of its history, these points are dense along the ground.

This time, the frozen road zigzagged uphill into the night, climbing between dark masses and vaguely bottomless drops. It seemed impossible that this terrain could yield a town within a thousand miles. But somewhere just ahead lay Nyalam, a provincial outpost, which I recalled as a garrison – raw concrete, iced-up streets, institutional buildings. A small café; cabbage soup and bamboo shoots. Suspicious soldiers, in slack green uniforms.

But the boot steps, the fast breathing overtaking me on the icy hill at night were those of a friend. He, too, was in a different country. His was the intense talk of an organiser who knew that everything that could be done had been done, and our expedition was in the hands of fate – but not in any arbitrary way. The Plan would carry us through.

He talked of home, of children's education in a Dublin suburb, on an entirely different planet fraught with school journeys and entrance exams. The March sky there would be thick with cloud and anyone on a mountainside would be ankle-deep in bog.

We skidded downhill into Nyalam, into the Rice and Cabbage Café, its steamed-up window throwing a square of light across the frozen slush of Dalai-Who? Street. Our host was a beaming Chinese officer who hadn't a word of any language we could approach with a shout, but surely knew how to organise a midnight feed, with a tousled Tibetan dragged out of bed, sweating away in a cupboard-sized kitchen.

I was glad to be in another country, whether it fitted a map or not. I liked to cut loose. But my friend's family concerns made sense, even to me, who had no such ties. In that dark night, I forgot the soldiers and their guns. I remembered another time, higher on the same Tibetan plateau, when I was newly in love and I watched a shooting star flare across the sky and fall on this remote facet of planet earth. I made a wish, and sent it burning home across thousands of miles of human space.

Wandering in far off mountains, we may not be sure where *we* are … But we always know where *you* are.

IL CAMINO

Kate Duignan

Sounds: sparrows chirp in the cities and towns, cocks crow in back gardens, and hens lazily cluck and scratch in dry warm dust; doves coo, coo, in church towers and dove cots, and storks clack, clack, clack from their messy tangled platforms. And one hoopoo bird makes its alien call.

So many bells. Bells ringing to mark the time and to mark the call to prayer. Bells around the necks of sheep, cattle and mountain horses. The murmur of families sitting in the evening squares after the working day, communing. Frogs croak by the river; wheat's dry hiss in the wind. A Gregorian mass. A Buddhist monk cooking dinner and singing opera in the kitchen. And, one day, I swear I heard the clanking of metal and the snorting of horses, the rumble of carts and the shouts of an army as I walked alone, on a long straight road. As straight and flat and without mercy as when it was built by the Romans.

Startling pop from MTV in a bar after the peace of the mountain.

And footsteps, constant percussion, on dry dusty roads, slithery mountain paths, glaring high ways, green ferny hills, on ancient cobbles, echoing in churches and swishing over grasslands.

Sights: On one very hot day I thought to myself, there are only three colours, terracotta of the earth, blue of the sky and gold of the wheat. Wheat as far as the eye can see, that moves like animal fur, stroked back and forth.

Then, like nothing else on that landscape, spires of dark green cypress trees, shading us from the stark, blue sky and unremitting sun.

There was a wood yard that we passed where every inch of chicken wire had been woven with crosses; wood shavings fashioned into crosses all along the fence.

Old men and women, outside their garden gates selling cherries, waiting patiently for someone to buy. The welcome sight of drinking fountains, and yellow arrows or arrows made with pebbles or scratched into the path telling us 'you're going the right way, keep on down this road'. Then, the sight of a bed for the night in a new hostel, showers and baths and simple creature comforts. Familiar faces in a new place.

Smells: The smell of fields of evening primrose, sweet, so sweet, or the smell of meadow grasses and tiny plants on a mountain plateau and then, suddenly, something acrid over the wind, and when we came over the brow of the hill we saw the pall of pollution of our first big city for 200 kilometres.

Then the shock of the modern world after walking on an old road and suddenly coming across cars and shops and phone boxes. And of walking beside busy roads. And thinking my feet hurt and I'm running out of money and why am I doing this anyway? And remembering that there are people at home gathering money, line by line, kilometre by kilometre for charity and I have to keep going – and I will.

PILGRIMAGE

Rosemary Quinn

It was a cold, wet morning and we trundled towards the coach in silence. Even our tour guide was subdued. In the previous days, we had chatted and laughed our way through the streets of Kraków and out to the salt mines, but today was to be a day of meditation. For me, it was a pilgrimage. I was keeping a promise to myself made a long time ago.

Our guide pointed out Kazimierz, the area where Jews had lived peacefully for hundreds of years, then Podgórze, the ghetto to which they had been moved in 1941. We passed Plac Zgody, Concordia Square, the area where the Jews were assembled in June and December 1942 for transportation to the death camps. A new memorial, thirty-three large chairs and thirty-seven small, with the marks of the ghetto walls on the ground, is a constant reminder of the 50,000 Jewish people who once lived there. And of the 1,439 women and children removed from there in 1943 to Auschwitz/Birkenau, where they were immediately sent to the gas chamber and their bodies burned in Krema II on its first day in operation.

Auschwitz/Birkenau is always crowded. Every nationality is represented in the orderly lines that trail through the museum buildings of the original camp where everything possible has been saved and displayed for our education. We are spared nothing of the horror. Photographs, clothes, suitcases, prayer shawls, human hair, prosthetic limbs, eyeglasses, shoes, even combs, shoe brushes and babies' chamber pots are all there in the glass cases. The SS wasted nothing. Everything sorted and catalogued for export to Germany.

Every form of torture is on display, every form of execution. Polish political prisoners died here initially as did gypsies, homosexuals, anyone with physical or mental handicap. But by far the greatest number were Jews.

We return to the bus. Within five minutes, we are at the entrance to Auschwitz 2 or Birkenau. Nothing has been changed here since the day of liberation. This is a much larger camp built to deal with the huge influx of Jews from all over Europe. Here are the rail tracks where the trains disgorged hundreds of thousands of people. There are the platforms where the selections were made. In the distance, through the mist, we can see the site of the crematoria where the majority would be disposed of immediately after selection. Behind this, barely visible to us through the misty rain, is the little wood where mothers and babies, the sick and the elderly waited their turn for the gas chambers.

We stand in the latrines. We enter a barracks originally intended to stable horses. The clay floors, the bare wooden bunks, the holes in the wooden walls tell their story without words. There are no words. As I turn to leave, I pick up three stones, not, as the Jewish people do, to place on the graves of the dead, but to carry home with me so that when I glance at them last thing at night or hold them in my hands, I will remember that plait of hair with a ribbon, those red party shoes, that basket trimmed with artificial flowers that signified for me a living, breathing person who had entered this place before me but who, unlike me, did not get the chance to leave.

MOSNEY

Donal O'Kelly

When I was about eight or nine, I was brought to Butlins holiday camp in Mosney for a daytrip. Around the corner of the last chalet, the vast panorama of amusement machines revealed itself. I can still remember the surging thrill of it. Then, an even greater shock: you could go on everything for free. It was like paradise. My sisters and cousins flapped into the middle of it like moths to a lamp. I wandered towards the tumbling, spinning machines. The choice was so enormous, I was paralysed. Paralysed by freedom. I just couldn't make my mind up.

There were carousels and swing boats, big, high, well-oiled swings, bumper cars, this kind of swingy-thing, that kind of bumpy-thing. They were like big, garish monsters having a party, legs and arms going up and down and in and out. The whole thing was so fantastic it was overwhelming.

I had to sit down. There was a little wooden kerb. I sat down to try to gather my wits and figure out what I should do. I raised my eyes to look up at the sky. And that was when I saw it. It was the most beautiful thing.

A window up high in a concrete wall. And people were swimming in it. They were underwater, whooping around and treading water, diving into view and swimming out again. It was mesmerising.

I couldn't drag myself away. I watched for hours. My mother and my aunt tried to encourage me to try a few things. But all I wanted was to look at the people swimming in the window. I figured out who was friends with whom; who was whose daddy; and that two of them were boyfriend and girlfriend because he kept smiling at her underneath the water. I think he was trying to talk because bubbles came out of his mouth. And they all bobbed around up there, under the water, doing some of kind of crazy slow-motion acrobatics and holding their breaths.

Recently, I had reason to go back to that holiday camp in Mosney for the first time since that day in the mid-1960s. It was to see the ballroom, with a view to putting on a performance of Roddy Doyle's play *Guess Who's Coming for the Dinner* by Calypso. Roddy's play is about a girl bringing a Nigerian asylum-seeker to her Dublin home to meet her father. It's funny. It's also timely and provocative.

What was Butlins Mosney is now the Asylum-Seekers' Dispersal Centre, Mosney. Five hundred people live there. No free monster-machine parties now. And I couldn't find the underwater window. But there were people of over forty nationalities. Every colour of the human rainbow. Some looking well-installed, making the best of it presumably. Some walking slowly like ghosts.

The disused ballroom echoes with the voices and big-band sounds of the 1960s and 1970s. The beautiful parquet oak floor is pockmarked with the swivels of countless stilettos. In the dim work-lights it laps in silence like a calm dark sea.

Outside, the involuntary residents from across the seas exist as best they can. They have full board, which means breakfast, dinner and tea, and television in every chalet. They also receive fifteen pounds per week for incidental expenses. And a bus goes to Drogheda daily, where the nearest library is. The atmosphere is a bit different from the throbbing excitement of thirty-odd years ago.

One of the residents I spoke to has been there ten months, with still no date set for an interview to assess his claim for political asylum. Apart from wanting a cap placed on the length of time one has to wait, his biggest worry is to be sent to another dispersal centre. The people who have been in Mosney for any length of time know that it's the best they can expect under the terms of the Department of Justice's direct provision and dispersal policy. They are afraid that they could be sent to a caravan in Kildare Barracks or in the middle of nowhere outside Athlone. Or worse. Word travels fast among people in trouble. Especially bad word. And there are dispersal centres in Ireland, far away from Mosney, far away from home, where vulnerable people dread to be sent.

THE CLADDAGH

Fred Johnston

In autumn, the light over Galway Bay is unique and mysterious. On a particularly magical day, the water glass-smooth, the air charged with an otherworldly silence, you wait with a growing feeling of expectation: something is about to happen at the edge of imagination's eye.

A door has opened, admitting this blue-gold light. It settles over the silver, rustling water. Over the bay, the hills of Clare tremble in their dreaming sleep. A seabird, unsure of itself, flicks over the water and climbs upwards quickly, secure in higher air. The elements of air, earth, water and fire have combined to reveal a new world: everything around you has changed; a sudden and natural alchemy has altered the colour and texture of grass, water, rock. Too soon, everything reverts to a quiet ordinariness – what we have come to consider as the real. But for that handful of moments, we had been given a glimpse of something eternal.

On one such evening, I walked under Spanish Arch, down Long Walk, the old harbour of the Claddagh on my right, the waters of the river rushing below me into the bay. Into the mouth of the harbour and the river came a small boat, a *púcán*, its sails tilting and full, gulping up every morsel of breeze out of the falling stillness. The motion of the boat, its full-sailed grace and dignity, made me stop and watch. Small voices drifted over the water. The boat curved and arced into the shelter of the harbour, coming home, natural in its every movement. The rust-red sails clapped in the breaths of wind, a sound of applause; the shiny, black hull slid like a black beetle over the skin of the harbour. I was filled with an excited sense of vision, as if I were seeing something of great significance; as if such a moment would never come again. I was grateful to the boat, to the unknown men who crewed her; I envied them. Later, I wrote a poem, 'Boat Dreaming', in which I gave the boat a human voice and let her explain herself.

> I am what is on the sea
> and below the sea and above the sea:
> the sun is roped to my shoulder,
> black my Pythagorean sail,
> the wind is the breath
> of the world in sleep –
> I am hailed by name from the stone quay.
>
> Now I lean over to let
> the last hour of light wash the air;
> nets of gulls are flung over me
> I snuggle under a soft lather
> of chimney-smoke:
> my belly is full of ballast-stones,
> I am closed up and put away like something holy.

Sometimes we are witness to small sacraments, ordinary things made extraordinary. How many, in our everyday, do we not see?

THE CARS OF CAPE CLEAR

William Wall

They bring dying cars to the island but they never bring them back. Why should they? Who would bring even a half-decent car out here to be eaten alive by the wind?

But, somehow, they keep them moving. Someone keeps them alive, a magic hand that reaches under the hood and fiddles with the innards, a car surgeon, an island ER specialist with a gift for keeping the heart going when the flesh has long since succumbed to decay.

Here the normal process of life is reversed. It is not the heart that goes first: the heart and soul live on after the flesh has become so frail that the Atlantic storms whistle through it unimpeded.

On a bad day, you could stay forever.

This is Cape Clear Island in November. The sea rears up and drops on the broken southwest shore and foam mounts the wind and balloons over the island, falling soft as snow on the Gascanane. You could be forgiven for thinking that no boat will ever again brave the maelstrom that is the channel inside Oileán na nÉan. Away over at Long Island, you can see a reverse waterfall of white water climbing into the air: and the Skeams have disappeared altogether.

The improbable cars come down the hill with all the aplomb of bar-room boys showing a card trick – BMWs, Fords, Mercs,

Volkswagens – held together by rust and willpower. They disgorge their drivers – mere children sometimes – and everyone waits at the pier, watching, talking.

The ferry *does* come because things are never as bad as they look from shore, and the sea is a way of life out here. There has always been a worse day, higher seas, heavier wind. Islands have long memories.

She slips into the calm of the harbour: a man in the bow makes a graceful gesture and a rope flies from his hands and is caught and tied off. The passengers are mostly children because this is Friday and they are coming home from school over in Ireland, what we mainlanders call the mainland.

They are taken into the cars and swallowed in clouds of blue smoke. The gears scream and the engines rev, and they throw themselves at the hills with ferocity. A car here will spend most of its life in second gear because the island is all climbing or falling, steep gradients that would break the heart of a mainlander in a matter of weeks.

Out here, you have to learn to live life in the lower ratio: slower, simpler, but stronger, more deliberate, deeper too.

There are dead cars everywhere, blocking gaps, slowly being absorbed into dry-stone walls, sheltering hens. Left long enough, we think they will calcify and become stone themselves. The island bears up under the burden of its dead but I can think of few places where the fabric that shelters the soul has been worn so thin.

The survivors are indomitable. Fewer than 100 people live here in winter. Their way of life seems unnecessarily simple, unbearably complicated. Nothing comes here that is not brought. There is no passing trade. The only stray visitors are migratory birds for whom the island is a staging point, a transfer on the air route to warmer climes. And an occasional demented writer and his family.

A VIEW FROM THE BRIDGE

David Rowell

I'm standing on the spectacular new suspension bridge which soars over the road junction at Dundrum. It's a wonderful view but, this morning, the wind coming down off Three Rock would skin you. I turn my collar up and look towards the long line of hills which frame Dundrum to the south. The hills have not changed over the years – except for the television and mobile phone masts, like the few last spikes on a balding hedgehog.

I turn as one of the new Luas trams full of commuters glides across the bridge, heading for town. I wonder whether the passengers are wearing their screen-saver faces. This 'touch me not' look seems to have developed in Dublin over the past few years, although maybe they'll be more open to social engagement on the journey home. I look northwards towards the city and see the Spire in the distance. This new view, hitherto available only to high-flying hawks, puts the structure of the village in perspective and shows its transformation. Forty years ago, it was one of the last outposts of Dublin with fields stretching out southwards; now it's a major suburban hub.

The main street has maintained its shape, winding gently uphill, but modern shop fronts have long replaced the more traditional ones. It was to this village that the mountain men and women came down on Saturday evenings to buy provisions for the following week. Shops stayed open late for the sheep farmers from Ticknock, the stone cutters from Ballyedmonduff, and their wives and families. Fulfilling the gender roles appropriate to the time, the men secured the horses and carts to lampposts while the women purchased the groceries, afterwards joining their menfolk in the pub. It is no surprise to learn, as in all similar stories, that the horses knew their way home. Today, bankers with BMWs live in the converted stone-cutters' cottages. Very few sheep farmers remain, and they probably do their weekend shop on the net.

The new bridge has ruined the privacy of the old graveyard which surrounds the little church of St Nahi. High walls used to keep the occupants in their proper degree of seclusion, but, now, there is nothing to protect them from the scrutiny of the curious, looking down on them from on high. We, the living, can keep a bird's eye on any improper or unusual events taking place, and make sure the inhabitants are getting enough rest. Even the gentleman of the roads, who occasionally props himself up against a sunny gravestone for a slug of *vin ordinaire*, must now feel vulnerable to the public gaze.

The Luas tramway, of which this bridge is a notable landmark, uses part of the route of the old railway line which ran from Harcourt Street in Dublin to Bray. The bridge is dedicated to William Dargan, engineer and founder of the railway system in Ireland, who was appointed contractor for the building of the line. While supervising the construction, he noticed the nearby Mount Anville House and estate was for sale. He bought it, going on to live there and farm it extensively for many years. On the site today is a school for girls.

Queen Victoria, in town for the Dublin Exhibition of 1853, visited Mount Anville and offered Mr Dargan a baronetcy. He graciously declined the offer – there are no reports on whether or not herself was amused.

FOOD AND NATIONALITY

Paolo Tullio

Perhaps the biggest difference between the Irish and the Italians is their attitude to food. In the almost entirely secular state of Italy, food is the nearest thing to a religion. It's as commonly part of conversation as the weather is here. It's all-pervasive, it's all-consuming but, most of all, it's very good.

Much of the time spent during the day is devoted to food, not just preparing it but also buying it. Watch an Italian woman buying fruit. She won't even contemplate picking up a ready-made bag with a kilo of oranges in it. She'll pick up oranges from a pile, one at a time, squeeze each one, check for blemishes and slowly put together her choice. This is repeated for all the vegetables that she needs. Everything is examined minutely; only produce that fits her exacting standards will be bought. Time spent on selection is not considered time wasted; it is important to ensure that food quality is of the finest possible.

Huge bakeries with fleets of vans supplying bread for a fifty-mile radius are unheard of. Even tiny villages have their own bakery so that fresh bread can be bought twice a day. Italian bread has the same property as French bread, it goes hard quickly, so supplies are bought little and often. Despite the fact that there is a bakery in every village, people still travel to find the best bread. There is a bakery in the next town to mine known as Cessinella which has a permanent queue. People from villages at the other end of valley come here to buy bread and pizza, passing four or five bakeries on the way. Quality is appreciated and no effort is too much to seek it out.

Living in Ireland, where fish is plentiful, cheap and almost completely unappreciated, I find the Italian attitude to fish remarkable. In Italy, fish is a treat, a special food for special occasions, and not a penance for Fridays. It is also expensive; a meal in a restaurant will double in price when fish is served. For an honoured guest at dinner, the menu will certainly contain fish, or will be entirely composed of it. Again, time and trouble are no obstacle when it comes to obtaining it. Although it can be bought frozen in supermarkets or fresh in the markets, it is not unusual for people in our valley to drive to Formia or Gaeta, an eighty-mile round trip, to buy their fish at the quayside. Nobody considers this exceptional or extreme behaviour. How else can you be sure the fish is as fresh as possible?

What it all comes down to is that Italians believe food is important. Its supply and preparation forms a large part of their day. They really believe that quality in the ingredients is paramount, and they'll spare no effort to ensure they get the best. And when you think about it, it makes sense. Food is the one sensory pleasure that can be enjoyed several times a day, right up to the day of our demise.

HUMAN WISHES

Gerald Dawe

The concluding poem in my book, *The Morning Train*, is called 'Human Wishes'. Living in Dun Laoghaire it is hard not to realise just how close we are on this island to Wales and England and further south, to the European continent. The seas bridge not separate.

On Sunday walks to Sandycove I often see the ferries come and go out of Dublin Bay, and the stroll takes us along Victorian terraces, villas and parades, many converted into offices and apartments, fast-food outlets, pound shops, some ugly facades and uglier shop fronts, until you reach the People's Park and the vista across the full Bay is stunning. The redbrick suburbia behind stretches into the Dublin hills but it could well be the north Belfast of my childhood in the 1950s.

'Human Wishes', a hymn to the everyday world we all inhabit, is mindful of those excluded from so much of what is taken for granted in the brave new Ireland. I imagine this suburban landscape as a kind of glorious place – its beauty concealed, its imagery splendid and, in its own way, its interior life both vulnerable and spectacular.

But we can be consumed by all this – as history and civic priorities are lost sight of in the brash egotism of the tigerish economy of today's Ireland. Language, poetry, dare I say, art, becomes just another product, bought and sold at the going rate and with, at times, a politics to match.

Human Wishes

Gulls have the best of both worlds here –
the last remaining trawlers ditch
the unsaleable back into the sea
and, when they're not out, skips are gone through.

Families unsure what to do for the day
walk about or stand along the east pier
convinced that all is well, pointing at Howth
to queries about what's over there.

The ferry crosses to the North Wall
but is it really moving? We brace ourselves
against this gusting wind and hail.
The DART shuttles under bridges like a toy train.

Ladies and gentlemen of the People's Park,
hooded lads beyond in the bus shelter,
those well-to-do and those who barely
keep their heads above water –

do we live our lives in vain?
A dog checks along the cold sea-front;
old married couples get on with it.
This is a homecoming of sorts.

Scuba divers at the Forty Foot
bob and duck like seals
caught in the drifting nets.
The coast is clear. Wales

and England ride on the tide;
the sky is laced with jet trails.
By the time we reach the Baths
the aquamarine has turned ice-blue

'Dear God, such a shocking murder.
How was he ever allowed out?
We're off to France this year. And you?'
And you? And you? And you?

Our selves dissolve into side streets,
arm-in-arm, ever so lightly, we go
past the buggy that's been left behind –
the supermarket trolley, the beer-kegs,

the fast-food cartons, the pavements
and kerbstones rooted up by trees,
the white carrier bag snagged in the breeze;
the artisans' cottages, the old lady's open door,

the turn-of-the-century family grocer –
we bring back in with us the brash air
as the gasmen's barrels take off down the street,
the wind bends back our strange mimosa tree

and smashes against these paper-thin windows.
Sun-burst is the breaking cloud-cover upstairs.
Myself and the shoemaker have curtains pulled,
not quite enough, so you can see what

movement there is, inside and out.
He, too, has the radio on, I don't doubt.

*

A squashed cider-flagon rattles around
the back-lane, the sky races overhead
and the churlish sea explodes;
we contain ourselves as best we can:

the green light of the deep freeze,
the microwave's skinny digits,
the mobile phone on its life-line,
the alarm panel keyed in, the cat's eye

dashboard of the answering machine
and whoever's voice is leaving word.

THE GROTTO

Mary Gilroy Johnson

The Grotto of Our Lady of Lourdes stood at the southwest corner of our parish church of St Patrick.

High in the rockery, standing in the nook with her eyes raised heavenwards stood the statue of Our Lady. In every season, the rockery was a cornucopia of colour: purple pansies, pink ground roses, evergreen of every hue, hyacinth, snowdrops in spring, viola and golden marigolds in autumn.

Surrounding the grotto was a white-painted stone altar rail, broken at the corner by a locked wooden gate, painted blue. To linger at the grotto was to be in silence. The passing traffic, the shouts of the altar boys playing 'tag' around the church never seemed to disturb the tranquillity of the sacred space.

Every year the May Procession in honour of Our Lady ended with the priest walking through the grotto; in through the open, blue-painted gate and out through the iron gate just beyond the shrine.

Only those who had made First Holy Communion were allowed to walk through the grotto at the May Procession when the girl First Communicants strewed the narrow path around the grotto with flower petals.

I had made my First Communion in early May and now the day of the May Procession was approaching. My parents were away on holiday, but I was quite sure I could get ready for the great event without the help of my cousins who were in loco parentis.

Patricia, who had also made her First Communion that year, and myself would get ready together. Gingerly, I lifted the box from the shelf, inspected the tissue paper wrapped contents and set out for Patricia's house. Her mother chanced to be out. Only the parlour was deemed good enough for our preparations and so the school uniform was discarded and the boxes opened.

We put on the white organdie dresses. We spat on the white kid shoes and wiped them with grubby handkerchiefs, stabbed each other with hairpins as we fixed the wreaths and veils on our uncombed hair. Everything seemed in order, but for both of us, two items were missing.

Carefully we pulled down our white vests, inspected ourselves in the over mantel and decided we looked perfect. Yes, we agreed, as we twirled in front of the mirror, no need to be concerned; we were quite perfectly turned out for the Procession.

In the schoolyard, milling with excited children, we joined the First Communion classes. The harassed nun-in-charge thrust a basket of flower petals at each of us and scuttled over to the restless male First Communicants.

At the procession, both of us took our places in the group in the vanguard of the parish priest who held high the Blessed Sacrament, encased in an ornate monstrance, followed by the altar boys. The procession began.

We recited the decades of the Rosary. We sang out the hymns in praise of the Virgin Mary, the Immaculate Heart, the Seat of Wisdom, the Mother Most Pure. We chanted the Litany of Our Lady of Loreto.

In a shimmer of bright blue and bright pink, Patricia and I tiptoed reverently through the narrow gate opening onto the narrow path which led past the shrine. The evening air was scented with the aroma of incense and flowers. The singing, the clinking chain of the incense thurible and the murmured prayers filled the air and seemed to waft backwards and forwards from grotto to church gable. Solemnly, we strewed flower petals to our left and right, preparing the way for the Blessed Sacrament.

I thought my heart would burst as I walked past the grotto, at last able to gaze more closely at the statue of the Virgin Mary, to walk close enough to touch Bernadette, who gazed upwards at her Heavenly Mother, the plaster hands clasped in prayer. Even the birdsong on that beautiful May evening was silenced by the prayer and the singing. It was a taste of heaven.

Patricia and myself chattered happily on our way home, talked of the thrill of 'going through the grotto', of being allowed 'strew the flowers' and of how we knew all the words of the hymns.

Patricia's mother was standing on her doorstep, waiting for us. Her facial expression did not auger well for us. She yanked up our white organdie skirts. 'The pair of you!' she exclaimed in horror. 'The pair of you! I tried to catch you before you went into the grotto but I was too late! The shame of it!'

Patricia began to giggle. Her mother hurried her indoors. I slunk home.

When my mother returned, I told her the sorry tale. She promptly produced the missing article, which, of course, had been right under my nose. I took my scolding quietly thankful that I had been not instructed to confess to my sin of desecrating the grotto.

The curate's ears could not be sullied with the words 'pink interlock knickers'!

THE HIGHEST PLACE ON EARTH

Pat Falvey

This was it. The last few metres to the highest place on earth. I was now about to cross the highest platform on earth. There were thousands of feet of fall-off on all sides, as I walked on this narrow ridge with the world below my feet.

A feeling of excitement rose from the pit of my stomach to fill my heaving chest. Approaching the last fifty metres, my emotions were running riot. Those few minutes were the most amazing moments of my life. Step by step, by lingering step, I inched my way to the top, stopping every few steps for a rest and taking in one of the greatest views on earth.

With about fifty metres to go, something very strange happened to me. I began to feel as if my soul and body had somehow parted company. It was as if I was having an out-of-body experience: my soul was hovering a few hundred feet above me as it watched my mortal body, which was under severe pressure due to fatigue, slowly making its way to the pinnacle ahead. Unsure whether I was alive or dead, I continued, like a moth attracted to the light of a candle, to the summit ahead.

Tears of joy streamed from my eyes and froze on my beard as the awesome Himalayan chain started to unfold below.

Glaciers, which, for hundreds of thousands of years, have been slipping down the sides of these enormous rock formations, lay spread out on all sides like fingers on the welcoming hand of the mountain.

I will never forget the last few steps, and there I was, standing on top of the world. I could have roared with joy but instead I prayed silently. Thoughts of those who had gone before me, and those who sadly never completed the journey back to Base Camp, ran through my mind.

My partners, James and Mike, and I just stood there in silence for a minute and then turned 360 degrees to take in the greatest view on this earth. I was conscious that this was not just another climbing exploit. After many years of dreaming, planning, fundraising, fretting, risk-taking – and, on occasion, being more single-minded than was fair to those close to me – I had stepped from dreamland into the bright, sharp light of reality.

It was quiet and peaceful as we stood on that patch of sacred ground, six miles high in the sky. There were no television cameras, no press and no roaring crowds to distract me. The time we spent there was very beautiful and gave me a personal, inner satisfaction that was calming and private. I was excited and elated beyond description. I was so proud to be an Irishman standing on the summit of the Goddess Mother of the Earth – Mount Everest.

NIAGARA FALLS

Peter Phillips

It is difficult to understand the magnitude of Niagara Falls. The words 'awesome' and 'natural wonder' are often overused, but here they can be applied together. However, anybody that has been there will confirm that after about three hours you will have seen the falls from the American side, the Canadian side, from a boat, from a cave behind the water and from the tall spiky building on top of the casino.

Now, if you have ventured there on day trip from Toronto or New York that's fine because you go back having seen just about enough spectacle. If, however, you are committed to be there for any longer period of time, you now have a problem.

This is why a tourist industry of secondary attractions has built up. If I tell you that one of the major attractions is the Rock 'n' Roll Waxworks and their window display consists of two identical tailors dummies – one adorned with a black wig, heavy eye make-up and a snake, the other a blond wig, large glasses and platform boots – you will probably have got a handle on the quality and depth of Niagara's tourist infrastructure.

Worry not. Half an hour's drive away is the scene of one of the most amazing, bizarre and little heard of events in Irish history.

I first came across it doing some research for a book set in the middle of the nineteenth century. When looking at a summary of the events of 1866, I read, virtually as a throwaway fact, that the year also saw the Irish military invasion of Canada.

After staring at the page for a while, I dropped what I was doing, compelled to immediately look into this in more detail. And it is true. More to the point, very few people seem to have heard about it and those that do have bought the generally delivered version that it was a minor event and can be summed up as a shambolic raid of no historic significance. Not so.

Having now researched and written about this extraordinary page of Irish history, let me share some of the highlights.

During the American Civil War, tens of thousands of Irishmen had fought bravely for the Union. With the war over, those who had survived were battle-hardened, experienced soldiers and also out of work.

Meanwhile, the Fenian movement was probably at its peak in America with its own Senate, backed by a well-organised fundraising machine. They considered themselves a government in exile. What they needed however, was a plan to bring the British government to its knees, leading to their goal of independence for Ireland. They had concluded that bombing the occasional police station was not going to achieve this.

At face value, the British military might would always succeed. However, when the wider picture is looked at, there were vulnerabilities. Britain was stretched around the world. Mutinies and wars in India and China had not been completely dealt with and decades of conflict had left the British Treasury empty. There was also an emerging threat from Prussia. Britain had one thing going for her: she still possessed the mightiest navy in the world. Where better to attack her than 1,500 miles from the sea?

A plan was conceived. An army of 30,000 men would be recruited in America. Two thirds would assemble along Lake Erie and invade Canada. The British troops dispatched from Toronto and reinforced from Montreal would be easily defeated. This would allow a third Fenian Regiment to invade across the Canadian border from Vermont, where the unprotected St Lawrence River would be secured, preventing any British reinforcements arriving by sea. Britain would have no choice but to grant Ireland independence in return for her North American property. The alternative was for the Fenian Senate to establish an overseas Irish Republic in what are now Ontario and Quebec.

General Tom 'Fightin', Sweeney, one of the most decorated soldiers in the Union army, and an Irishman to boot, was recruited to mastermind the operation, and on 1 June 1866, the plan swung into action.

Looking back, it is difficult to see how it could go wrong, but wrong it went. However, not before the spearhead troops invaded across the Niagara River from Buffalo, New York. Near to the small town of Ridgeway, they engaged the British army and won the resulting battle. This remains the only time an Irish army has inflicted a defeat on the British outside of Ireland and raised the Tricolour on British territory. It is, in fact, the only time Ireland has ever invaded another country.

And it is all there to see. Twenty miles down the road from Niagara Falls is the little town of Ridgeway. It has a wonderful museum and the original building, which was used as a field hospital, has been converted into a heritage centre. If you go there, buy a booklet written by David Owen, a local historian. It will give you a fascinating tour around the area, highlighting all the events surrounding the invasion. Even if military history is not your cup of tea, you get to see some great views across the river to Buffalo.

Trust me, it's far more interesting than the Rock 'n' Roll Waxworks.

STRANGERS ON A PLANE

Grace Wynne-Jones

When I step onto a plane, my concern about whether it will arrive at its destination can make me a bit brazen. I start to chat to the person next to me. Who are they? Where are they going? Are they scared of flying too?

The high point of my aeroplane encounters involved an author of books on 'meaning of life' matters. I was travelling to New Mexico. Shortly after I arrived, I would be going on a watered down version of a Native American 'Vision Quest'. This would involve spending hours alone in the wilderness. I'd read that the Vision Quest is amongst the oldest tools tribal people use to seek direction for life. But, suddenly, the attractions of a package holiday seemed incredibly potent.

Once on the plane, I noticed that the author was sitting nearby and that I had an empty seat beside me. I rose and approached him. Why should I be shy? After all, I had chosen to spend much of the day hurtling through the air in a huge piece of machinery and needed distraction. Not only did I tell the man that I admired his work, I added that I had an empty seat beside me if he wanted to talk further. I was far too anxious already to care if he rejected my low key, though clearly eager, invitation. But if he did accept it, we could discuss his work and it might help me to forget I was on an aeroplane.

In fact, this is what happened. The kind man joined me, probably sensing my fear. We had a great old chat about all sorts of things, including the lows and highs of authorship and the weirdness of the human condition. When he pointed to a notice that said 'coat hook' and said 'that does not say goat hook', I almost fell off my seat in semi-hysterical giggles. I was laughing so much, I forgot to think about eternity, and I don't mean the aftershave.

By the time we reached London, the prospect of getting on a plane to Chicago and another one to Albuquerque did not seem so daunting. The man went on his way, but the protective feel of his company had lightened my journey. The Vision Quest was wonderful, if challenging. And I fell in love with New Mexico's red rock country.

And, later on, I realised that the next time I felt embarrassed about approaching someone I really wanted to meet … I should simply pretend I am on a jumbo jet.

NEW YORK

Sean Hogan

There's a particular sort of New Yorker who flusters me: the ones who bob their heads in rhythm with speech. It's not the kind of casual nod of assent which you or I might give. It's a mechanical shift which puts me in mind of Offenbach's 'Doll Song'. And, as with dolls, nodding New Yorkers also have a basilisk stare.

It's most apparent when they're obsessing, as all Manhattanites seem to do. But then, living on a thirteen-mile-long by two-mile-wide island, surrounded by about one and a half million people would occasionally tip anyone into neurotic self-absorption. Today's 'yap, yap, yap' is about the new deli on 14th Street, where the bagel and lox are to die for. Seriously die. Yesterday, 'twas getting front circle seats for opening night at the Metropolitan Opera. Tomorrow – and forever – 'twill be moral relativism, upward mobility, *growing* hedge funds and getting Junior and Janey into Miss Burlington's prep school.

'Tis escape time. The barouches and vis-à-vis lined up on Central Park South might seem a bit tacky, but both jarveys and horses know their way about and even the most cynical have a bit of harmless fun.

Now that the World Trade Center is in oblivion, one of the best vantage points for Manhattan's skyline is the Hudson and East

River. A Circle Line boat trip is the fifth business. It takes two and a half hours or so and, viewed from this angle, massed on-shore concrete and glass towers give a sense of the upward thrust of commerce and power which is both the ideal and idea of essential New York.

For me, this also is exemplified at the United Nations headquarters and on Ellis Island. All that is symbolic of consequence, glory and conquest is on view at the UN. For here you'll find, in its modest glass case, a bit of moon rock which Armstrong and Aldrin brought back from the heavens in 1969.

Irrespective of views of the organisation and its works or pomps, you also can lay modest claim to being part of 'We the peoples of the United Nations, determined to save succeeding generations from the scourge of war...' by eating in the delegates' dining room. Amazingly, this is one of New York's better kept secrets. We'd all know Kofi Annan, but would we recognise Ban Ki-moon at the next table? This recognition factor does not apply to Ellis Island, its Statue of Liberty and the kindness to strangers which it exemplifies. Extracted from the poem 'The New Colossus' by Emma Lazarus, the inscription on the statue's plaque reads:

Give me your tired, your poor,
Your huddled masses yearning to breathe free,
The wretched refuse of your teeming shore;
Send these, the homeless, tempest-tost to me,
I lift my lamp beside the golden door!

She sure does ...

LANGUAGE

FACEBOOK
Éamonn Ó Catháin

As an Irish speaker, you'll always get someone coming up to you enquiring about the state of the language or asking why, at all, do you bother? It's been a hard one to answer; most of the time it is true, I can go for days without speaking a word of the language and unless I make a deliberate detour to the Ceantar Gaeltachta here in Belfast, I can cross from one side of the city to the other without speaking a word of Irish or, indeed, walk from Connolly Station to Stephen's Green without needing to use the classic *cúpla focal* so beloved of people south of the border. I can get away with just one *focal*. Luas.

Time was that the situation appeared just a tad grim and possibly terminal.

Except that something has happened and I now find myself using the Irish language in a different way, every day and just about all day long. You see, Irish is not only not dead nor invisible, it's simply wised up, regrouped and changed location. Irish is alive and well and hanging out online. It not only hangs out online with its own sites but has embraced one social phenomenon in a big way and that, *a chairde Gael*, is Facebook.

I think Facebook is a lot of fun and I throw my hands up and admit to its addictive quality, the necessary fix being rendered simple and easy by virtue of it being available on most mobile phones and, in the case of the all-conquering iPhone, sublimely slick. *Agus glic*. But the reasons I started using Facebook in the first place have gradually changed, with the emphasis now thoroughly on the Irish language, and each and every day it is in that language that I express myself, with the result that increasingly my status updates, more often than not, are in Irish. Oh and I'm assuming you know what I'm talking about.

But we Irish speakers – well, the internet is bringing us together in a way that the gold *fáinne* could only dream about ... I don't have to justify myself or walk out of my way just to have a conversation in the tongue ... we come together in cyberspace no matter where we are globally speaking and *'cha dtuigim do chanuint agus cha labhraim leat béarla'* has never seemed more irrelevant. Indeed, speakers of Scottish Gaelic are muscling in on our act and the non-existent barriers to mutual comprehension are being exposed as fiction.

I think it started with a group on the social networking site called 'Don't ban Irish on Aer Lingus' – in fact, I might just be the administrator of said group, but I've forgotten in the whirlpool of related groups I'm now a member of: *'Éistigí le seo'*, *'Nós iris, Comhdháil Náisiúnta na Gaeilge'*, *'Conradh na Gaeilge'*, *'Gaeilgeoirí Mhanchain'*, 'Gifts as *Gaeilg*', the oddly named 'agelic is not a language but *Gaeilge* is', *'tá mé ag foghlaim na Gaedhilge'*, 'South Park *as Gaedhilg tá sé go h-iontach*, and our beloved *'Seachtain na Gaeilge'*, and, of course, *'Cúpla focal'*. It had to get in there somewhere.

It's a huge and impressive selection and that's only a few of the more popular examples. Indeed, Facebook itself, after a defiantly monolingual and anglophone stance, has been translated into most of the world's popular tongues – including Irish. And here we see the power of technology at work for a few cent more; most of the facilities once deemed too costly are now available to us, from

ATMs to railway station readouts; from the far-eastern handset maker who introduced texting in Irish to Mac OS 10 and Facebook.

So don't expect an anti-Facebook rant from me like the doctor who exhorted us all last week to drop our mice, abandon our keyboards and, in the immortal words of William Shatner, 'get a life'. The truth is, the future has never been more rosy for speakers of minority tongues thanks to the like of Facebook – *deir siad go bhfuil an fhírinne searbh ach ní searbh atá sí acht garbh, agus sin an fáth a sheachantar í* – in the immortal words of Seosamh Mac Grianna.

MYLES

Phyl Herbert

He emerges from the water, my little sister's boy, her Apollo. He is in his element, the blue sky above his crown of curls and the Atlantic Ocean licking his feet. He walks towards me, all seventeen years of him. I hardly recognise him, the youth who was a boy just days ago.

Myles has no fear of water, but he does not like the world of noise, of harsh sounds that shatter his silence. Myles has no words; his inner thoughts are a mystery to all who encounter him. He can understand what is said to him and about him. He has a finely tuned radar system that registers the decibels of his universe.

During the time of his father's wake a few short weeks ago, the many voices in his house rose in pitch with the clinking of the glasses. The waves of sound swept him to his bedroom in fright. His sister soothed him with quiet tones and gently asked us to keep the volume down. The roar of the Atlantic does not faze him, but the roar of the human voice does. He is deep like the sea with a language all his own.

Voices have colour, texture and tone. The human voice can signal our inner fears and prejudices screeching to the world. Myles has no words; they have dwindled down to a trickle; they come out like a thin, slow stream in single drops. Single utterances. When his voice comes to the surface, it is a sweet voice and I wish with all my heart that, some day, he would burst into song. But this is my fantasy, my selfish fantasy. Another dream is that by some magical intervention his Apollo-like body would blossom into a dancing rhythm and, by a series of osmosis, release his inner world into movement that would bring him the joy of expression. These are but wistful thoughts.

Myles has taught me a lot. Without uttering a word, he has corrected my tone. He has taught me not to be careless with words. He has taught me to be mindful of my body language, particularly my facial expression. He has taught me not to entertain negative thoughts because he can pick them up on his radar beam.

Myles is not afraid of water or the Atlantic Ocean. He is afraid of the harsh, heartless human voice.

As I look again at him emerging from the sea, I know his father is looking at him, too, from his chair up there beyond the sky.

OUGHTERARD LEMONS

Moya Cannon

I am addicted to place names and to the stories embedded in them.
A few years ago, I was told by a musician acquaintance of mine
that the housing estate on which he had grown up in Oughterard,
County Galway, bore the improbable name 'The Lemon Fields'.
Allegedly, a local landlord, returned from Spain, had once tried to
grow lemons there. My informant claimed to have seen the last
remaining stunted lemon tree, complete with miniature lemons,
growing in a neighbour's garden in the early 1960s.

I loved what I first saw as the extravagance of the venture – the
audacity of trying to grow lemons in Galway's rain and wind. I
then began to think about the impulse in most of us, particularly
after a *first* journey abroad, to bring back something of the savour
and the colour of the place we have visited.

This is, after all, how language, culture and agriculture have
always travelled – by people bringing with them what they love as
well as what they need. Silk, spice and amber carved out some of
the great trade routes of the Middle Ages. There is so little, if
anything, which is really native to any area. Even the bedrock has
usually travelled vast distances. It is hard for us to believe, for in-
stance, how very recently gigues and quadrilles were brought back

to this country by some travelling musician or other. They quickly became naturalised as jigs and reels – the exotic becoming apparently indigenous.

If there is truth in the story of 'The Lemon Fields', it is worth considering that lemon trees may have seemed a reasonably sensible import and no more exotic than the potatoes which Raleigh had brought to the south of the country some centuries earlier. Lemons were known to prevent scurvy on long sea voyages, they tasted wonderful and they were extremely decorative. Trial and error are as essential to our survival as our more measured endeavours. I wrote the following poem as a celebration of the quixotic impulse, which is central to our humanity and, indeed, to our survival.

In Paup Joyce's garden in the sixties
in a council estate called 'The Lemon Fields',
they say there was a bush
with small lemons growing on it.

An O'Flaherty of Aughanure Castle
had once shipped the trees from Spain
and had planted his land with them.

Stranger things had rooted,
had almost gone native –
tubers from the Americas some voyager had brought back –
so why not this counterpoint to honey,
like honey, a love child of the sun.

A whiff of spice roads
and we drag dreams home from our journeys –
necessary evidence of other climates,
other ways of growing –

And some dreams do take root in the quotidian,
as surely as fuchsia rampages along a side-road,
and some sustain us totally, then fail us totally

And some hardly take at all
but survive in the tang of a place name,
in a crazy bush tilted by the wind.

THE GRAVITY OF POETRY

Iggy McGovern

Richard Feynman once remarked that a Martian observer might reasonably conclude the following: the reason the earth spins is the feverish, collective brushing of teeth by earthlings located at the light/dark boundary on the earth's surface. Our Martian might also speculate that the reason the earth goes around the sun is something to do with school summer holidays. Of course, the real reason is gravity.

Gravity is a very serious word. We speak of the gravity of the situation; mention of the school summer holidays registers high on my gravity meter. And gravity is the cause of much anxiety among the physicists. Gravity is the last big puzzle (for the moment at least), the one of the four fundamental forces in the universe that cannot be unified with the others. And yet, when it comes to poetry, gravity, as Myles would say, is your only man.

The proper answer to the question 'What have physics and poetry got in common?' is *rhythm*. The easiest way to demonstrate rhythm is with the simple pendulum: suspend a small weight on a length of cord and set it swinging; the period of swing varies with the length of cord and is, in fact, proportional to the square root of the length; the other parameter needed for this calculation is the acceleration due to gravity. Indeed, one writer has poetically described gravity as 'the pendulum's silent partner'.

The properties of the simple pendulum were first investigated by Galileo, including the suggestion that the pendulum could be used to construct a clock – moreover, his great contributions as an astronomer paved the way for Newton's theory of gravity. However, Galileo's espousal of a sun-centred universe also brought him into conflict with Church authorities, leading to the threat of torture and, upon his recanting of his work, a sentence of house arrest. The eventual apology was a long time in coming.

Gravity and politics are never far apart; the race to put humans in space was a feature of the Cold War; the sputnik that crossed the skies of my childhood had more than one political context. Back then, we did not know that in a satellite the dust accumulates on the floor *and* on the ceiling. The net force on dust particles is in the opposite direction on either side of the zero-gravity line, but then the politics of housework was sub-surface in the 1950s.

More relevant portents, perhaps, have come the other way, that is, from space to us. In the same period, a sizeable chunk of meteorite fell to earth in County Tyrone. That it crashed through the roof of an RUC station seems now like a harbinger of three decades of political violence.

And we are all sky-watchers, on the lookout for extraterrestrial visitants. In his marvellous poem 'Exposure', Seamus Heaney describes himself as the inner emigré, grown long-haired and thoughtful:

Who, blowing up these sparks
For their meagre heat, have missed
The once-in-a-lifetime portent,
The comet's pulsing rose.

PRAYER

Mark Roper

One New Year's Eve, I met up with some friends in a pub. We spent the night there. It was, in retrospect, a strange night. Other people kept coming over to talk to us. It seemed all these other people wanted to do was to pour their hearts out. They would sit down with us and, next thing we knew, they'd be deep into a long confession.

What did their confessions have in common? They had all had terrible Christmases with their families. Rows, tears, recriminations – it seemed a wonder that anyone had survived the so-called festive season. They all swore they were never going to endure another family Christmas again. New Year's Eve became a kind of group therapy session.

I was reminded of the joke about Einstein's Second Law of Relativity: time passes more slowly with your relatives. But it wasn't all that funny. There was a sense of relief, but it wasn't a case of being able to enjoy New Year's Eve and to look forward to another year. It was a case of having survived Christmas. At the same time, families hadn't really been escaped. There was a kind of desperation in the way people were talking, as if they were really talking to themselves. It was as if a tape was playing inside their heads, which they were powerless to stop.

I suppose that we all carry around something like that inside us. Sometimes, it's referred to as 'baggage'. Certain things that have happened to us we can never forget, and sometimes our whole life gets based around them. At worst, we blame someone else, as if things could somehow have been different. I don't mean in any way to make light of such feelings. In fact, I'm really trying to stress how strong, how deep, how unalterable they can be. Sometimes, our minds are like washing machines. The same old stories go round and round. We can do nothing to stop them.

When such feelings are at their worst, they're very hard to bear. But, if we're lucky, there are moments when all the 'baggage' falls away and gets revealed as something that exists only in the mind. In this poem, 'Prayer', I've tried to put those two states of mind together.

How we survive, Lord. Twenty-two homes,
sixteen schools before we were ten.
Those blind uncles touching us up.
Our wounds wide open, our words not heard
until we wept, but were not allowed to.
O the tears uncried, strained against
the eyes, the good conduct medals.

It's no wonder, Lord. Fingers at
the underwear, fists in the stomach,
stories spooled inside us, pleading
to be repeated. Look at us, crawling
from the wrecks of our childhoods,
begging any stranger for a hug.
O what happened. And what happened.

Let us praise, tonight, ourselves.
Our flesh, bones, eyes, hands, hair,
the brightness of our being.
How should our light not shine?
Look at us, Lord, praise us,
real tonight as each other,
as real as can be. Beyond belief
our beauty, our right to be here.

INSPIRATION

Louis de Paor

September 1973. Our first week above in the big school, and we have no idea who he is or what he's supposed to be teaching us. It doesn't matter. The class is an education.

We had boarded, he told us solemnly, 'the academic bandwagon', bound for Inter Cert 1976, that notorious Limerick Junction of the mind. Some of us wouldn't make it. Boys who failed to keep up, who fell off the bandwagon, would be 'crushed, crushed, by the academic juggernaut' that followed behind. 'The wheels of the juggernaut grind smooth.'

The bell that sounded every forty minutes was not, as we had imagined, a sign that the end of class, or the end of the world, was nigh but a signal to Pavlov's dog inside each and every boy that it was time for his 'subsidised bun'.

There was no such thing as mathematics, advanced or otherwise; only sums and hard sums. If homework wasn't done, it wasn't our fault. The mothers of Ireland had their sons ruined, out all night playing Bingo. 'Tell your mother I want to see her in the morning.'

If you misbehaved you were a 'targe'.

'What are you boy?'

'A targe, Sir.'

'You're being recalcitrant. What are you?'

'Recalcitrant, Sir'

'A bitter fellow. A masochist. You want me to beat you? You're being naïve, boy.'

He taught us Latin ('La *tin*, Mac Uí de Paor. La *tin*.') and forbade us speaking of television as though it were a reality. No one was stupid. Or thick, for that matter. Only 'heavy' or, worst of all, 'bitter'.

Verbs, nouns and all the glorious mysteries of grammar and syntax were to be learned off 'like the proverbial pop song'. Invariably, we were 'too slow. Next boy. Too slow. Next …' With each failure, his raised and practised hand failed, by the proverbial whisker, to clip our ears. The disturbed air around our spinning heads was enough to put the wind up most of us.

We translated sentences never heard by the people or senate of Rome as if the best Latin ('La *tin*, boy. Say it right.') were spoken in the Marsh. 'Andy Gaw says you should drink Dairy Bawn because its good for you. Enoch Powell says all the Paddies should pack up and go home.' His pronouncements became proverbs. 'The adjective chaperones the noun.'

What we learned was not for a day or a year, for passing exams, getting jobs or getting ahead. 'Ye'll be on yere deathbeds. Dying roaring. After a debauched life. The priest will be there and the doctors. No good. "I can't go," ye'll say, "till Mr Dennis comes in to examine me in my irregular verbs."'

Stories clung to him like Colmcille or Jonathan Swift. The day he left, or so the story goes, he stood, chalk in hand, gazing out over Murray's Farm as far as the water tanks on the hill, the limits of the world as we knew it. 'Lads, there has to be more than this.' And he went. Just like that. It felt good that he was out there, ahead of us as always.

The Palace Bar, December 1988. I'm waiting for someone else when he rushes in, crouched like a prop forward, ready for anything.

'Mr Dennis,' I said.

He turned quickly. 'Conjugate tango, boy,' he said.

'Tango, tangere, taxi tactum,' I said, delighted. And wrong.

'Too slow, boy. *Tetigi* tactum.' And he stood on tiptoe to almost clip my ear. 'I thought you'd waltz through it.'

I can still feel him breathing down my neck. An inspiration. Literally. You should have been there.

HOME WORDS FROM ABROAD

Bernard Share

The obvious sources of our colloquial speech are Irish, English and, in the North, Ulster Scots, but that is by no means the whole story. Over the centuries, words have crept into the vocabulary from many other sources, some of them now virtually unrecognisable as anything but the familiar vernacular. It is hard to credit the fact that, for example, the 'hooley', an accepted feature of the Irish way of doing things, has its origins in a word describing a Hindu festival and was possibly brought back, some suggest, by Irish soldiers in the imperial British army. The same source has been held accountable for 'conjun box', a familiar term in Cork for a small moneybox. A Tamil word, it was possibly imported at some stage in the nineteenth century by returning Munster Fusiliers.

I say possibly, because in the matter of word origins it is very difficult to be positive beyond argument, unless you can catch them almost at the point of entry. Thus we can hazard that the Dublin word 'gurrier' is somehow related to the French *guerrier*, a warrior, but we are far from sure how and when it entered our colloquial speech. On the other hand, we can be pretty certain that 'to disappear', deriving from the Troubles in the North and meaning to execute and bury in an unknown grave, owes its presence in our language to the *desaparecidos* who suffered a similar fate in

Argentina. Similarly, the term 'mingi man', a kind of itinerant salesman who catered to the needs of the Irish troops in the Congo in the 1960s, not only entered the language at that time but also was brought by the same troops – or their colleagues – to the Lebanon where there was, and probably still is, a flourishing band of mingi men. An interesting question, of course, is whether the term will survive in popular speech or disappear like a host of once common colloquial terms. Only time will tell.

Language, particularly colloquial language, is two-way traffic, and, in this respect, Ireland has been in the export business since our people began to leave our shores to travel the world, whether voluntarily or otherwise. Thus, the English of Australia is rich in Irishisms, from the familiar phrase 'Good on you' (compare the Irish *rinne sé a mhaith orm* – literally 'he did good on me'), to the Kathleen Mavourneen, an indeterminate prison sentence, from the ballad which includes the words 'it may be for years and it may be for ever'. Then there are words like 'sheebeen' which turn up in American speech and, in the colloquial Spanish or Cuba, a word that appears in their dictionaries spelt b-a-i-l-i-j-ú. If you know enough Spanish to try pronouncing it, it comes out as 'bailijú', the Caribbean equivalent of our 'ballyhoo', but with the meaning slightly modified to indicate self-importance.

I once met an old lady in Argentina who was fourth-generation Irish. Her daily language was, of course, Spanish but when she spoke English, it was in a pure Westmeath accent and with a vocabulary and turn of phrase that echoed that of the nineteenth-century writers such as Charles Lever or Samuel Lover. No wonder that the manner in which language lives and reproduces itself is a source, to me, of endless fascination.

FOUNDATIONS

Hedy Gibbons Lynott

They come, this unlikely corps de ballet, sidling, one by one, through the gaps in the stone walls, brown rumps to the wind, white faces bent to their task. There's a patient grace about these cattle, this daily procession; a tranquillity that reaches me through the filigree of stone that makes up the boundary wall between us.

The presence of these gentle creatures somehow engages, inviting me into this world of limestone terraces that climb out of the purple shadows into the morning sky. Many times, since moving to this new house, to these wide-open spaces, I have found myself hankering after the comfort of clothesline conversations, the revving of morning traffic, even the sound of heavy metal through an open window, the thud of football in the long evenings.

Here, early-morning silence blankets everything, so that the soft plod of the cattle, munching their way across the grass, draws me to the back wall. The occasional brown glance in my direction becomes more purposeful as their leader moves closer to our boundary, and stands in quizzical regard, chewing rhythmically. He is joined by another, then another, until a line of twenty-one large, brown animals is shoulder-to-shoulder along the wall, a kind of exotic chorus line, eyeing me intently.

We stand there, my new acquaintances and I, regarding each other with equal curiosity. Finally, the leader decides he has more important things to do, and turns away. The herd follows.

Reluctant to part company with them completely, I let my eye run along the tracery of limestone between us. 'It all depends on the *bun figiní*.' The words of PJ, a dear friend recently deceased, come back to me, recounting how, as a boy, he built many of these stone walls with his father. Work for a winter's day; when they were no longer cutting beet and it was too early to sow potatoes; when their fingers felt like they would fall off from the cold, and the light was low and harsh, the scraw silvered by winter. It was then they gathered the smallest stones from the fields, laying them cheek-by-jowl, level with the ground; foundations for the walls they would build come spring, when they'd plant a patch of ground with spuds and carrots, and construct these adaptable walls to corral their few cattle. *Bun figiní*. Bottom markers. Foundation stones.

And then there was the other group of stones. 'Tightenin' stones' PJ called them. They lie somewhere in this wall, sustaining and re-enforcing it, occasional points of strength, enabling it to stand firm against the worst the Atlantic can throw at it. Unlike the open lacework of rounded stones that totter and lurch in wondrous serendipity, this cluster of upright flattish stones is inserted at intervals, each tightly packed against the others' curves.

'When you understand, you know where to look.' PJ's words come back to me. My gaze roams slowly along the wall; slowly, and now more patiently, as I wait for the wall to reveal its mystery; for me to discern its pattern. For a long time, I stand there searching, like a child learning to read, for the characters of this new language; the language of stone walls.

ALL IN A LANGUAGE

Patricia Nolan

Expressions like '*le shopping*', '*le parking*' and '*forwarder un email*' are invading the French language. The French, once resistant to English, have now embraced globalisation. They are flocking to English-language schools.

Maybe due to this new openness, the French government has recently approved the teaching of certain regional languages in French schools. The Bretons and the people of the Languedoc have campaigned for this right for years. This new law could eventually include Berber, the language spoken by over one million Berber emigrants from Algeria. Not Arabs, they speak their own language and have a rich and ancient culture. Famous Berber kings like Massinissa once reigned over northern Africa from Libya to Morocco. They fought the Romans and the Carthaginians. The Berbers in Algeria are known as the Kabyl. They are wonderful musicians, poets and writers.

Until recently, in France, few people spoke English. One could speak freely in public knowing that relatively few understood what was being said, whatever the language.

However, some years ago, a younger sister and my overweight English cousin sat opposite two girls in the Metro. It's rare anybody speaks in the Metro. The movement of the train rocks everybody into a state of semi-consciousness.

Suddenly, one of the girls said to the other in Irish, '*Tá sí ana ramhar.*' My sister glared at the two girls opposite.

They wriggled in embarrassment. One said to the other, '*Tá súil agam nach dtuigeann sí.*' My sister simply said, '*Tuigim.*' My cousin never knew she had been the subject of a conversation in Irish.

But to come back to the Kabyl of Algeria. They have been looking for official recognition of their language and culture for decades. In 1998, the Algerian regime imposed Arabic as the official language of the country. Their law did not take into account the cultural diversity of Algeria. The result has been continual social disturbances and deaths among the Kabyl.

In June, Kabylie commemorated the third anniversary of the assassination of their outspoken singer Matoub Lounès. He symbolised his people's struggle for recognition of their culture. We Irish can emulate the Kabyl by putting a greater effort into preserving the Irish language.

Now that we are prosperous, we could invest more in our native language. I am privileged to speak French and English. I can read my poetry in both languages in Francophone and Anglophone countries. But I miss being able to read in Irish although I used to be fluent when I was younger. I had a wonderful teacher to thank for this. Her name is Sister Margaret Mary from Gortnor Abbey in Mayo.

Some time ago, I met her after many years. I was introduced in my Anglicised name. She said to me, 'Cad is ainm duit?'

I replied, 'Pádraicín Ní Nualláin is ainm doim.'

Immediately, she knew who I was. I wonder now why I never kept my Irish name. When I tell Kabyl friends my Irish name, they can't understand why I'm called Patricia Nolan. They are literally dying to preserve their language. Every language is unique; it connects us to our history, our myths, our own vision of the world. Future generations will thank us for preserving this richness.

Postscript: In 2002, Berber was recognised as an official language in Algeria, alongside Arabic.

LETTERS

Mary Coll

The postman calls to our house almost every day, and, every day, I still pick up the post expecting to find an actual letter among the ever-increasing pile of catalogues and bills. It's not that I'm waiting for some special letter in particular. It's just that it's been so long since anyone wrote to me, personally, other than a financial institution, that I actually can't remember who my last letter came from or what it was about.

I have two telephones, each with some form of answering machine, I have email and I have a serious weakness for text messaging; this means that, on an average day, I communicate with a frequency that keeps at least one satellite orbiting the earth. However, I haven't written a letter in so long that I'm not sure if I have notepaper and envelopes that match, and, what's worse, I'm no longer even certain that matching stationery is in vogue.

Without giving away too much information, I will admit to coming from the 'Insert coins now and press button A' era of communication, which was also still the era of the letter writer – it had to be, because very few of those telephones ever worked properly.

I accept that my letters from Irish College did not mark the beginning of a golden age in correspondence, but, from around then to some ill-defined time recently, I was consistently writing to friends and family, and getting replies from all over the world at a level that made at least one half-decent stamp collection possible. I also kept most of these letters, because it was unthinkable to throw away personal letters and dispose of that unique link between two people, when, like a photograph, it enables the possibility of a brief return to moments that capture the absolute cadence of your life. Moments that seemed ordinary or unremarkable at the time, until the people you shared them with are no longer there to tell you who won the match or what the weather was like or who got a job. Letters that came faithfully to me every week in Ohio full of details I thought were a little unimportant then. Somewhat more exotic letters from Florence, from the first of my friends who really went to live in Europe before travel became incidental. Small, pale-blue, wafer-like letters from Africa, as brief and composed as the life they represented, and then the long, neatly typed letter describing a funeral on a hillside above the convent hospital for a family who would never visit the grave. Some stand out, most I have forgotten, but they are all there somewhere in boxes, under beds, up in the attic, all the highs and lows along with a few that might even raise an occasional eyebrow.

Perhaps it's sentimental of me, but I suspect I may not be the only one who double checks the post. I used to recognise handwriting as quickly as I now recognise the numbers that flash up on my phone. I also think, or perhaps just hope, that I had something more to say than the telegram-style sentences I now send in quick response to receipt of same. When I was still writing letters, and letters were still being written to me, I have a feeling we were all able to read far more between the lines.

STARS

Pat Boran

I've been thinking about the word 'star'; you might say I've been considering it. People, when they consider, put their hands under their chins and look up at the heavens, the kind of pose you see in Roman statues. In fact, that's exactly what the word consider means, the 'con' part meaning 'with' and 'sider' coming from *sidus* meaning 'star'. Musing on the heavens. It's the way words often tell a physical history like that which makes them so addictive.

It's 1993 and I'm in Enniskillen, County Fermanagh, for a month as writer-in-residence. The room I'm in, in the local library, fills up with twenty or so school boys and girls, aged about twelve or thirteen. Some Protestant, others Catholic. The ones in grey are the Protestants – or is it the Catholics? Either way, it's important to know they're different.

'Say the word "star",' I say to the nearest girl. 'Stor,' she says, somewhat puzzled. Then I have them all say it. 'Stor', 'sthor', 'store', 'sthair', until there is a night sky hovering above us, the library we're sitting in has vanished for the moment and we can be ourselves again, children who like to play with words beneath the sky.

The dictionary says the word 'pupil' comes from the Latin *pupila*, meaning little doll.

'The wolf,' I say, 'represents the dark, the hidden side of the pigs.'

We've been discussing my favourite fairytale, my favourite story, actually, the *Three Little Pigs*. There's something incredibly satisfying about hearing it yet again. We've been talking about how, when the wolf and the last little pig finally meet, the pig finds a tiny version of himself in the wolf's eye and the wolf finds himself hiding in the pig's! As if on cue, two soldiers in camouflage pass by the window. We are in the pupils of their eyes, as they are in the pupils of ours.

There's a picture of a ship run aground stuck up on the felt board at the front of the room. It's an impressive sight: the enormity of this man-made vessel against a line of men who look like little more than insects trying, if you can believe your eyes, to drag it over the land.

My students have to write about this ship, this beach, these tiny ant-like people. They have to write and read out what they write to the rest of group, often doing so in the voices of strangers.

'My name is Chang,' one says (it's not), 'and I am Chinese and I come here every day to try to pull this ship.'

'And my name is Stavinski,' another says, and gives another explanation.

And there are Irish men and women, and English men and women, and Martian invaders caught without reserve fuel, their great hulk of a ship stuck fast in the surface of an alien planet, and as many other stories as we have time for.

But the Catholics, Protestants, Chinese and Martians are pulling the same ropes now – word ropes – not only as if they had to shift this rusting hulk we have to deal with, but also as if their common efforts might draw out more stars in the sky.

SILENCE IN WICKLOW

Ellen O'Toole

Whenever I'm in Wicklow, travelling the road from Aughrim to Greenane on my way to Glenmalure, I let down the window of the car just before I reach Greenane and broadcast Radio na Gaeltachta – quietly. It is, at one level, a ridiculous gesture. At another level, it is all someone like myself can do to send a message back in time, to tell the ghosts that there are still people around who speak the same language, who care.

On the right-hand side of this road, as you go towards Greenane, there is the museum of farm implements, well signposted. There are signs for it from as far away as Calary Bog. And it is well worth a visit.

On the left, on private land, there is a ring fort, once the *dún* of the O'Byrne Clann. Fiach Mac Hugh O'Byrne was the 'firebrand of the Wicklow hills', who held out for so long against the forces of Queen Elizabeth I and who won the battle of Glenmalure in 1580 – one of the very few battles that the Irish actually won. There is no sign to indicate the presence of this *dún*, nothing to preserve or protect it. Lucky for us that the present owner has a sense of history and can recite the ballad of Fiach McHugh that she learned at school some seventy years ago.

It was in this *dún* that the *Leabhar Branach* was compiled. Because the O'Byrnes were among the few Irish chieftains who could still afford patronage in the sixteenth century, everybody who was anybody in the *Poetry Ireland* of the time turned up on the doorstep in Baile na Corra.

Tadhg Dall Ó hUiginn came here and left a poem behind him – by his own account, he found it a rather wild place and only came to let a political situation he had created at home quieten down a little. Feargal Óg Mac an Bhaird came to the *dún*. Feargal Óg might be considered the first modern Irish poet, since he braved bardic convention and composed poetry in the open air – actually on horseback! – his critics claimed.

Poets would have been rewarded with Spanish wine, gold, silk, perhaps a horse – the proceeds of a dawn raid on Arklow or Wicklow or even a longer strike as far away from Glenmalure as Tallaght or Crumlin.

The *Leabhar Branach* has been called a 'jewel of late Bardic poetry'. In it, there are conventional court poems, dedicated to the chieftains of the O'Byrne clan over several generations. There are poems in it that throw an interesting light on the women of the clan. Most famous of these was Fiach Mac Hugh's second wife, Róis Ní Thuathail. Róis was a 'political activist'. She was confined, at least twice, in Dublin Castle, where she was condemned to be burned as a witch. She escaped that fate and lived a long life, continuing to the end to conspire against the English, as the State Papers complain rather peevishly. There are a number of harrowing poems in the *Leabhar Branach*, composed when Fiach Mac Hugh was finally defeated, beheaded, quartered and exposed on a rail outside Dublin Castle. The best-known one is by Aonghas ó Dálaigh:

A cholann do-chím gan cheann,
sibh d'fhaicsin do shearg mo bhriogh.

How many Irish people know anything at all about the *Leabhar Branach*, about the *dún* where it was compiled, about Feilim's castle on the hill above, now swallowed in forestry?

It is a silence that grieves me. So just after passing the farm museum, I open the left-hand window and, if it is a Sunday afternoon, let Seán Bán Breathnach give the ghosts the latest sports news – *as Gaeilge*.

LUNAR LANDING

Vincent Woods

Poems can have a strange genesis. A few years ago, I was driving from Sligo to Leitrim at night and, as I turned a bend in the road, the moon was huge on Lough Gill – in it, almost. For a moment, I felt this pull, this surge to drive the car into the moon in the water – to land, splash on the moon – drown in it.

I resisted, but a poem came by a short time after – and this is the thing, poems *do* come by. We're not sure where they come from, we can dream them, almost remember them, conjure them – but sometimes the poem seems to conjure itself through us. And there's the rub – how do we rationally explain inspiration? The times when words flow through us, when the artist's pencil or brush or pen moves with speed and certainty out and beyond what is planned or anticipated. It's one of the joyful mysteries of life and I do not believe science will ever explain it. Not fully. Never.

Like the feelings we get sometimes in a particular place – feelings of pain or suffering; of well-being or great love – the *'fear gorta'*, hungry grass of life-force thwarted or exalted.

So from the moon in a lake on a winter's night comes a narrative, and a character or two, and a story that is a true lie – something that never happened, yet must have happened; that may never happen, yet occurs each time this poem is read. Each time,

the person who never existed, Francie McPadden, sits into his car
and the barman looks up at the moon and remembers:

Lunar Landing

You all think, the barman said,
You all think that Neil Armstrong
Was the first man on the moon.
Well, you're wrong –
Because he wasn't.
You see Francie McPadden
Was going home this night
And a good fourteen or fifteen
Pints in his belly.

There was a full moon
(It was July)
And there's a hoor of a bend
In the road out there be the cross.

Francie took it in top
And it seems he was blinded
By the moonlight
And the old Cortina went splash
Into the lake –
Right into the moon
In the water.

So you could say Francie landed
Well ahead of Armstrong.

Only he didn't come back.

HOME AND TIME

THE JAR

Vona Groarke

Say you go back to Ireland, to the place where you grew up. It's a beautiful March morning. You decide to take a walk around the old farm. There've been changes, of course: a new house built, an old house knocked – every step asks you to notice something different but to remember what has stayed.

The old kitchen garden is no longer tended, though you remember the rhubarb that used to grow there, stalks thick as your wrist, and the tarts you made with it that even to this day are the very taste of young summer on your tongue.

The daffodils are just coming into their own all along the garden's earthen banks. You wander over to where they are brightest, and, as you go, your foot catches on something. It appears to be a small pot that you prise free from the soil and brambles and there it is, perfectly, marvellously intact.

You're given it to take back with you to America. Weeks later, when you know it inside out, the feel of it, the chip on the underside, the letters of the maker's name: weeks later, when you still haven't washed it out and soil from home still clumps under the lip, you give it words, you write it up. Weeks later, it is a poem.

The Jar

Flush with the ground now, this gate I pulled behind me,
    Saturdays,
my bouquet of rhubarb tied high with baling twine, bars even
    light.
The low branch of the crab apple tree yields an habitual
    shrug.
I bend to unpick a rust petal from my skirt and notice it, as I
    would
any yellow flower that had survived my step. It is, instead,
    what
would have been an unremarkable jar: buff ceramic, glazed,
    homely;
sunk to the neck in umber earth that falls, when I tip it over,
    on boots
I polished sometime south of yesterday. For butter maybe. Or
    preserves.
The sound of soil on leather is like spit on a warming iron, or
    the sputter
of two pheasants shook out of mountain ash. Tomorrow, half
    a world away,
I will rub what's left of home between foreign fingers, unpick
    the primrose
I pressed in my notebook and leave in photographs to be
    developed.
Perhaps then, other things will make some sense, like the
    kitchen garden
buried in its own soil, or the tyre tracks, stiff and
    compounded, that point

every which way to those who left and those who didn't; those
   who think
of nowhere else, or those who visit and take away what little
   remains.

THE REAL MEANING OF HOME

Ann Bree

Home is where the heart is. Home, that word with so many meanings – warmth, welcome, security, love, familiarity, ease, identity.

Home, forever connected with where I was raised, where my parents lived, still home in my mind even though I have had my own home and family for nearly thirty years.

When news of my father's death came, I still thought of it as home. After the funeral, the house was full of people. People who insisted on telling us about our parents, how Dad had been so brave over the last four years, how much he had missed Nell, how now, if there was any God, they had to be together. In the flurry of activity, we somehow got through those days. Now, in accordance with my father's will, the house had to be sold.

The house after the funeral … was such a different place. No response to my walking in, no 'Oh there you are', or 'It's great to see you'; no, just an oppressive stillness. I walk from room to room. The photos I had proudly sent, of graduation, wedding, first grandson, first communions, the gifts carefully chosen … still adorn the living room. Thoughtfully placed, on the mantelpiece, by the television … what was I to do with them now? Taking them back would feel very strange.

The house – for now it is a house, no longer home – feels empty, bereft of any human warmth, it is just a building, a house … nothing is what it was … it is lonely, cold even with the heat on, the task of sifting through decades of living and all that goes with it now staring me in the face.

I have come prepared: tea, milk and biscuits in my bag, a roll of black plastic bags, yellow post-its, a notebook: it seemed straightforward enough yesterday when I left Galway. I am not a hoarder in my own life. I know all about decluttering, bags for charity, bags for the dump, bags for what is to be retained … it seems so straightforward. Now, however, I am besieged with memories, I feel like an intruder, everything is familiar, yet it is not mine.

I walk around the house, everything is too tidy, it is too quiet. I put on the radio for company. A neighbour, seeing my car, drops in to say hello and to enquire how we are getting on. 'We miss them so much too,' she says. The tears come. I make some tea. Sitting at the kitchen table, drinking from the familiar cup, I think of all the problems that have been sorted out in this same fashion. Shortly afterwards, she continues on her way, offering a kind invitation to pop by for something to eat before I head back.

Once she's gone, I decide to be businesslike about it all. This job has to be done. I've got more time than the others. Where will I start? I decide on wardrobes and, for a while, I make good progress; so many items are old fashioned, worn, it's easy to relegate them to the pile for the dump. Then on a shelf in the wardrobe, I find an old box. I wipe off the dust, gently open the lid … and there it is, the faint but unmistakable trace of 'Blue Grass', my mother's favourite perfume. I lose track of time. Coming out of my reverie, I realise I can't do this on my own.

My sister comes in answer to my call. Together we are stronger, our combined memories bring tears but also laughter, we sift through presses and drawers, we start so many sentences with 'Will you look at this?' or 'Do you remember when…?' The moments are truly bittersweet. We select little items that have special memories for us. My mother's small jewellery box proves too much for us. We put it aside until we are less raw.

Gradually, we realise that the clearing out is of things, that our memories will always be with us. Whatever the new owners do with the house, even if they demolish it, the home we knew will live on in our hearts and minds. In a certain way, we can always go home.

SUBURBAN IDYLL

Leland Bardwell

I am being ironic. The suburb in which I found myself was far from idyllic.

In 1981, I was evicted from the small house I rented in a lane behind Adelaide Road. The landlady wanted to sell the property and in no way had I the wherewithal to buy it from her.

So, there I was with three adolescent sons with nowhere to go. So, I had no choice but to throw myself under the aegis of Dublin Corporation.

Around this time, what was known as 'Tallaght' was spreading into the foothills of the Dublin Mountains. New housing estates – Killenarden, Fettercain, Jobstown – were mushrooming out into the hinterlands and the old buildings in the city were being de- molished to give way to offices. Fine old Georgian houses were being knocked down overnight.

So, every week, I queued in the Corporation buildings, with hundreds of others, mostly in the same boat as I was, all of whom begged not to be sent out to Tallaght or Coolock. Strong men wept and babies howled. We executed Danses Macabre, but all to no avail. I was told that when finally my furniture was out on the street, we'd be given the key to our new abode.

When the sheriff came, riding on his Honda 50, he furnished me with my eviction papers.

I do not wish to go into the inconvenience caused to my family by this move, with the secondary school the other side of Dublin, no jobs for young people if you gave that address, no public transport, no telephones. Nor do I want to go into my own feelings of disorientation. But what saddened me most was the fate of the young married women who had been uprooted from their families, their neighbours, especially their mothers. These young women, already burdened with one or two children and a husband out of work, were suddenly expected to settle in these half-built surroundings bereft of all other human contact. Even the Travellers, of whom there were many all around, with their horses and jalopies, seemed happier and ironically more settled with their freedom of movement.

When the snows came that January, the roofs leaked; the houses, subcontracted by the Corpo, were unable to stand up to this type of weather and mud ran down from the hills.

With great difficulty and many weeks of queuing at head office, I managed to get an exchange back into Dublin, but most of these poor families, unable for the fight, remained.

A few years after I left, still saddened by the memory of it all, I wrote this poem for them.

Them's your Mammy's pills.

They'd scraped the topsoil off the gardens
And every step or two they'd hurled a concrete block
Bolsters of mud like hippos from the hills
Rolled on the planters' plantings of the riff raff of the city.

The schizophrenic planners had finished off their job
Folded their papers, put away their pens
The city clearances were well ahead.

And all day long a single child was crying
While his father shouted, 'Don't touch them,
Them's your Mammy's pills.'

I set to work with zeal to play, 'doll's house'
'Doll's life', 'doll's garden'
While my adolescent sons played music
In the living room out front
And drowned the opera of admonitions
'Don't touch them, them's your Mammy's pills.'

Fragile as needles the women wander forth
Laddered with kids, the unborn one out front
To forge the mile through mud and rut
Where mulish earth removers rest. A crazy sculpture.

They are going back to the city for the day
That is all they live for
Going back to the city for the day.

The line of shops and solitary pub
Are camouflaged like checkpoints on the border
The supermarket stretches emptily
A circus of sausages and time

The till girl gossips in the veg department
Once in a while a woman might come in
To put another pound on
An electronic toy for Christmas.

From behind the curtains every night
The video lights are flickering butcher blue
'Don't touch them, them's your Mammy's pills.'

No one has a job in Killenarden
Nowadays they say it is a no-go area
I wonder then who goes and does not go
In the strange, forgotten world
Of video and valium.

I visited my one-time neighbour
Not so long ago. She was sitting
In the hangover position
I knew she didn't want to see me
Although she'd cried when we were leaving.

I went my way
Through the quietly rusting motor cars and prams
Past the barricades of wire, the harmony of junk
The babies that I knew
Are punk size now
And soon children will have children
And new voices ring the leit motif

Don't touch them, them's your Mammy's pills.

BED

Dominic Cogan

Some time ago, my wife and I went shopping for a new bed. The salesman helpfully explained the advantages of different types of mattresses to ensure a good night's rest. It was only when the bed arrived home and was assembled that it crossed my mind that this might well be the last bed we would buy. After all, a good-quality bed could last a lifetime. And this led on to the rather morbid thought that we might spend our final hours on it.

A bed is a very versatile piece of furniture. What can you do on a bed – practically everything? For children a bed is the original bouncy castle. They may also be the site of our first introduction to the magic of fairytales.

At all stages in life, when we are sick we take to the bed. When life overwhelms us and the tears flow, the bed is a place of comfort, a place to gather our energies. Beds can also, of course, be the setting for the most intimate moments of lovemaking.

New life may be conceived in a bed and it is most typically in a bed, albeit a hospital one, that the newborn infant makes its first appearance.

And I haven't even mentioned a bed as a place to go to sleep in. What is this thing called sleep? We all know that sleep enables the body to rest and replenish its energies. But within sleep, there is the mysterious other world of dreams. Where do we go to when we dream? Wherever we go, the bed, tangible and real and four square upon the ground, takes us there. In sleep, it transforms from being just a piece of furniture into a vehicle that transports us between worlds.

But in waking time, a bed can also act as a café or a library, or both. Breakfast in bed is one of the great creature comforts. But the bed for me has always been the place, par excellence, to read a good book. It would be no declaration of promiscuity for anyone to say that they had gone to bed with some of their favourite writers.

Perhaps salespeople, when engaging customers in furniture shops should give the wide range of uses of a bed more consideration. It could lead to some very interesting sales talk.

LIVING IN THE IRISH SEA

Carl Tighe

When you live at the edge of a community, alliances and identities are always uncertain. You can feel the world shifting under you, like an irregular sea swell.

My granma lived in the fishermen's cottages on the sea wall at Ringsend. It was with her we stayed. The cottage was very crowded and once Granma, to get us out from under her feet while she prepared dinner, asked my brother and I to step into the garden and pluck up a bunch of her home-grown carrots. We sprang to it and returned a few minutes later, having carefully shaken off the dirt, with about a dozen carrots, and we presented them to Granma. Looking back, I realise she wanted us out of the cottage because she was having some kind of a confab with my dad. She took one look at the carrots and began to slap us about the head and face. She chased us from the kitchen. My father jumped into her path shouting, 'Ma, what are you doing? You asked them to pick the carrots.'

Granma was having none of it. She snatched up the carrots and shook them at my father. 'See,' she yelled. 'See! That's exactly what I'm talking about.'

My father was silent.

'You've brought a little tribe of Brummies into the world. Little Brummie savages. What were you thinking of, over there? Did you take leave of your senses?'

My brother and I retreated to the sea wall. My brother was wheezing with asthma. This was hard for us. I was nine, he was seven. We always found it difficult to understand why our Dublin family called us their English cousins. It put us at a distance. Englishness was not something we felt comfortable with, though, yes, we had Birmingham accents. But we were brought up in an Irish Catholic environment. We were surrounded by other Irish Catholic families. We went to an Irish Catholic school with nuns and priests and Irish Catholic teachers. We went to mass where our priest, Father Murphy, was a fierce Texan Irishman. And we did the penance he dished out. In what way were we less the real thing than him? If anything, our upbringing had been intensely Irish, but in a complicated immigrant way.

But what made it hard was that I was still limping from incidents the previous week. I was limping because I had been attacked in the playground by a gang – the James Boys, they called themselves – who said my brother and I were English. In fact the James Boys, like me, were Irish kids with Birmingham accents.

That same afternoon as I was going home, because I could not run I was cornered by another gang. They punched and kicked me until I slid down the wall and then kicked me in the chest, screaming, 'Irish Scum Bastard! Irish Scum Bastard!' My brother, unable to help, watched from a distance. When they had gone, he helped me home. After a week, the bruises were ripe and yellow.

After two beatings in one day – one for being English, the other for being Irish – Granma's revelation that there was some ambiguity about us did not come entirely as a surprise. That it came from Granma, that she blamed my father, that somehow my mother was nowhere in this picture – these were real, lasting, painful messages. My brother and I were here: we were facts. That we were not what was required, well, there was nothing I could do about that.

HOMECOMING

Geraldine Mills

This is what we do to retrieve half-lost, half-remembered pieces of ourselves. We hold on to a fragment of story, of personal history, something that connects us with what has gone before and brings us back. That weekend, my sisters and I looped our way into the past after the death of another of our sisters because she dreamed of doing it herself and we hoped to retrieve pages of our own history. We had already recovered three houses in which our family had lived in north Mayo and now we were looking for another. We drove through avenues of gorse and rhododendron, roads that knew no traffic, to find a shell of a house where my eldest sister was born. Only three of the walls remained, but she knew it was called the forge then because the local blacksmith worked from there. She recalled horses coming from all around, their hot, sweaty equine scent, the ferric smell and singe of metal on hoof, this was our door into the dark. A bird sat on a branch. This landscape hadn't changed since she had lived there, the way the moor grass turned the whole mountain purple when it was in its season or the copper reeds turned the area to a holy monstrance of fire.

There was something in the earth that we heard, half-heard as we drove down side roads, turned along the cliffs to see waves breaking off the headland. There was something so intrinsic to us in the area and, though we hadn't lived there, it had come down to us nonetheless, roots that came to us without our knowing.

We walked to the harbour where a man was checking some lobster pots and, in the way of country things, was curious about five middle-aged women not from the place. In no time, he had our seed, breed and generation. He pinned names together like a necklace, naming those who were cousins or second, those that carried the music in their veins, fiddlers in pubs, concertina players from my mother's side. We could understand now why our great-grandmother came back to this. She left after the Famine, took her family off to Massachusetts thinking they would make a life there. She went believing that the streets were paved with gold but she never settled. She was choked by the rows of brownstone houses that were hiding out the sky for her, no gold of hay at saving or gorse that blazed all over the countryside, scenting the air with its sweet coconut smell. Against the tide of all the hardship in Ireland, she took the boat back home, back to places that she hungered for. Kept hidden in her shawl, her dead baby daughter who died on the journey, until she could bury her on Irish soil. She returned to this land that had so little but the poor land itself and never again went farther than Belmullet on Fair days when she went to sell milk, eggs or apples and with that money bought herself a stretch of cloth to make a dress finer than anything she ever saw in America.

THE SEWING MACHINE

Mary J. Byrne

There was a Yugoslav couple on the train back to Paris from Vienna. He was anxious to exercise his French. His wife just sat and smiled. They'd been back home in Yugoslavia for years, retired now on a small French pension, but still kept a little room in Paris that he'd bought years ago, a tiny space in which he and his wife had brought up their daughter. Like all Yugoslavs, they had sent money down home and, little by little, machinery was bought for the farm and the house was improved. In Paris, he and his wife worked in sweatshops, kept an industrial sewing machine in the small room to make extra money, washed at the sink and used the toilet on the stairs. When they retired, they went home to help on the farm. 'My wife's a good woman,' he said, 'she cooks and sews.' His wife smiled and nodded, with little French despite the Paris years. The farm was ten hectares, about twenty-five acres. His brother bred white cows with yellow patches that produced up to twenty-five litres of milk a day. I wondered what lay in store for such a farm, in the new global economy.

It appeared that Yugoslavs never leave their country behind. His daughter left France as soon as her schooling was finished and married a young man down home. Sometimes, these marriages were arranged in Paris. One girl had refused to return to the village.

'Too proud,' he said. That marriage had broken up. Yugoslav family solidarity seemed remarkable, as was the willingness of the children and grandchildren to follow their parents' ways. When a livelihood had to be found for his newly married daughter and her husband, the whole family sat down together and asked themselves, 'What is it that people always need – war or no war, prosperity or not?' The answer, they decided, was bread. So they opened up a little bakery on the farm, regular orders, people came to collect. 'It isn't easy,' he said. 'You have to work nights, seven days a week.' The grandson will take it over when he's finished his military service, so that their daughter and her husband can take a rest after twenty years. I thought it didn't sound like a family to rest much.

'That Slobo,' he said. He waved his arm in the air, then stopped. 'But Yugoslavia will pick up again. We're Europeans. Tito knew how to hold us together. It was Communism that ruined all those other countries,' he said. 'They all became robbers, even their new politicians.'

When the tirade was over, we enquired, by way of conversation, what they were planning to do in Paris. 'Only staying two days,' he said briskly. 'Collect the pension, dismantle the sewing machine, hit the road again.' They were bringing the machine to a young granddaughter in Vienna, who was to be set up in the sewing business. 'Give us three years,' he said, 'and we'll show you a new Yugoslavia.'

I wondered how many natives, in Austria or anywhere else, had any idea of the industry and energy foreigners use in order to keep several families going, in two countries. And I was instantly reminded of a woman on an Irish bus last year, who had only uttered one sentence as various foreigners boarded the bus in Navan, 'Too many of them foreign nationalists here now,' she said. And I knew it was something she'd heard somewhere, not something she really believed herself.

SHEEP PENS

Máiríde Woods

Somewhere a geography text called *Contours of Northern Ireland* is languishing – and in that book is a photograph of sheep pens on the side of a hill near Glenravel, the village next to my own. I think the photograph was meant to illustrate mountainy agriculture. The geography book had nothing about my home town, Cushendall – although it was much more photogenic with its curfew tower, its steep hills and curved strand but, in those days, tourism was on the sidelines of geography.

Sometimes, in the interminable grey study periods in boarding school, I would open that book and gaze at those sheep pens, trying to establish the connection, to keep my map of home alive. I had never set much store on sheep pens before; I was your average would-be urban country child who had reckoned without homesickness, that slightly ridiculous emotion that bolts your heart firmly to the things you've lost.

Of course I hadn't really lost my home; I went back there every few months. But I didn't fit in any more. The stairs had got narrower, the kitchen smaller, the wild field muddier. The joint fantasy land my sister and I had slipped in and out of so effortlessly, now felt silly. Fishing for shrimps was unbelievably childish. Yet I wasn't sure what to do instead; my school friends were all miles away.

At school in my cubicle, I yearned for our house, for our bedroom with its sloping ceiling and its dormer window, its reddish damask curtains. The funny thing was I had never belonged in the world I now yearned for. We were outsiders, blow-ins in the tight-knit glens community; and my parents spent a lot of time looking towards their home in the South.

After the eleven plus, I had been ready for escape to new pastures. We thumbed through the brochures for the different convents and schools with their promises of musical and academic opportunity. My parents took me at my reasonable best. 'It's up to you,' they said. But when the pain of that choice overwhelmed me, they couldn't help me remake it. In our world, exile was a one-way street and going back on things was called reneging.

Like many an exile, I had taken no account of the ties that bind. At eleven, I didn't understand my own tearfulness, my longing for my mother. Homesickness is a staple of boarding school and you dealt with it by describing your home and family to anyone who would listen. All the girls were the same – they had apparently perfect families in bungalows and houses all over counties Antrim and Derry. I know intimate details of places in Kilrea and Swatragh that I've never set eyes on.

By the holidays, you almost believed home was truly like that. When you got there, the process of disillusionment set in; the house was shabby; your mother wore funny hats; your father grumbled. Yet, once back at school, you tried to hang on to shards of home: the smell of Lux that lingered on your cardigan for the first week, the jam your mother had made which was different from that of the other girls, the trinkets that helped define your personality in a world of uniforms.

And, wherever you went, it would be something the same. Even boarding school itself now evokes the odd sentimental twinge when I remember the good parts – the midnight feasts, the companionship, the inspiring teachers, the sound of sheep in the back field. Sheep – real and biblical – were the backdrop to my early life and when I think of those sheep pens – now vanished in reality – I feel that old ridiculous sorrow for the worlds I cannot re-enter, pens that will never again hold me.

THE JOYS OF LETTER WRITING

John Quinn

When I was in boarding school, some fifty years ago now, the hour from eleven to twelve o'clock every Sunday morning was devoted to letter writing. The study hall was hushed as we diligently wrote home – or to siblings, to an uncle or aunt or to friends – but mostly to home. The letter home was in my case mostly a pretence – everything was fine; I was doing well in my studies and enjoying boarding-school life. No mention of loneliness or homesickness. 'How is Roy, the dog?' 'Did you see any of my friends lately?' Occasionally there might be a hint that funds were low and we were hoping to go to a match in Tullamore …

We handed up our letters unsealed as they would have to be read by those in authority before being posted. Why? Well we might be … writing to *girls* … or something awful like that. Or playing a trick on someone like poor old Wally McNamara. Somebody wrote to Charles Atlas, the bodybuilder, for details on how to have a body like his – and signed Wally's name to it. Let's face it, Wally wasn't exactly the fittest boy in the school. Brother Oliver was not amused.

I doubt if such an hour exists in the timetable of today's boarding schools – the few that remain in existence. There probably isn't even a 'texting' hour. Sure you could do that during science class, or – God forbid – at the back of the church. Letter writing is a lost art nowadays – and that's a pity.

Writing a letter requires concentration and organisation of thought. A letter is personal, intimate and it reveals the writer's personality. It can inform. It can amuse. It can comfort. Of course, in those bygone boarding-school days, we were instructed in the art of letter writing and you could be guaranteed a letter as one of the choices in your English exam paper.

I have always enjoyed writing letters. One enters a special relationship with the correspondent, adopting a particular tone and a specific approach, depending upon the time and the theme. There is an even greater joy, of course, in receiving letters. There is the delight in the recognition of the familiar handwriting, the anticipation of the news within and the sheer pleasure of absorbing the contents in a relaxed state. And if the writing is unfamiliar, there is the added puzzlement and intrigue. Who might this be? And why are they writing? And, of course, a good letter can be read and re-read over and over – and filed away for future delight. I speak, of course, of personal letters. Let's not linger on those formal, typed letters – 'It may have escaped your notice that your account is overdrawn …' or 'With regard to your letter of the 12th ult., I regret to inform you …' – I'm talking about the letters that inform, delight and entertain – wasn't that what they used to say about television?

I was lucky in my youth to have the benefit of parents, uncles and aunts who wrote newsy and amusing letters and who wrote regularly. How important that was in boarding school – to receive news of home and family – and there was the added delight of seeing, 'ten shillings' or 'one pound' written in red on the envelope. Yes, the incoming mail was censored too (well there could be *girls* writing to one!) but the red marks indicated that a hint had been taken, money had been sent, had been retrieved by the authorities and safely lodged to the tuckshop account.

Yes, I'm conscious of the warning 'Never put it in writing', but that refers to archaic notions such as 'slander' and 'breach of promise', and is an argument for another day. For now, I must conclude. As my father would write: 'I hope this finds you well as it leaves all here ...' And, of course, he was always 'rushing to catch the post'. I'm so glad he did catch it.

It's mid-morning now. The postman will be coming by soon. I'm hoping ...

SMOKING

Frank Marshall

When my filing cabinet refused to open because of the quantity of stuff I had jammed into it over the years, it was clear it was time to face the fact that I was a hoarder. The decision was a long time coming, but, eventually, I brought some humour to it and was actually smiling at my weakness when I discovered a voluminous file marked 'Donnelly Visas'. This resurrected some very unsettling memories.

In the late 1980s and early 1990s, thousands of Irish people emigrated to the USA under a quota system introduced after much lobbying by a few US congressmen. There is little doubt that the famous green cards opened unlimited possibilities for many who would otherwise have been confined to the humiliation of the dole queue.

The outbreak of the Gulf War in 1991 raised some serious issues for the holders of green cards, when it was revealed that there was a possibility of being drafted into the US forces. What had seemed a harmless paragraph now loomed as a stark reality. It is unclear just how many were actually aware that they could end up in the Middle East opposing the forces of Saddam Hussein.

My two sons were working happily in New Jersey when the awful truth dawned. The phone lines were buzzing nightly across the Atlantic for a few weeks. I will never forget the night of 21 January when I heard a newscaster announce that Mr Bush had authorised the calling up of 20,000 extra into the armed forces. I was unable to sleep that night and, at 4 a.m., I sat downstairs, smoking my pipe, wondering what was going to develop. It happened that I had just enlisted in a poetry group, so I tried to commit my troubled thoughts to a blank page. Eventually, this emerged as part of the first poem I published:

Two Donnelly Visas equals two sons
Equals two US Marines
Masters' Degrees and Leaving Certs
Are excellent weapons, designed to kill.

The crisis passed. My sons were not drafted and went on to become naturalised US citizens. Over the following decade, I travelled over to visit them, almost every year. Once I had cleared US Immigration at Shannon, I treated myself to a glass of Irish whiskey to set me afloat across the Atlantic. It always seemed the right thing to do.

The first year that Kevin was installed in his own home, I had negotiated a smoking room for my odoriferous pipe. The following year, when I assumed the same arrangement would apply, he told me that as his wife, Deirdre, was pregnant, it would not be possible for me to smoke in the house. His manner was very apologetic and he seemed quite embarrassed. I can still remember his expression and the concern it revealed. This was a moment of some significance. The boy had become a man and the father had become, well, not an errant child, but he was taking the directions.

Kevin came outdoors with me. It was a warm, balmy September evening in Boston and it turned into a pleasant interlude in the fading light, once the initial embarrassment had softened. Our relationship had always been special but had undergone a perceptible transformation once he was married. 'For this reason a man shall leave his Father and Mother and cling to his wife.'

On subsequent visits, I settled happily on a bench in the garden and smoked quite contently. There was an apartment block visible from my position and my imagination was given plenty of scope as the tenants moved about. There was even a group on the top storey who had clearly gathered to smoke.

There is a change of location now. Kevin and Deirdre and three lovely grandchildren have relocated to Greystones. Boston is no longer on the map and smoking is less attractive outdoors in this climate. I stick with my addiction. However, there has been one unexpected development in that my four-year-old granddaughter, Heather, is not too fussed by my pipe. The refrain of 'No smoking in the house, Granddad' is often heard in an imperious voice, followed by her screeching, mocking laughter. Even on the phone she scolds me, but the laugh raises my heart like nothing has ever done before.

A non-smoker would never have heard that beautiful, lifting, mocking sound of joy.

CALL TO ADVENTURE

Isobel Mahon

I watch the warm water ooze through my fingers no matter how hard I try to squeeze them closed. I'm trying hard to hold on to something that keeps slipping away. Time. The time it takes to make a cup of coffee, the time it takes to think a thought. And I want to shout 'stop', 'wait', 'freeze', 'Press the pause button, I'm not ready yet. I haven't got my life in order, I'm wasting time.' But, of course, this doesn't happen and time chuffs on whether I'm ready or not and I clutch on to the back of the time-train and Do My Best to keep up. My Best. What would that be like? Well, for a start I wouldn't be writing about myself but about other people, proper 'characters', the bread and butter of any writer. And these would move obediently in a Story Arc. They would walk out the door one day in answer to The Call To Adventure, encounter two major setbacks on pages twenty-five and forty-three, recognise and overcome their Fatal Flaw, get the Boy/Girl/Labrador dog, have an epiphany by page seventy-five and then obligingly return to their home place but see it As Though For the First Time.

That's all.

But that's a shocking amount to expect from any human being.

That is not my call to adventure; my call to adventure is the shrill drilling of my white cubic digital clock at seven thirty. My co-protagonist is not Brad Pitt but my five-year-old pixie daughter with her extravagant love and her sharp little elbows.

My story arc is not some graceful structure that spans a tidy adventure. More like a scuttling rat run, really. Woolly-jumpered and blue-jeaned, school running, huffing, puffing, bag rattling, grocery shopping. And rushing home to find transcendence. Wherever that may be.

I begin to despair, perhaps there is no call to adventure for me. No story arc. Then I listen a little harder and, after a while, begin to hear the self-confident warble of a fat blackbird and his homely little mate who has always known that brown is the new black. The twittering of a long-legged robin in his middle-management office on the apple tree. The exquisite apricot finch, beauty queen of the garden.

These are my calls to adventure. Small calls. And hard to hear in this busy, busy time-short world. But calls nonetheless. Calls to the journey inwards, to a quiet place and that, perhaps, is where the real adventure begins.

FATHERHOOD

Dermot Bolger

Let me tell you a story told to me by a novelist friend. It occurs in the remote northern part of his native Sweden several years ago. Winter, a desolate snow-bound road, subzero temperatures and a car that breaks down a hundred miles from the city he is returning to with his family.

Whatever brief light exists is fading as he trudges to the nearest village with his wife and two small children. Naturally, there isn't a garage. Real men fix their own cars up here, he is told. There isn't a bus or a hotel either. Eventually, he is told that if he can find a certain barn in the woods somebody there might take pity on him.

When he finds it, he's not so sure. It's where the local hard men hang out, souping up their jeeps, spending the long winter tinkering with pistons and spark plugs. They observe him in silence as he tells his story, enjoying his discomfort. Shaved heads, arms thick as the walls of Limerick jail, eyes like hard sweets from Bray that would break your teeth. The rural/urban animosity is the same the world over. Nothing much happens up there in winter but, by God, the night the city slicker got stranded, unable to fix his own bloody car, will be a story to savour on many evenings to come. He is on his own, they let him know in no uncertain terms. He drove the car, he can fix it.

He opens the barn door to leave, muttering something about getting back to his children. Children? What children? Why the hell didn't he mention children before? The hard men suddenly surround him. What age is his little girl? Is she frightened, cold? One man is producing a photo from his wallet of his daughter who is the same age. Other men are reaching for their coats, a hub-bub of male voices laughing companionably as they jostle him out the door, grabbing their tools, demanding directions to the car.

He walks among them, looking at their open faces. They have ceased to be men, he realises, suddenly they have all become fathers.

Ever since being told of that incident, I think of it a lot when I am with other men. Maybe Masonic lodges are the same with their secret codes and handshakes, but fatherhood is a strange, invisible bond, linking the most unlikely of people.

People look back at society thirty and forty years ago and say that it was a man's world. On almost every practical level they are absolutely right, most especially when the most obvious symbol of fatherhood today, all too often, is the shabby bedsit a few miles from the spacious family home. Forty years ago, men certainly held all the cards, with property rights, women forced to leave many jobs when they married, biased inheritance laws and the unwritten law that women were meant to suffer in silence behind closed doors while authority turned a blind eye.

The marvellous poet Michael Hartnett once summed up a chilling portrait of Christmas Eve at that time as being a night when 'in pubs the men filled up with porter and in the homes the women filled up with apprehension'.

And yet – for all that – they were prisoners too, trapped within the hard circle of their own maleness. Perpetually in fear of the public ridicule summed up by The Citizen in *Ulysses*, who, upon hearing that Bloom was once seen buying baby food for his son that died, snorts and remarks scornfully, 'Call that a man?'

Even in literature, Irish fathers seem trapped in the same boat. The silent, sour, tyrannical head of the family runs through Irish fiction right up through John McGahern and Shane Connaughton and even into very recent novels by the likes of Kate O'Riordan and Colm O'Gaora. What makes Roddy Doyle's *The Snapper* such a radical book isn't just having an unmarried mother as the heroine, but the fact that the book's hero is her own father, a bumbling, well-meaning, slightly bewildered figure, who doesn't chastise but learns to celebrate and bears his grandchild home in triumph.

Irish writers could well argue that, up to now, there were too few of Roddy Doyle's Mrs Rabbitts in real life and too many of John McGahern's Michael Morans.

Maybe they were right, but on summer evenings in playgrounds or wet mornings in adventure centres, I see other fathers now. Clambering down narrow slides after their laughing children, pushing prams proudly, rocking teething infants on their knees, immersed totally in the second glimpse at wonder that is given to them by being fully a part of their children's childhood.

Sometimes, our eyes meet for a second and I think we are thinking the same thing. Not that it was a man's world for our fathers and grandfathers, but just how much of this short-lived (and never to be repeated) wonder did they miss out on, in that cage of manhood which society trapped them into.

My own father was at sea for all my childhood. His homecomings were joyous events. But, too often, the coming home of a father was something for children to be threatened with. They were the breadwinners, the rule enforcers, the hard men out in their barn in the woods waiting for one chance to let the mask slip and produce the photographs of their children, which they carried close to their breasts.

A TEENAGE BAND

Josephine Molloy

We have all heard of shell shock suffered by soldiers at war and of seismic shock felt in earthquake zones. But have you ever heard of Heavy Metal Shock? Believe me, it is real. I am the mother of a drummer. It does exist. And my house must be suffering from it. Like myself, the walls, ceilings, floors and furniture must be neurotic wrecks. We have endured five years of ear-shattering shrieks from souped-up guitars, thundering decibels from a drum kit, roars from raucous singers and the noisy antics of a group of teenagers. The practice sessions were frenetic, the performances passionate and the laughter contagious.

To achieve 'The Image', gear could be any shade so long as it was black. And splashed with images of ghouls, skeletons, gravestones or dripping blood. Not for the fainthearted! Apparently, it is impossible to have 'drum cred' without sporting long, lank locks that flip and fly around like a mad Muppet! I have also learned that no self-respecting guitarist can perform without the dreaded bandana glued to the brow.

Early on, when I was asked how I thought they sounded 'on the last number', I would dutifully reply, 'Great! Cool! Brill!' – not really knowing one number from another. But, gradually, I began to recognise music by Metallica, Green Day, Slipknot, Satriani, among others. The metal heads were more shocked than I when I got a title right.

The groupings changed over the years. New guitarists came, singers were replaced. But my drummer was a permanent fixture. Gradually, the bangs and screeches and squawks modulated and came together very well. It actually became a pleasure to stop and listen to the music and be amazed by the talent, skill, energy and discipline involved. Nights before gigs were frantic. Leads, plugs, amps, microphones, control panels, pedals, spare drumsticks were all gathered and loaded with the instruments into our trusty old jeep. Joy divine if the gig went well.

Now my drummer is in college and, for the first time in five years, the drums are silent in what was once the toy room. Dust dares to rest on the snoozing drum kit. Lonely looking drumsticks, with chips and gouges bashed out of them, lay exhausted across the snare drum. When I go into that room now, the silence reverberates louder than the music ever did. The sofa looks bored and depressed. The drums sit dozing in the sunlight.

My drummer comes home at weekends. The drum kit is awakened with delight and joy. But I know the day will come when my drummer will move his drums to another place. I'll be sad. But memories will linger forever of the laughter, melody, harmony, pizza crusts, mashed chips, coke bottles and odd socks. And the sheer joy of it all.

FORTY-FOUR

Michael Murtagh

Today, I celebrate my forty-fourth birthday. I begin my forty-fifth year. My birthday happens to fall on Lady Day, or Annunciation Day. I was christened Gabriel on this account. I became known by my second name, Michael. Gabriel was considered a little pretentious. It was also subject to all sorts of unpleasant abbreviations. It could have been worse. I might have been called Annunciato.

The New Year began on this date in England until the middle of the eighteenth century. It was called Lady Day. All leases and contracts were dated from that day. In the wider world, it had been considered the beginning of the year until the Gregorian calendar reforms in 1582 changed the date to 1 January. In the year 1958, Lady Day, for me, was the beginning of my contract with the world, my lease of life.

The very mention of the year 1958 makes me feel like a relic of the middle of the last century. Sometimes, I try to remember how the fortysomethings of my childhood appeared to my infant eyes. They seemed to be parent-like and very old, I suppose. Though my elders tell me that I'm still 'only a child', I realise that from the perspective of a child, I am something of an antiquity, being able to remember the beginnings of cultural disorder in the 1960s. I slept through the last years of the 1950s, thankfully, so I escaped the great whinge as a writer's theme. The 1960s arrived in the 1970s where I lived.

In spite of the protestations of those of more mature years, I recognise the signs of wear and tear. In fact, my dentist told me some time ago that my teeth were uncommonly worn for someone of my years. I wondered on the reason and found comfort in telling myself that it could be worse. If I had been a horse, my valuation would be significantly decreased by worn teeth. There is a crease too that used not to be there and that appears at a right angle to my jawline in times of tiredness or weakness. It goes away, but, one of these days, I expect it to carve itself permanently into my features. My hair has gone grey, or just gone, and no amount of bottled promise can regain the dark brown or the blond of my earlier and earliest years. I genuflect in an empty church and my knee cracks loudly. I hunch at a hospital bedside and cannot rise without pain and stiffness in my knees. I can no longer sleep the marathon of my student days, lazing and turning till dinnertime. Daybreak finds me awake and late nights leave me shattered.

There is a process of development to be gone through by those who reach these years. It is sometimes called trans-valuation by psychologists. It simply means that the outlook and values of youth are left behind or sought to be left behind. The youthful focus on the future, the fearlessness and the idealism of early adult life, usually give way to compromise, conservatism, conformity and pragmatism. Reputation may increase but ability declines. People who have difficulty negotiating this change or accepting the inevitable call the syndrome a 'midlife crisis'. Those who deny the reality or fail to negotiate it safely often end up the butt of ridicule or may find themselves lying on the psychiatrist's couch, unable to accept their limitations and their mortality. There is the recognised figure of the 'oldest swinger in town', the bald male with the ponytail and earrings, wearing a jean-jacket and bovver boots and boasting of his latest conquest or purchase, occasionally meaning the same object. As the country song has it, 'the only difference between men and boys is the size of their shoes and the price of their toys'.

To whom does the term 'middle-aged' belong? I have no desire to claim it, as it reeks of cardigans and Brylcreem and Deep Heat. The psalmist tells us that the span of man is 'seventy years, or eighty for those who are strong'. He adds pessimistically, or with realism, that 'most of these are emptiness and pain. They pass swiftly and we are gone'.

Without claiming the labels of middle age, I have to admit, as Bill Clinton said some years ago, that I have, in all probability, more yesterdays than tomorrows. 'Only a fool celebrates getting older,' said another American, so, on Lady Day, I will celebrate life and say with one of my favourite writers, Dag Hammarskjöld, 'for all that has been – thanks – to all that will be – yes'.

DANCING ON
THE EDGES OF TIME

Geraldine Mitchell

She is a boarded-up house,
a leaking ship,
a blindfold woman,
an empty shell.
Windows broken through neglect,
slates fallen,
birds nesting in the chimney stacks.
She's a door left open in the storm,
rain blowing leaves through the kitchen
to the hall.

She is turning down a corridor and finding all the doors are
    locked.
She is turning down a corridor and finding that it isn't there.
She is looking in the mirror and seeing a lost child.

They say procrastination is the thief of time, but I say it's memory
loss. It thieves on all fronts: present, past and future. Worst of all
is having to watch helplessly as the burglar ransacks your house. It

happened to my best loved aunt. In the early, terrifying stages, she described the inside of her head as just that: a ransacked room with everything thrown randomly about the floor. She said it was like swimming and suddenly finding that the familiar rocks to rest your feet on had been taken away. She said, 'It grows inside you, grows to a great big tree and fills you.'

The trees grew slowly at first,
just one here and there.
It was the mess she objected to most,
twigs and leaves all over the place,
tap roots tripping her up, branches
catching at her clothes and hair.

Then the wood thickened,
taking away her light, her air.
She tried to pull it up, break it down.
Her hands tore.

When there was no way out
she grew quiet. Distant sounds
– a bird, an airplane, children laughing –
bounced fitfully from leaf to leaf
into her hollow.

But sometimes for a moment,
maybe two, a shaft of sunlight
cleaves the canopy, bathes a smiling girl.
Then she sees you, laughs,

and grips your hand.

I, MY FATHER,
ON ACHILL ISLAND

John F. Deane

It was late summer, we were on holiday on Achill Island and the weather was, to be kind to it, demanding. We had brought my father, then some seventy-nine years old, and, on that day, we decided we would eat lunch and then go to Keem Bay and see what was what. So, we had a delightful meal of fresh salmon and brown bread while the slow mists continued to move by, like a procession of silent ghosts, outside. By the time we got back from the beautiful Keem Bay, the mist had eased but the world remained grey and damp. We waited a while and then, perhaps out of sheer bravado, my daughter and I decided we'd brave the Atlantic Ocean and swim. We pronounced the water tolerable and then, to my wonder and delight, Father decided he'd try it too. He undressed, braved the waves, got down and got out very quickly indeed and I could see him dress rapidly, then lean back against a rock to smoke. He was shivering with the cold and I felt very guilty indeed. That was, in fact, the last time he ever went in for a swim.

But it all came back to me as I watched him gaze vacantly out to sea, towards the mountains of the west, towards Croagh Patrick. I remembered those games he had initiated for us when we were children, games on that very beach, thought up to help us get dry and warm again after our swim. He would draw a great circle on the sand with a stick, then criss-cross the circle with easy paths. Right in the middle of the circle he placed a stone. The game consisted of running as fast as we could, keeping always to the lines he had drawn, trying to get to that stone before he tipped us with a seaweed stick. We loved the game and, of course, it dried us quickly and warmed us up. So, that day, I found myself doing exactly the same to help get myself and my daughter dry and warm, although, this time, my father would take no part. But that smile on his face, that proud stance, told me he was pleased and I saw myself at once as growing into my father, the way we all, over the years, grow into our parents, assuming their idiosyncrasies, their ideas, their lives almost.

And does not this awareness remind us how circular our living is? Even though we think we are moving forward in a straight line, as an individual, as a nation, as a race. How circular everything is, how the ending of our lives seems to join up full circle with our beginnings and how we are taught that, while time can be represented as a straight line, eternity is a circle.

You came into the game from a starting point near the rocks and ran, trying to reach the stone placed at the centre, the den, the safe house, home; and there I go – screaming round the outermost circle, father pounding after, a switch of sea-wrack in his hand. Eternity, he told me once, is like the letter O; it has no beginning and no end, or like the nought, perhaps, and you could slither down and down through its black centre. With a silver pin, he would draw the periwinkles from their shells, that soft flesh uncoiling from the whorl; he would scoop out that gravelly meat from the barnacle and we swallowed its roundness whole with that black mucus-like blob at its centre. And see me now, following, the way you became your father, that same diffidence and turning inwards, that same curving of the spine, the way the left shoulder lifts in emphasis. See me where I run, my father watching from the distance as I go pounding round the outermost circle, a father myself, my child racing and laughing in front of me, and a switch of seawrack in my hand.

GROWING OLDER

Ann Henning Jocelyn

Like many others, I dread the prospect of growing old. Old in the sense of becoming obsolete, past it, consigned to the scrapheap of society. With a body steadily losing its functions, a mind going increasingly blank. Who wouldn't be worried by the less-than-pretty picture, often presented by the media, of old age as a series of drooling mouths, trembling hands, swollen feet in felt slippers ranked along the walls of a nursing home?

Having said that, I quite enjoy growing older – the way we all grow older, day by day, starting from the moment we are born. Becoming ever more enriched and experienced, approaching the fulfilment that comes from understanding more and more of the mystery of life and the strange goings-on in the world around us.

Also, I look forward to the freedom that beckons beyond the sometimes stifling demands made upon us during our most active years. The promise of an entirely new lease of life, once the efforts of pursuing a career, raising children, building up security, can be safely left behind.

I consider myself lucky in not having to look far for inspiration. My mother, at the age of seventy, lost both her legs in a traffic accident and, confined to a wheelchair, discovered the joys of writing. Now, at eighty-five, she is a prolific novelist – when not writing, she lectures on the topic of rehabilitation.

A Swedish friend, a popular singer-songwriter, in sparkling form at seventy-eight, tours the country performing to packed houses. An elderly actress I know is blossoming with her one-woman shows. Another friend, an art connoisseur, spends his old age travelling the world seeking out its best museum collections.

They all vow, convincingly, that their life has never been sweeter. Not for them to let physical frailty, poor hearing or dimming eyesight come in the way of their enjoyment. Even a defective memory can be of help, apparently, in sorting out what really matters.

It's probably no coincidence that their vitality is closely linked to art and creativity. Creativity, after all, taps the source of life itself: in all its guises, it's what personal growth is all about. What's more, it is freely available, to all of us, if only our society would do more to encourage it.

I wish there were many more such role models, in whose footsteps the rest of us could follow. We need the incitement to keep adding to ourselves, for as long as we are able, sustained by the belief that, as long as we keep growing, we will remain, happily and vibrantly, alive.

CINEMAS

Gerry McDonnell

The cinema is now a place where we experience movies, respectful and informed, educated in film studies. Not so in the 1950s! A deafening cheer rose from the kids as the lights dimmed and the heavy drapes parted like the Red Sea. Ushers tried to calm things down, but another cheer rose when Abbott and Costello, or Laurel and Hardy appeared.

Some bizarre memories stay with me. The time the boys from the industrial school, The O'Brien Institute, came to the Fairview cinema. This institution for orphans and other unfortunates, which provided the music of the Artane Boys' Band in Croke Park on a Sunday, filled us with dread. The thought that fate could conspire to arrange the unthinkable circumstances whereby we would be sent there terrified and humbled us. Half a dozen rows had been reserved for the boys. The film was *Darby O'Gill and the Little People*. Presumably, on the say so of a Brother, the boys opened their packets of Clarnico Murray sweets in unison. The tearing of plastic and unwrapping of sweets drowned out any sound from the screen for at least five minutes.

Some Sunday afternoons, we went to 'the Blind', a makeshift cinema in the school for blind boys in Drumcondra, where a Brother operated the flickering projector behind the screen. We sat on wooden benches, albino boys in the front row, and thrilled at the adventures of Zorro and the Lone Ranger; emerging from the dark into the daylight with a blinding headache. The irony of having a cinema in a home for the blind was lost on us.

Back in the real cinemas, like the Fairview or the Strand, and more especially in the Savoy and Adelphi in town, the ushers possessed a daunting power. In their impressive uniforms, they stood sentinel at the doors to the Promised Land. To be refused admission was equivalent to the social deprivation in being barred from an 'in' pub in adult life. Like barmen, ushers ranged from surly and cranky to welcoming. Dealing with a sometimes-troublesome public, no doubt they had their own side of the story.

Willie Sandford

I finished up Head Usher
in a cinema in town.
That uniform counted for something.
You could bar someone for life.
The cinemas were rough in those days.
It could take three of us
to throw a fella out.
No one knew, but all the time
behind that uniform
I was terrified.
The drink gave me Dutch courage.
I had a right skinfull one night
and didn't see the car coming.

That ended my career as Head Usher.
The uniform was sent back,
blood and muck all over it,
property of the cinema.

Bridie Sandford

My Willie was so proud
of his Head Usher's uniform.
I had my work cut out
keeping it pressed and immaculate.
When he was killed that time
we had a photo of him in it
blown up and framed.
I used to get a laugh
out of visitors
when they saw the photo
and asked,
'Was Willie in the army?'

'No,' I used to say,
'he was in the Adelphi.'

TIME,
LIKE AN EVER-ROLLING STONE

Mike Absalom

If it is true, as I have heard, that the universe is a knotted net of pearls and we are all it and it is all God, then it seems logical to suppose that if I were mischievously inclined enough to untie one of the knots, I might stand a chance of finding out something important about the nature of things. And indeed, I once did just that.

When I was a boy, fifty years ago, my father was a country vicar, and it was one of my chores to help him in the parish. At Holy Communion on a Sunday morning, I served at the altar and it was my duty to pump the organ at evensong while he officiated and my mother stumbled through the hymns. There was a little cubbyhole, a kind of tiny second vestry, hidden away behind the stacks of magical silver pipes where I would ensconce myself. It was an enchanted place, lit by thin daylight from a huge leaded window and there was even a pew for me and a thick embroidered hassock.

Evensong, I remember, was often close to sunset, and a particular pale orange light would fall across the back of the wooden organ and, at the signal to begin (a loud thumping on the panelling from my mother's side), I would seize the great oar that filled the bellows and pump away two-handed with the vigour of a Roman galley slave.

A small, lead weight descended on a cord like a slow-motion bullet as I pumped and, when the bellows was full, it stopped and hovered in the air in front of my face. I had time to think then, in that moment of balance, in the orange sunlight, among the flying dust motes, in this holy unseen place, hidden and secure, until the lead weight, now returning to the top of the wall as the bellows emptied, came to a halt, and it was time for me, once again, to put my shoulder to the oar and pump away.

And if I failed to notice the position of the receding lead, a horrible wail from the organ and the dying gasp of a strangled hymn would call me back to red-faced duty and the apprehension of imminent stern, or at least embarrassing, admonishment.

Each week, I made a small mark in pencil on the back of the organ and every fifth week I crossed the marks out and started a new tally.

And, one day, there in that orange glow, breathing in the incense of old sun-warmed timber and ancient leather, and making my pencil mark on the back of the organ, the world suddenly stopped dead. I had, not in a blinding flash, but in a crystal clear moment of revelation, a vivid and lasting understanding of the nature of time. The pencil marks might change every week. But the back of the organ did not change. And I myself stood still. I did not pass from yesterday into today and on towards tomorrow. There was no road of life down which, as my teachers had taught, I would walk. I had only to stand and watch life pass me by. I had undone my first knot.

THE CANAL

Mick Ransford

When I was eleven years old, two of my brothers almost drowned in the Grand Canal.

We'd only moved to the canal a year before and we were still ignorant of its hazards.

One morning after breakfast, we decided to swim in the Barrow on the other side of Lord's Island: myself, my older brother Pat and our younger brother Johnny. We were crossing the lock at the tip of the island when Johnny's foot caught in the gap between the catwalks and he tumbled into the water.

I turned around and he was gone. Pat was staring at a bubbling circle of black in the sheet of sudsy detritus that had collected against the lock gates.

A moment later, Pat was gone too: he'd jumped in after Johnny. He resurfaced with Johnny held under his arm but the two of them sank again almost immediately.

I started screaming; my father came running – he'd been mixing cement in front of our house farther along the canal. He leaped into the water, boots and all, when he was still yards from the lock. He came up with Pat first. He stuck him to the gates and dived under again. By the time he surfaced with Johnny, Mrs Quinn had emerged from the lock house with a bargepole.

Then my mother arrived.

'Where's Joe? Where's Joe?' she kept screaming. I told her Joe hadn't been with us. 'He was playing in the garden when we left,' I said. Joe was the very youngest. Pat and Johnny and I had sneaked off on him earlier; we thought Joe a sissy; all those girlish blond curls. 'He followed you!' my mother insisted, shaking me by the shoulders. 'I saw him following you!'

She didn't believe my father either when he told her Joe hadn't been behind us. Only when Joe showed up minutes later did my mother calm down. She remained convinced though, she'd seen him following us, even though Joe himself denied it. Pat and Johnny had rolled onto their bellies and they were coughing up dirty water when Mrs Quinn began to speak about a boy who'd drowned at the lock when she was a child.

'Some bargemen brought the body into our house,' she told us. 'They laid that little boy out on the hearth. He had curls like a girl,' Mrs Quinn said. 'I'll never forget the water running through those blond curls.'

We never crossed that lock so cavalierly again, convinced that our mother had seen not Joe trailing behind us on that bright summer morning, but the ghost of a boy who'd waited forty years for a playmate to walk over the spot where he had drowned.

GRATITUDE

Dolores Whelan

Meister Eckhart once said if the only prayer you ever said in your lifetime was Thank You it would be sufficient. Gratitude is a powerful spiritual quality that, together with acceptance, enables a person to live a deep and richly abundant life no matter what the outer circumstances are. Gratitude is an attitude or frame of mind that emerges from the open and grateful heart. A story in Peig Sayers recalls her saying, 'I was after thanking the good God for everything, even for the suffering itself, because it would make a person ask deeper questions.' Once, a friend of mine, telling her life story, divided each chapter with the refrain, 'If I keep a green branch in my heart the singing bird will surely come, and a quote in my current diary boldly states that there is eternal summer in the grateful heart.

May-time, the season of Bealtaine, is, for me, not only a season but a state of mind. A place where I can risk bringing something out into the world of form and allow it to blossom into its fullness. It is a place where I step boldly into the world, like all of nature does in May-time, regardless of what lies ahead. To know your own May-time requires a deep and sensitive listening to yourself and a willing to be true to your process. I have often tried to force May-times in my life, to force a piece of work out of its inner space before it was ready to force myself to be in May-time because some aspect of my ego thought I should. What I have learned is that when I do that to myself nothing blossoms!

I am also learning to recognise the many Bealtaine moments that are available in my life every day. These opportunities that happen at unexpected times each day are moments when I say yes to my life as it is this moment and allow the moment to blossom into its fullness.

So let us give thanks for the beauty of Bealtaine in the world around us and for the blossoming energy of Bealtaine wherever it is within us. Let us also honour the journey that begins in Samhain and moves through each of the seasons until it reaches Bealtaine because, in truth, there can be no Bealtaine without Samhain.

BEFORE AND AFTER

Kevin McDermott

I am five and the sky is blue
And there is no before and no after

And my mother is in the kitchen,
Her bare arms flecked with flour.
And she catches me in a floury embrace
That seems to last an hour.

And I pour the currants into a cup
And I stand on the kitchen chair
And I empty them into the mix
With my mother standing there.

Oh I am five and the world is blue.
And there is no before and no after.

And grandfather is in the garden,
Searching out the weeds.
Lost in his own twilight world,
To me he pays no heed.

And I am five and his hands are blue
And there is no before and no after.

And I run to the chicken run.
And I slip through the make-shift gate
And I catch a small white chick
And feel her frightened heart beat.

Oh I am five and the sky is blue
And there is no before and no after.

And I search out the eggs
And I carry them as gifts into the house,
And my mother smiles and lifts one up
And taps it on my nose.

Oh I was five and the sky was blue
And there was no before and no after.

CHRISTMAS

BEARS ON THE HORIZON

Noreen Walshe

In the Tundra, in North Manitoba, outside of the town of Churchill, I saw my first live polar bear. This is where they say it takes two trees to make a Christmas tree, due to the winter gales that burn the windward sides of the fragile Spruce.

It's day three, early morning and we're already jolting about in a huge Tundra buggy, scanning the horizon for the creamy white of even one bear. I am in the company of a group of naturalists. While they search for the perfect photo, I dream of line, shape, pattern and colour, all the elements that will make an interesting painting.

There is a moment when we approach an oasis of aubergine-coloured willow bushes and we see the back of a prone white figure. The driver cuts the engine and tension fills the truck as cameras are lifted, focused and everyone is trying to not explode with excitement. We're as close as is possible to see the hairs of its coat and the coal-black eyes slowly open. The round shape of a female's head rises above the bushes and watches us.

Winter is closing in, as we wait in suspended animation to see what happens next.

With the first few flakes of snow, a memory comes out of the arctic sky, gently at first, then tumbles down the stairs of so many years. It lands on the fourth step of my childhood and settles like the quiet world within a snow globe.

I'm standing behind my mother inside the front door. She has a sprig of holly in her hand that has fallen off the Sacred Heart picture and I have the measles. As she opens the door, the snowflakes blow in onto the lino and the postman hands her a bulky, brown-paper parcel tied with white twine. She puts her hand into her apron pocket and takes out a half crown, the Christmas box. She hands it to him, they exchange greetings and he is gone.

My father said that Christmas began with his birthday on 26 November. My mother said it began on 8 December when the country people came to town to do their Christmas shopping.

Christmas began, for me, when the parcel came.

Every year, that parcel came from my Auntie Tess in England and, every year, the Queen of England came with it stamped in several images across the front. And written in my aunt's hand writing on the side was 'Old clothing, personal belongings'.

There's a jumble of pictures in my head of the things that came over the years; hand-knitted socks, willow-pattern plates, a tiny, china jug with a hole in the bottom of it and jelly babies ... but, this year, it's different.

There's a jacquard waistcoat, a pipe with a packet of tobacco, a wraparound black coat 'for the opera' and a child's pea-green sweater.

Stuffed into one of the sleeves is a small package wrapped in tissue. It's hard in the centre. I find three tiny figures hidden in there; a mother polar bear, her cub and a penguin, each standing on their own piece of ice, silent in an eternal winter of frozen porcelain.

I am juggling the details of this memory when the gasps of excitement in present time, call me back and I steady myself and my sketchbook and look out onto the arctic desert.

My childhood memory has come alive. In front of my eyes, a small cub's head appears above its mother's back. Mother bear looks to the left, turns, looks at us and leans over on the other side, deliberately and slowly moving four massive paws in the air. She settles on her haunches.

Baby is missing for a minute but, soon, its head is seen nuzzling into its mother's belly. In a consorted effort of accommodation, the cub finds its milk, thrusts and pushes and then there's a visible relaxing of the smaller cream body. Mother, with her left paw, pulls her offspring closer and nurses it while sitting.

In that space between thoughts where dreams are born, I want to call my mother. I want to remind her of that parcel and tell her about the real bears in the Arctic and the magic out there in this far off place with the pea-green sea.

She is beyond phones and spruce trees and lives in her own world, far beyond the Arctic Circle.

There are moments, though, when I'm drawing and painting great white bears, I sense she is around me, helping to capture beauty in the wildest of natural spaces.

THE GIFT

Kate Thompson

Running away from Christmas was an inspired idea. The first time we did it, we fled to Jamaica. Paths lined with palm trees stood in for Dundrum Town Centre; a bungalow on a beach was our home from home; and reggae obligingly nudged Noddy Holder off the soundtrack. Jamaica was laid-back, slow-mo, uncompetitive and unglossy, and we wondered how Christmas in Ireland could ever be endured again.

We met up with a Dutch family – kindred Christmas spirit escapees – and together we explored the island's northeast coast by bicycle and jalopy, and its underwater world courtesy of scuba. We partied in a shanty town outside Port Antonio where we danced to the lazy strains of mento, where we were served goat soup, and where an infant burst into shocked tears because we were the first white people she had ever seen. We set up a tiny, token Yule log on our veranda, and toasted absent family and friends. We bathed in the heat and chilled in the sea, and on the stroke of midnight on New Year's Eve, we plunged into the Blue Lagoon, because we were told that to do so means you'll come back one day.

We haven't been back – yet. But we will. Because that Jamaican Christmas gave us a taste of freedom. Like jailbirds, or seasonal turkeys granted a reprieve, we were hooked on escape. From then on, every few years, we'd slide out from between the claws of the Celtic Tiger and go off and dive a reef somewhere temperate – or somewhere not so temperate. There's some magical scuba-diving off the Atlantic coast, and Connemara at Christmas time is many air miles closer to heaven than Grafton Street.

Over the course of those Christmases spent AWOL, Malcolm and I made a vow that the only gifts we would exchange would be small ones. Our daughter, however – as befits an only child – got something priceless. Not something you'll find in a chichi window display or on eBay or in the pages of a glossy shopping catalogue. Because you don't need posh luggage to go travelling, you can't wear couture on a beach, and jewellery looks silly teamed with walking boots. I like to think that Clara got something more valuable than diamonds. She got wanderlust.

THE TOYS THAT WAIT

Thomas F. Walsh

It was early on Christmas morning in that suburban cemetery and the rising sun had not yet wiped away the hoar frost that whitened the tops of grey monuments and headstones. The grass beneath our feet crackled in wonder that anybody would venture here on this day of all days. The faint smell of smoke from the houses all around the cemetery reminded us of another life beyond our own.

This year, we had decided to make our visit in the early morning, so that we would be home again before the grandchildren opened their presents, before all that explosion of joy and surprise bore us away like a great wave from the bleak backwater of memory. Then, all would be well again in the full flood of organised excess. Life would return again to what might still be called 'normal'.

As we move along, quietly thinking our own thoughts, we cannot help but notice that, because it is Christmas, there are more toys than usual. They are placed assiduously here and there, at once incongruous and appropriate; a cuddly dog with floppy ears, a rag doll, an old and battered teddy bear. Propped with care against cold stone and petrified in the frosty air and no doubt our passing forms are reflected in their glassy eyes as they lie silently watching.

And then I see a fleck of red and green that has fallen in the white grass beside a marble kerb. A tin soldier! And that poem learned in childhood suddenly flickers in to my mind's eye like a still scene from an old silent movie. The screen before me is the well thumbed open page of an old schoolbook. 'Land of Youth' it was called. Land of Youth, with the blue cover and that old line-drawing of the soldier beside his drum with his high helmet and his shouldered gun. And, suddenly, my old brain is racing with words sprung from the baited trap of memory.

The little tin soldier is red with rust,
And his musket moulds in his hands …

I seem to hear the children chant in unison, their faint voices rising and falling in the way that only children's voices can rise and fall:

The little toy dog is covered with dust,
But sturdy and staunch he stands;
The little tin soldier is red with rust,
And his musket moulds in his hands.
Time was when the little toy dog was new,
And the soldier was passing fair;
And that was the time when our Little Boy Blue
Kissed them and put them there.

And, as he was dreaming, an angel song
Awakened our Little Boy Blue –
Oh! the years are many, the years are long,
But the little toy friends are true.

And I think of us learning this poem as children and how our parents nodded sadly by the fire and how it strangely meant more to them than to us. And I think, too, of the toys that wait in warm sitting rooms everywhere this Christmas morning and those waiting here through dark nights and slanting rain: the one a testament to love's beginning, the other a monument to that powerful, resolute, parental conviction that love never ends.

When we get back to the house that is all lights and the mayhem that is our own sitting room, to the toddling grandchildren, to the smell of hot milk, to the tinselled tree, to the sweaty nearness of new life, to the scattered wrapping and the almost already-discarded new toys, our perky four-year-old grandchild asks me where we've been.

'We were visiting your auntie.'

'Where is she?'

'She is in heaven.'

'Where is heaven?' she asks.

And I can only take a deep breath and look around and answer quietly to myself, never mind, heaven is here and now. I need you to hold on to my old hand. Heaven is here, now.

SONGS OF HOME

Mae Leonard

When my Uncle Theo moved to Canada sometime in the 1950s, I really missed him. Being the youngest of my father's family, he was more like a big brother to me. But he appointed me guardian of dog-eared cowboy books and promised that he would write often and said that he expected me to reply. His letters told tales of Toronto and the adventures – real and imagined – of himself and his friend John Lynch – who was better known by his nickname, Buller. I lapped up every word. These lads were living their dream. Or were they? When Christmas came their thoughts turned to home and family – to the Christmas Social at Athlunkard Boat Club; to walking up the hill to welcome in the New Year with the chiming of the Bells of St Mary's Cathedral. He wrote of trudging home from work through inches of snow in Toronto on Christmas Eve to find Buller Lynch lying on the couch with the tears streaming down his face as Nelson Eddy sang on radio the 'Old Refrain' – 'I often think of home dee-ol-ee-ay when I am all alone and far away.'

That severe winter in Canada had them longing for the softer clime of Ireland or the sunshine of California. So while they were still young enough to make choices, they headed for Los Angeles. Between them, they drove a car across the United States, taking several weeks and visiting places that they had read about in cowboy novels. Postcards came to us from the Wild West – El Paso, Tombstone, The OK Corral, New Mexico, Dodge City – and, having reached the Pacific, they settled somewhere in the San Fernando Valley. At Christmas, they were invited to a party somewhere in Beverly Hills. The sunshine and a host of gorgeous blondes somewhat distracted them from homesickness until someone began to sing 'Mona Lisa … Mona Lisa men have named you …' It was like an electric shock to the two lads – tears began to stream down the Buller's cheeks. Mona Lisa was the party piece of their friend back in Ireland – Joe Mullane.

'The best crooner in Ireland.' Buller sobbed and, in order to console him, my Uncle Theo decided to call Joe Mullane. The only thing was, Joe Mullane had no telephone but there was one in the garda station on Mary Street. Can you imagine the guard on duty there at seven o'clock on the morning of Christmas Eve being asked to go down two streets and bring back Joe Mullane?

But fair play to him, he did.

It must have been some shock to the poor Joe himself thinking that something terrible had happened. However, as soon as he came to the phone, all was made clear. Well, as clear as could be expected. 'Would you sing "Mona Lisa" for us, Joe? asked Buller Lynch. 'Myself and Theo are at a party here and nobody in the world sings it as good as you do.'

And in the dark of a very early Christmas morning, sometime in the late 1950s, Joe Mullane crooned all the way across the Atlantic for those gathered in that house on Beverly Hills. The guard on duty in Mary Street station joined in the encore of 'Galway Bay' and the partygoers in California agreed, yes, indeed, that Joe Mullane gave the best rendition of both songs they had ever heard.

They say that the telephone call cost the two lads a week's wages each, but agreed that it was money well spent – the best Christmas present they ever received.

THE HOGGET

Sylvia Cullen

A few years back, one of my research trips took me to the home of an elderly man. It was during Lent, so my biscuits were politely set aside and our conversation was, instead, sustained by strong tea and home-made brown bread.

Of his own accord, the man began to describe what food meant to him and all the other labourers as they went about their work for the big farmer. Each task was achieved with an accompanying fantasy, the dreaming and conjuring up of food. One, as he milked, would picture a plateful of salted herrings. Another, doing heavy work in the stables, called forth glorified visions of an egg. For himself, the be-all and end-all, was 'a meat tea', the mere words alone capable of bringing on a flood of saliva … It was all too much for the pair of us. More tea had to be made, another square of bread cut and the home-made damson jam spooned thickly over the slices.

Sated, our talk turned and, suddenly, the room was filled with 'the lads', the Wicklow word for fairies. The man's voice dropped lower and his shoulders shook with giddy laughter. Descriptions flowed of fairy football matches and the dangers of getting them vexed. Take care should I do anything involving a *sceach*, for the lads wouldn't like it – and they'd have ways of letting me know.

Then, a silence came over the room. Something seemed to be bothering the man: his manner changed, he was edgy and unsettled. At last, he announced that he'd have to talk about a certain Christmas … There had been one particular December when the hunger was fierce. But all eyes were fastened on the twenty-fifth because the big farmer, his father's employer as well as his own, had given a promise to pay money that was owed. The family could put up with a lean, mean month because the prospect of having meat on the table on Christmas Day was a glorious and a joyful one. Agitated, the man moved his blue cup around on its saucer; struggling, he continued describing how Christmas Eve drew near. His father and himself finished all their labours and approached the big man with great hopes … Tears appeared on the face in front of me before the words could be forced out. 'We got nothing. Only the promise of a hogget. Turned away so we were, out into the bitter cold.' I watched as he relived every step of the way home, crying out his anguish as he described that desolate Christmas table and his parents' sorrow and helplessness, watching their children go hungry. The hogget was never handed over.

When I left the house, I drove around the corner and pulled in, hesitating, weighing up. Not for long. I turned and went back to my previous interviewee, a descendant of that same big farmer. Straight away she understood, said the man had been on her mind a lot lately, that was why she had recommended him to me. She hadn't been aware of the promise of a hogget but she did know there was some wrong to be righted from way back, explaining that the big man's treatment of his workers had often been less than the best. Before ever I came on the scene, she had already resolved to make some kind of a gesture to the old man. Land, a field, was what she had in mind. And now, after hearing the story of that Christmas more than fifty years ago, perhaps a few hoggets to graze it.

COLD TURKEY

Cyril Kelly

My father was a commercial traveller. His assigned area was the border counties. Before he'd leave Listowel early on Monday morning, my mother would get me up to say goodbye. Crouching down till his face was level with mine, he'd declare, 'And who's the man of the house till Friday?' For me, his words had the solemnity of a pact but, as days darkened into December, such resolute responsibilities began to bother me greatly. Then, with Advent counting down the hours and forlorn strings of festive street lighting coming on earlier each day, I began to have vague feelings of foreboding. My eighth Christmas was approaching but memories of my seventh still lingered.

Behind the counter of my mother's millinery shop, I was kneeling at the stool of the old Singer sewing machine, tracing the headline 'Christmas is coming and the geese are getting fat'. The blotting paper under the heel of my fist whispered over and back across the red-and-blue-lined page. Every time I dipped the pen into the Quink ink, the nib pecked the base of the bottle. My mother was sitting at the counter, ceaselessly stitching. Working in silence, she was struggling to have a gown ready so that Mrs O could make a stunning entrance to the Hunt Ball on St Stephen's Night. Engrossed in my lessons, I was still aware of the protracted sigh from the thread with every stitch. My senses were on high alert. Now and again, the stove would give a contented murmur, like a lullaby.

In the backyard, the condemned turkey was under a tea chest. Even though she was supposed to be fasting, I sneaked out every chance I got to slip food in to her. On the pretext that our backyard was too small, I was not allowed have a dog so the annual turkey from the wild fields of Clownmacon was the nearest I came to having a pet. On arrival, one wing had been clipped to prevent flight and she was allowed to roam the yard. Each afternoon, I used to rush home from school and straight out to watch her. She had a funny way of standing on one leg, the other one gathered up into her plumage as if, like old Mrs Wilmot, she was going to produce a pinch of snuff any minute from the warmth of her drawers. And her gait, it was so innocent, ungainly, the neck cranking back and forth in a sort of syncopated rhythm with the feet. Sometimes, the slanting, midwinter sun glanced off her feathers, highlighting pewters, coppers, bronze.

Suddenly, exasperated with the intricacies of forty-minute buttonholes, my mother snapped, 'Aw, here!' and, in a flurry, the gown was tumbled in a heap onto the counter and the shop door was shut for the night. I had to hoist the iron bar and clunk it into the sockets of the door jamb before hurrying after her.

In the kitchen, it was cold. I saw that my mother was holding the bone handled knife. The blade was already concave from strenuous sharpening, yet she began to hone a new gleaming curve and the noise set my teeth on edge. My first duty was to open the curtains so the corner of the yard would get some light. Peering out, I could barely distinguish the rusty outline of the tea chest. All thoughts of the cosiness in the shop were gone.

In the yard, I could not stop shivering. Upending the tea chest, there was a bit of a schumozle as my mother hauled the turkey

towards the shore. My job was to grasp one warm wing and the –
by now, bound – feet. The other wing was secured between my
mother's knees. Gripping the beak, she stretched the scrawny neck
low over the grating. I squeezed my eyes shut and braced myself
for the inevitable. At the best of times, I was barely able to hold
my footing in that part of the yard because of the slope and the
slippery film of moss.

For days after, the cold turkey hung by the feet from a rafter in
the back porch. Plucked and pale, she wore a muffler of congealed
newspaper. Every time I passed, she was staring at me through
slits in her slate blue lids.

My father arrived home on Christmas Eve, excited already by
the extravagant Santy hidden in the boot of his car. Duly he was
regaled with accounts of my heroism. We were standing around
the kitchen table where the turkey lay trussed, stuffed and stitched.
But even when he joked, 'There'll be many a bird at the Hunt Ball
who won't have such stylish needlework decorating her craw,' my
effort to join in my parents' laughter was only half-hearted.

HEALING

Sarah Ní Riain

Two years ago, after an autumn of bereavements, my mother decided that Christmas was best avoided for once, so my family headed for our usual corner of the south of France, in the hope that the festive frenzy would have passed by when we peeped our heads out again.

The little resort town where we stayed, normally packed to the gills with sun-seeking holiday-makers, was almost deserted. The few year-round families, and presumably the other seasonal escapees, made do with one little shop for their daily bread and evening wine, and the beach was a place to be solitary, not sociable, in the bright winter sunshine.

When we got there, it was cold, so cold, and quiet. Our house, abandoned since the summer, felt like it would never be warm again. The bustle and rush of Christmas at home; shopping in the city centre … wrapped up against the cold, dazzled by lights and deafened by carols piped from every shop … was replaced by a feeling of stillness and emptiness. We had no friends or relations to distract us, or long-lost acquaintances to bump into in the street and promise to visit in the New Year, 'please God'.

But in the peace of our little refuge, and in the bright, chilly sunshine, our four broken hearts began to grow back together.

There were long talks, and longer walks, and hugs and tears and smiles here and there. And as the days went on, the deck of cards was used less for lonely games of solitaire, and more for raucous episodes of Lives and 45. My mother disappeared into nearby Béziers one day, and returned with a Christmas crib, and I dug some fairy lights from my luggage, where I'd packed them – just in case. We even ventured as far as Montpellier to their Christmas market, and bought each other little gifts from the craft stalls, and drank mulled wine and told each other we should come back next year to do all of our shopping there.

In the end, we had Christmas Eve mass in the local church, where we tried out the new French carols with all of our new French neighbours, a full Christmas dinner next day with almost all the trimmings, and a stroll on the beach *en famille* in the crisp Mediterranean morning. Not quite 'just like home', perhaps, but definitely just like Christmas.

CHRISTMAS 1987

Anthony Jordan

I have had a haven of privacy I can repair to for the past thirty years. It is not a place, but rather a person I briefly knew. There, anywhere, I am alone with her; we are alone as we once were, alone amid a crowd of people going about their work. In a way, I feel myself vulnerable to her presence and yet I welcome it. I would not change it even if I could; I welcome it, I welcome her. She is a refuge for me. In times of intense happiness, I seek her most. I want to include her in the ecstasy, though knowing that cannot be. It is painful, too, very painful, and the tears will flow on my cheeks. I remember the letters I wrote to her, the hopes expressed, the promises, the lack of bargaining, the acceptance of whatever materialised. She was mine; I saw her struggling; I saw her pain; I felt my own pain. And whether paradoxical or not, pain does purify; it scours the soul as well as the body.

I disputed with a good bishop once, on her behalf. I told him that his theology was mistaken, that he was ignorant of the reality that enveloped her.

And so I revisit her quite regularly during all these years, often by choice, but sometimes out of necessity. Always the tears cleanse me as a *douche* when I think of what might have been and what was. Though she passed me by in a flash, she, like nothing else, has given me a means to repair, recover, recuperate, in a painful interlude which I would not trade because it brings us together until the next time. Oliver Gogarty wrote in his poem 'Golden Stockings' how he stored up in his memory many thoughts that would last if he were blinded. My thoughts of one particular visitation on Christmas Eve some years ago went like this:

Christmas 1987

The stars shine brightly on this cool Christmas night.
A red candle flames from our window.
I wave to my wife and daughter as they pass to Midnight Mass.
A white stocking hangs limply, a young girl sleeps expectantly.
Happiness wells within me, unwished for, unwanted.
So soon, by thought of you, my first born,
My cross, my joy, the swell is overtaken.
Thrice I saw you, yet you are the measure of all I am.

The eyes fill; the tears fall on my cheeks.
It is a sacrament I receive from you.
My girl in the incubator, who was not there when last I called.
But removed, transferred to a cold loose wet clay,
In a wooden shoebox, beneath a tree, beside a stony path,
In nineteen seventy.

CHRISTMAS

Mary P. Wilkinson

THE PROLOGUE

It is in a steam-filled November kitchen that I first come to know Christmas. I am the child standing on a chair alongside my mother. I am slipping almonds from their brown skin. Mountains of flour and fruit and candied peel line the counter top. Pyramids of golden sugar glisten. The only sounds are of stirring and grating, cutting and mixing. I notice how my fingertips have puckered and dimpled from the warm water of the steeping almonds.

When I decide that this activity bores me, I go to stand at the kitchen window and use the condensated pane as my easel. The sun shape sketch starts to trickle down the glass before I have time to finish it. A gloom settles over me like the grey blanket of winter that sweeps across the garden and tells me that, perhaps, I do not like all this activity. The dim, chaotic kitchen. My mother's flushed face. Her distraction. It confirms the event to come when I will have to surrender my bedroom to the maiden aunt who demands the pope's nose be served to her on a platter and hints at how it would be nice to put a bow in my hair. That day, when I must smile at the jokes, wonder at the lighted pudding and marvel at the little silver fish that curls in the palm of my hand.

THE EVENT

It is Christmas Eve and, all day, I have waited for my brother to come from his bedsit somewhere in a big city. The house is ready. Scented with spice and clove. The fires are lit. The tree laden. I linger by the telephone, stand at the door – waiting and watching. Toasts are made in the living room. There is the magic sound of the kiss of crystal. Laughter. My mother, so proud of the cakes and puddings on the sideboard, calls me to come in and sit with her. My brother has not come. Disappointed, I go to my temporary bed. In the morning, I waken to see him standing there, yawning and rubbing his eyes. The gift is wrapped in sea-green tissue paper. Jade as smooth and cool as ice. I slip it onto my wrist.

THE EPILOGUE

It is only when the windows are opened and the first tentative rays of white sunlight fall into the room that I feel like I am able to breathe all over again. Peace has descended on the house. The aunt gone home. I kneel in front of the grate and watch my mother as she tosses the blackened holly into the flames. It blazes wildly, crackling and spitting until, quite suddenly, it dies. Then, as my mother makes to leave the room, she sighs, wipes her hands on her apron and says, as if to no one in particular, 'That's it now for another year. Thank God.' It is all over. The jagged collage that was the event leaves me and something else takes its place. It is an anticipation of things to come, from the turning to the first clean page of the new calendar to the slow but unstoppable greening of the garden and after that, the days, long and seemingly infinite, to come tumbling in, abundant with promise. With my head full of these dreams, I take off the jade bracelet, close my eyes and run its seamless perfection across my face. Then, on hearing my mother's voice, I run to where she is calling out my name.

THE PIG

Maggie O'Kane

In these last days coming up to Christmas, I went looking for a pig on the internet.

A pig for my husband – perhaps one for Rwanda – to help families rebuild their lives after the genocide.

A Trócaire pig for Christmas so that all year – if he chose to think about it – he could imagine a struggling farming family in Kigali sending their children to school on the back of his Trócaire pig.

I live in Scotland, in Edinburgh, a city that deserves Christmas.

The frost is shining on the banks at Princes Street Gardens and up on the hill the castle is built in the frame of an icy, winter night sky. The air smells of punch and cinnamon and, well, the Scots do this thing well.

But back in Ireland, I'm told, there were ads for the Trócaire pig – no more last-minute presents of jumpers that didn't fit, bad aftershave and boxes of boxer shorts. Buy a pig and change lives.

The idea of the pig began in Argos two weeks before Christmas during the frenzy of present buying. I looked around at our morose little Christmas queue. Shoppers strained, grey, waiting for their numbers to be called. Hassled mothers with purses melting in their hands against our backdrop of ads for cheap credit that would crucify us by June.

Out in the car park, it was worse – Christmas road rage in the Argos car park. A bullying Volvo and a battered red car duelled for space. Was there room for any happiness among our sad, motorised nativity mob? Was there no escape?

My sister, Una, provided the answer in body and in spirit.

My sister, Una, who, as I write, is straining and pushing a boy and a girl into the world in Galway Regional Hospital.

In the run-up to Christmas, weighed down with her fourth and fifth child, she went shopping for the world on the internet and phone. The brother in San Francisco got a field of seeds in Angola, the one in Skerries a set of school books for Oxfam. She was reclaiming the life of Christmas and I would follow her.

I am, this morning, without want. Surrounded by my husband's family and my two children, I will have made midnight mass in St James' Church on Edinburgh's Brighton Place to listen to the sounds of Christmas, sounds I haven't heard since childhood in Skerries.

St Patrick's on Skerries, Church Street with the murmur of the chuntering drunks at the back catching midnight mass on their way home from the Bus bar. Inside, the smell of wax, the blaze of heat from the laden tables of candles.

It has taken me twenty-five years to find my way back to the candlelight. Not necessarily back to God but to a place far from Argos and B&Q. To the spirit of Christmas – a modern one with that cute internet pig. It feels good in some way that the spirit has been reclaimed. Happy Christmas.

CONTRIBUTOR
BIOGRAPHIES

MIKE ABSALOM: Irish writer, painter, printmaker and musician. He was born in England and raised there and in Canada and Sweden. He has lived and worked in many parts of the world, and now lives in County Mayo. He writes a daily blog, *Blog from the Bog* (*mikeabsalomart.blogspot.com*).

LELAND BARDWELL: *The Noise of Masonry Settling* is the latest of Leland Bardwell's six collections of poetry. She has written five novels; a memoir, *A Restless Life*; a volume of short stories, *Different Kinds of Love* and plays for stage and radio. She is a member of Aosdána and lives in County Sligo.

DERMOT BOLGER: Born in Dublin in 1959. The author of nine novels, including *The Journey Home*, *Father's Music* and *The Family on Paradise Pier*. His many plays include *The Lament for Arthur Cleary* and *In High Germany*, and he is the author of eight volumes of poetry, including *External Affairs*. He has also edited many anthologies, including *The Picador Book of Contemporary Irish Fiction*.

PAT BORAN: Born in Portlaoise in 1963, Pat currently lives in Dublin. He has published a dozen books of poetry, prose fiction and non-fiction, including *New and Selected Poems* (Dedalus Press, 2007). *The Invisible Prison*, his memoir of growing up in Portlaoise, is due in winter 2009. He is a member of Aosdána.

ANN BREE: For many years she combined a busy family life with teaching French. An avid reader since childhood, she has in recent years begun to write. Attendance at writing workshops in her local library in Galway has opened new vistas for her.

LOUIS BRENNAN: An electrical engineer who worked for a Waterford exporter of high voltage equipment to Iceland and other countries, he is a member of the British Shakespeare Association, and collects first editions and rejection slips.

KEN BRUEN: The author of 26 published books and the winner of 10 awards for the Jack Taylor series, he also has a Ph.D in Metaphysics. Films of two of his novels, *London Boulevard* and *Blitz*, are being shot in London in 2009. Ken has one daughter and lives in New York and Galway.

STEPHEN BUCK: Shortlisted for the Francis MacManus award four times, Stephen has had many radio plays broadcast by RTÉ and in the US, and his work for stage has been produced by Red Kettle. He is co-founder – with his wife, the novelist Marian O'Neill – of the publishing company, Pillar Press.

DECLAN BURKE: Born in Sligo, Ireland, in 1969, he is the author of *Eight-ball Boogie* (2003) and *The Big O* (2007). He lives in Wicklow with his wife Aileen and baby daughter Lily, and hosts a website dedicated to Irish crime fiction called *Crime Always Pays*.

PADDY BUSHE: Born in Dublin, Paddy now lives in Waterville, County Kerry. He writes in both Irish and English, and has published eight collections of poetry, the most recent of which is *To Ring in Silence: New and Selected Poems* (Dedalus Press, 2008). He is a member of Aosdána.

MARY J. BYRNE: Mary J. Byrne was born in County Louth, has worked in Ireland, England, Germany and Morocco and now lives in France. She has had short stories broadcast and published in Ireland and internationally. She is a Hennessy Literary Award winner and recipient of the Bourse Laurence Durrell de la Ville d'Antibes.

MOYA CANNON: Born in Dunfanaghy, County Donegal in 1956, Moya now lives in Galway. She has published three collections of poems and has been an editor of *Poetry Ireland Review*. A recipient of the Brendan Behan Award and of the Lawrence O' Shaughnessy Award, she is a member of Aosdána.

MAURICE CASHELL: Maurice has worked in Switzerland and Belgium as well as Ireland. Nowadays he divides his time between Malahide and France's Loire Valley. He has been involved with creative writing groups in the People's College and has published short stories and travel features.

MICHAEL COADY: Michael's publications from Gallery Press include *All Souls* and *One Another*, both books integrating poetry, prose and photographs. He is a member of Aosdána and lives in the place of his birth, Carrick on Suir, County Tipperary. A new book, *A Litany for Monsieur Sax*, is forthcoming from Gallery Press.

DOMINIC COGAN: A teacher and healer, Dominic's ex-periences of living in Ghana, Oman, Japan and Nicaragua continue to inspire his writing. He was First Prize Recipient in 2007 for the BBC Breathing Places Poetry Competition and has also broadcast on *Sunday Miscellany* on RTÉ Radio 1.

MARY COLL: A poet, playwright, freelance broadcaster and arts critic, Mary lives and works in Limerick. She contributes regularly to a wide range of RTÉ radio and television programmes including *Sunday Miscellany*, *The Tubridy Show* and *Artszone*. An area of particular interest for her is the work of Limerick novelist Kate O'Brien.

KEVIN CONNOLLY: Kevin Connolly grew up in England and Bailieborough, County Cavan and is the founder of The Winding Stair bookshop in Dublin.

FRANK CORCORAN: Frank Corcoran comes from Tipperary. He studied ancient classics, philosophy, theology and music in Dublin, Rome and Berlin. A noted Irish composer, his First Symphony premiered in Vienna 1981; he has been awarded many prizes and distinctions. Frank lives in Italy and Germany and is a member of Aosdána.

ENDA COYLE-GREENE: Published widely and a frequent contributor on RTÉ radio, Enda lives in County Dublin. Her first collection, *Snow Negatives*, won the Patrick Kavanagh Poetry Award in 2006 and was published in 2007 by The Dedalus Press.

SYLVIA CULLEN: Sylvia Cullen is a playwright. Her work includes *Crows Calling*, *Bedazzled*, *The Legend of Lola Montez* and *The Thaw* which is published by New Island. She recently edited an anthology of new writing, *From the Hill of the Wild Berries*.

PJ CURTIS: Born in the Burren, County Clare, PJ Curtis is an award-winning broadcaster, record producer and writer. A winner of three national awards for his radio programmes on RTÉ Radio 1, Century Radio and Lyric FM, PJ has also had four books published to date, including *The Lightning Tree* (Brandon Books).

ITA DALY: Ita Daly was born in Drumshanbo, County Leitrim. She has published five novels, one collection of short stories, two children's novels and two re-tellings of Irish myths and legends. She has won many prizes, been translated into several languages and is a member of Aosdána.

GERALD DAWE: Gerald has published seven collections of poetry including *Lake Geneva* and *Points West*. A volume of selected prose is due out in 2009 along with *Country Music: Uncollected poems 1974-1985*. He is a Fellow of Trinity College Dublin where he is director of the Oscar Wilde Centre for Irish Writing and Senior Lecturer in English.

PATRICK DAWSON: Patrick Dawson is an actor and scriptwriter. He has worked in theatre, TV, radio and on film. He lives in Bray, County Wicklow.

JOHN F. DEANE: John F. Deane, poet, was born on Achill Island. He founded Poetry Ireland, *The Poetry Ireland Review* and The Dedalus Press. He has published several collections of poetry, most recently *A Little Book of Hours*.

CELIA DE FRÉINE: Celia de Fréine is a poet, playwright and screenwriter. She has published three collections of poetry: *Faoi Chabáistí is Ríonacha* (Cló Iar-Chonnachta, 2001), *Fiacha Fola* (Cló Iar-Chonnachta, 2004) and *Scarecrows at Newtownards* (Scotus Press, 2005). Arlen House have recently published a collection of her plays *Mná Dána*.

KATE DEMPSEY: Kate lives in Maynooth and writes poetry and fiction. She is widely published and has been nominated for and won many prizes including The Francis MacManus and Hennessy New Irish Writing Awards for both Poetry and Fiction.

DIANNA ROBIN DENNIS: An American expat writer, poet, and composer, Dianna Robin Dennis lives outside Athenry, County Galway. Her work has been published in a number of magazines; her two horse books are considered standards in the genre and have been translated into five languages, so far. She still plays her 1975 Gurian guitar.

CARMEL DENNISON: Carmel lives in North Staffordshire in the UK but has strong links with Ireland. She enjoys presenting tales of the history of her locality, with slices of Irish culture, humour or oddity thrown in.

LOUIS DE PAOR: Louis de Paor is Director of the Centre for Irish Studies at NUI Galway. His latest collection *'agus rud eile de/ and another thing'* will be published by Cló Iar-Chonnachta in 2010.

PAT DONLON: Former Director of the National Library and curator at the Chester Beatty Library, Dr. Pat Donlon is now Director of the Tyrone Guthrie Centre in Annamakerrig.

DERBHILE DROMEY: A native of Clonmel, County Tipperary, Derbhile lives in Waterford City. She is a freelance journalist and broadcaster. Her work has appeared in numerous national publications, including *The Irish Examiner*, *The Evening Herald* and *Irish Theatre* magazine. She also has an active interest in creative writing.

JOHNNY DUHAN: Johnny Duhan's life-work as a songwriter has recently been condensed into four albums – *Just Another Town*, *To The Light*, *The Voyage* and *Flame* – which correspond to the four chapters of his recently published lyrical autobiography, *To The Light*. His website is *www.johnnyduhan.com*.

KATE DUIGNAN: Kate Duignan moved to Galway in the early 80's to join the Dandelion Theatre Company. Here she had her two children, Seán and Réalt. She has just completed first year in a new BA programme with Creative Writing as one of its strands. *The Quiet Quarter* was very much a starting point for her published work.

PAT FALVEY: Adventurer, explorer, motivational speaker, team trainer, environmentalist, author, photographer and film producer, Pat Falvey's website is *www.patfalvey.com*.

JOHN FEEHAN: A Senior Lecturer at UCD, John is well known for his television work on the environmental heritage and history of the Irish landscape and has written extensively on it. His books include the highly-acclaimed *Farming in Ireland: History, Heritage and Environment*.

TOM FINNIGAN: 'I moved to Inishowen from England in 2001. From a studio above Trawbreaga Bay I try to write stories. The view distracts me, so I mostly stare.'

GABRIEL FITZMAURICE: Born in Moyvane, County Kerry, where he still lives, he has published more than forty books including collections of poetry in English and Irish as well as several collections of verse for children. He has translated extensively from Irish and edited a number of anthologies of poetry in English and Irish.

IAN FOX: Ian celebrates 40 years as a writer/presenter on RTÉ in 2009. For over 20 years he was quiz-master for *Top Score* and has been writing programme notes for the RTÉ Symphony Orchestra. He is a Governor of the Royal Irish Academy of Music, a Council Member of the Wexford Festival and a director of the Dublin International Piano Competition.

GERRY GALVIN: A widely published writer and retired chef/ restaurateur, Gerry is a native of Drumcollogher, County Limerick, and is now living in Oughterard, County Galway. He has just completed a novel, *To Die For*, about a food critic who is also a serial killer.

CARLO GÉBLER: Born in Dublin in 1954, he now lives outside Enniskillen, County Fermanagh. He is the author of several novels, a short story collection and several works of non-fiction. He is currently writer-in-residence in HMP Maghaberry and Royal Literary Fund fellow at Queen's University, Belfast.

HEDY GIBBONS LYNOTT: Born in Cork, writing found her in Galway. Her prose and poetry has been broadcast nationally and internationally and published in several anthologies. She continues to write and conduct creative non-fiction workshops.

MARY GILROY JOHNSON: Mary settled in Kerry but her 'heart remains ever in Galway'. Her husband retired early but she describes herself as 'far too young for the Joan role of the retired couple'. She has worked for Radio Kerry on *Bookmark* and the religious affairs programme *Horizons*. One of her present projects is writing yarns about knights, dragons and enchanted forests for her grandson.

VONA GROARKE: In 2008, she published *Lament for Art O'Leary*, a version of the eighteenth century classic Irish poem. She teaches at the University of Manchester. Vona's latest publication is *Spindrift* (Gallery Books) which was a Poetry Book Society Recommendation for Autumn 2009.

ROWAN HAND: Rowan describes himself as a 'Voyager on the ocean of life. Seeker of the course to the next land. Broadcaster (how ordinary). Traveller, lover. "To give and not to take". A labourer for "God". A Beggar. Same thing really.'

MICK HANLY: Singer/songwriter Mick Hanly had a major hit with his song 'Past the Point of Rescue' in the US in 1992 and picked up three BMI awards. His songs have been recorded by artists Hal Ketchum, Mary Black, Delbert McClinton, Dolores Keane and Christy Moore. *The Collected Mick Hanly* was released in 2009.

BRENDAN HARDING: A native of Carlow town, Brendan is an award-winning writer of both travel-related fact and fiction. Currently he is working on a novel based in East Africa. His work has been serialised in newspaper and online.

MICHAEL HARDING: Michael Harding is a playwright, novelist and columnist, currently living in Mullingar.

ANN HENNING JOCELYN: Swedish-born author, playwright and broad-caster Ann Henning Jocelyn has been living in the West of Ireland since the early 1980s, and is best known for her best-selling *Connemara Whirlwind* trilogy and for *Keylines for Living*, broadcast on RTÉ and available in six languages, including Chinese.

PHYL HERBERT: Phyl Herbert lives in Dublin. She has a background in teaching and theatre. In 2008 she completed the M.Phil in Creative Writing in Trinity College. 'Lunar Ladies', her short story, was published in *Sixteen After Ten*. She is presently working on a stage play.

RITA ANN HIGGINS: Born in Galway, she is a playwright and has published eight collections of poetry. She has been Green Honors Professor at TCU, writer in residence at the National University of Ireland and an honorary fellow at HKB University. The recipient of a Peadar O'Donnell award, she is a member of Aosdána.

SEAN HOGAN: Former *Irish Times* Letters and Obituaries editor, Sean has been a regular visitor to Manhattan for over thirty years. In a sequence of pieces for *The Quiet Quarter* he spoke of the swank and swagger, consequence and compulsion of this great city.

SHARON HOGAN: Irish-born and North America-raised, Sharon is a film, television, theatre and radio actor who frequently contributes to RTÉ reading her own and others' writing. She is also a mask-maker and holds an MA in Dance from the University of Limerick.

FRED JOHNSTON: Fred Johnston was born in Belfast in 1951 and is a writer and critic and founder of the annual Cúirt Literature Festival in Galway. More recently he founded the Western Writers' Centre (Ionad Scríbhneoirí Chaitlín Maude), Galway. He is also a musician.

ANTHONY JORDAN: Anthony Jordan is a native of Bally-haunis, County Mayo. He has written biographies of Major John MacBride, Seán MacBride, Conor Cruise O'Brien, Winston Churchill, Christy Brown, and W. B. Yeats.

JOE KEARNEY: A writer, broadcaster and independent documentary maker, his memoir and short fiction work has been shortlisted for the Francis MacManus award. His award-winning documentary, *No Cure for Mickey Finn*, was RTÉ's entry for the 2008 Prix Europa. He teaches creative writing and is currently working on a PhD in Creative Writing at UCD.

CYRIL KELLY: 'Born Listowel. Taught in Dublin. Now retired. At present, apprentice scribbler.'

MARTINA KING: Martina King comes from Athenry, County Galway. A classically trained musician, she taught in Dublin before moving to County Clare. She is a member of the Killaloe Hedge-School writers group.

CHUCK KRUGER: Author of five books, all set on Cape Clear Island, Kruger has won the Bryan MacMahon, The Dubliner, and the Cork Literary Review's Short Story Competitions, and several poetry contests. For further details, unexpurgated reviews, and fun photos, browse his website: *www.chuck-kruger.net*

MARGARET LEE: Margaret Lee was born in and grew up near Ballingarry, County Limerick. She has now retired from Social Work, writes occasionally and lives in Newport, County Tipperary with Jess where they both walk the hills.

MAE LEONARD: Originally from The Parish, Limerick, now living in County Kildare, Mae is an award winning writer and poet, broadcaster, local historian and writer in schools and libraries.

BRIAN LEYDEN: Brian Leyden lives in County Sligo. He is the author of the bestselling memoir *The Home Place*, the novel *Death and Plenty* and the short story collection *Departures*. His radio work includes *No Meadows in Manhattan* and *Even the Walls Were Sweatin'*.

CLARE LYNCH: A native of Cavan, now residing in Sligo, she has published two collections of short stories: *Short Steps in Long Grass* (2002) and *Life Through the Long Window* (2007). Her work was also included in RTÉ's *Sunday Miscellany: a selection from 2006-2008* and other collections.

FERDIA MAC ANNA: Novelist, playwright, journalist, television producer/ director, musician. Among his novels are *Cartoon City* and *The Last of the High Kings*, the film of which was released in 1996. He has published two memoirs. In the early 1980s he was known as Rocky de Valera, lead singer with The Gravediggers and later The Rhythm Kings.

JOHN MACKENNA: John MacKenna is a novelist, short-story writer, playwright and documentary maker. Winner of the Jacobs Radio Award, the *Irish Times* Fiction Award, Cecil Day Lewis and Hennessy Literary awards, he is the author of thirteen books. He lives in County Kildare.

MARGUERITE MACCURTIN: Marguerite MacCurtin is a travel writer and broadcaster.

COLETTE MCANDREW: Colette spent most of her early life in rural Oxfordshire with strong links through her parents to the Glens of Antrim and North Mayo. She has lived and worked in Dublin for many years now, occasionally writing poetry and short stories.

KEVIN MCDERMOTT: Kevin McDermott lives in Dublin. He has written novels, radio plays and poetry as well as a number of radio documentaries.

GERRY MCDONNELL: Born and still living in Dublin, he has written for radio, stage, and for the RTÉ television series *Fair City*. He has had five collections of poetry published and has a long- standing interest in the poet James Clarence Mangan about whom he has written a libretto for a chamber opera. He is a member of the Irish Writers' Union and the Irish Playwrights' and Screen-writers' Guild.

IGGY MCGOVERN: Born in Coleraine and living in Dublin, he is Associate Professor of Physics at Trinity College. Widely published at home and abroad, he is the recipient of the McCrae Literary Award and the Hennessy Literary Award for poetry. His first collection received the inaugural Glen Dimplex New Writers Award for Poetry.

MANCHÁN MAGAN: A writer, and documentary maker, his travel programmes for TG4 explored remote cultures. He has written six books in English and Irish including *Angels & Rabies* (Brandon, 2006) and *Truck Fever* (Brandon, 2008). He writes the 'Magan's World' column for the *Irish Times*.

CARMEL MAGINN: Since being short-listed for the Hennessy New Irish Writing Award in 1998, Carmel has had several short stories and non-fiction articles published. Other achievements include broadcasts on *Sunday Miscellany*, *The Quiet Quarter* and local radio, and a novel completed but not yet published. She teaches at Ballyfermot College Dublin.

AISLING MAGUIRE: Aisling Maguire has published short stories and reviews in several journals and anthologies and her first novel, *Breaking Out,* was published by Blackstaff Press in 1996. She works in the Debates Office in Leinster House.

ISOBEL MAHON: An actress and writer living in Dublin, she has worked on stage and in television for most of her life. Writing for stage includes *So Long, Sleeping Beauty*, *The Life and Times of Selma Mae* and *The Born Again Virgin*. Isobel has also been a regular writer for RTE's *Fair City*.

FRANK MARSHALL: Frank Marshall has had drama, prose and poetry broadcast on RTÉ Radio 1, RTÉ Lyric fm, Radio Kilkenny and KCLR. His poetry has appeared in a number of obscure journals. An occasional contributor to *Spirituality*, he was the first editor of *Rhyme Rag* for Kilkenny Arts Office.

GERALDINE MILLS: A poet and short story writer, she lives in Galway. She is the author of two books of poetry, *Unearthing your Own* and *Toil the Dark Harvest*, and two short story collections, *Lick of the Lizard* and *The Weight of Feathers*. She was awarded a Kavanagh Fellowship to work on her third collection of poetry which will be published in 2009.

GERALDINE MITCHELL: Geraldine Mitchell started writing poetry when she moved to Louisburgh, County Mayo, ten years ago. She was the winner of the Patrick Kavanagh Poetry Award in 2008. Her publications include two novels for young people and a biography.

JUDITH MOK: Judith Mok was born in Holland and lives in Dublin. She travels the world working as a classical singer. She has written three novels and three books of poetry, articles and short stories. She was shortlisted twice for the Francis McManus award on RTÉ Radio 1.

JOSEPHINE MOLLOY: Josephine is from Thurles, County Tipperary, 'a wonderful town where I taught English and Geography at Secondary School for forty years. I retired recently and now have more time to enjoy writing, reading, attending book clubs, taking another degree and gardening.'

JOHN MORIARTY: John taught English literature in Canada for six years, before returning to Ireland in 1971. Lecturer, broadcaster, gardener, mystic, writer and philosopher, in 1997 he hosted a major RTÉ television series, *The Blackbird and the Bell*. He is the author of many books but his story for *The Quiet Quarter* was never in print until now. He died in his native Kerry on 1 June 2007. Ar dheis Dé go raibh a anam dílis.

EAMON MORRISSEY: Eamon Morrissey, born in Dublin, has acted and written for theatre, television and radio, at home and abroad for over forty years.

MICHAEL MURTAGH: Born in County Down, he was ordained in 1986. He studied psychology and has published several works on local history as well as articles in local history and theological journals. He has broadcast for national radio and was a columnist with the *Dundalk Argus*. He is editor of the magazine *Lann Léire Review* and previously edited and published community magazine *Deeside Doings*.

NÓIRÍN NÍ RIAIN: Nóirín Ní Riain is an internationally acclaimed spiritual singer who has performed worldwide. A theologian and musicologist, she was awarded the first ever doctorate in theology from Mary Immaculate College, University of Limerick. Her autobiography, *Listen with the Ear of the Heart*, was published by Veritas in October 2009.

SARAH NÍ RIAIN: Sarah Ni Riain's favourite word is *popty ping*, which is the Welsh for microwave 'Isn't that wonderful?' says Sarah. She lives on the Internet, and enjoys crafting, baking and playing the ukulele with more enthusiasm than aptitude. This is her first published work.

PATRICIA NOLAN: A Dubliner, Patricia lives in Paris. Her poetry collections, *Travelling* and *Striptease* were published by Le Castor Astral. *Gros Cactus* and *44 Poèmes Pour Mon Père* are due out in 2009. Educated at Cape Town University, she teaches at the Université de Pantheon Assas.

ÉAMONN Ó CATHÁIN: Born in Belfast, he lived for some 20 years in Dublin and various parts of the world abroad. After running his own restaurant for many years in Dublin he has been better known as a broadcaster in Ireland on all platforms on a variety of topics, mainly music and food, presented in Irish, English and French.

BRIGID O'CONNOR: Brigid O'Connor was raised on Dublin's northside. She owes her interest in the world of literature to her parents, Tom and Sheila, who supplied her with her first pencil and jotter and a Marino library card. She lives in Meath with her husband and two children and is attempting to fulfil a lifelong ambition of becoming a writer.

CONOR O'CALLAGHAN: Conor O'Callaghan has published three collections of poetry and one prose book, *Red Mist*, which was adapted into a documentary for Setanta TV.

JOE O'DONNELL: Joe O'Donnell has written for radio, tele-vision and theatre. He produced and directed many programmes for RTÉ television. His short story, 'Valediction', won the 2009 Francis MacManus Award.

MARY O'DONNELL: A member of Aosdána, her five collections of poetry include *The Place of Miracles: New and Selected Poems* (2006). Her fiction includes the bestselling literary novel *The Light-Makers*, the critically acclaimed *The Elysium Testament* and a collection of short stories, *Strong Pagans*. Her latest collection of short stories is *Storm Over Belfast* (2008).

MAGGIE O'KANE: A former foreign correspondent with *The Guardian*, she is editorial director of Guardian Films, the Emmy award winning company which specialises in investigative films for *guardian.co.uk* and British and international TV. Her awards include British Journalist of the Year and Foreign Correspondent of the Year. She has three children and lives in north London.

JOHN O'KEEFE: Dean of the Law School at Dublin Business School, he was educated at UCD and Cambridge University. He also works as a journalist where he writes on legal matters for both the *Irish Daily Mail* and the *Mail on Sunday*. He is a weekly con-tributor on national radio and television and presents a weekly legal TV slot on TV3's *Ireland AM*.

DONAL O'KELLY: Donal O'Kelly is a writer and actor. His plays include *Catalpa, The Cambria, Vive La, Jimmy Joyced!, Bat The Father Rabbit The Son, Operation Easter*, the music-theatre piece *Running Beast, The Dogs, Judas of the Gallarus, Farawayan, Trickledown Town* and *Hughie On The Wires*. He was elected to Aosdána in 2007.

MARY O'MALLEY: Poet and essayist. The latest of six books of poetry, *A Perfect V,* is published by Carcanet Press UK. A frequent broadcaster, she reads her work at home and abroad. Mary was born in Connemara and is a member of Aosdána.

MARIAN O'NEILL: The author of three books: *Miss Harrie Elliott* and *Daddy's Girl* were both published by Townhouse and Country House. Her third, *Seeforge*, was published by Pillar Press, the publishing house that she and her husband, Stephen Buck, founded in 2004. Marian currently lives in Thomastown, County Kilkenny.

ELLEN O'TOOLE: Ellen O'Toole lives in Wicklow, has three cows, fights briars and cultivates bumble-bees. She writes when it is raining.

THOMAS PAKENHAM: Thomas Pakenham has written 4 books on trees. He has also written three history books: *The Year of Liberty*, *The Boer War* and *The Scramble for Africa*, as well as a travel book, *The Mountains of Rasselas*. He lives in County Westmeath and is Chairman of the Irish Tree Society.

PETER PHILIPS: Writer and broadcaster, Peter Phillips' first book was *Humanity Dick*, the biography of Richard Martin. Among his other publications is *The German Great Escape*.

JOHN QUINN: John Quinn is a writer and a former teacher & broadcaster. He retired from RTÉ in 2002. He has published six children's novels, one adult novel, two memoirs and a number of books based on his radio work. 2009 sees the publication of *The Curious Mind*, an anthology of items selected from his 25 years of broadcasting.

PATSY QUINN: Born in 1936, he left school without having learned to read or write very well. Years of voluntary youth work and part-time study led to teacher training. He taught history and physical education in County Down, and is married with three grown up sons. 'Just myself and my best friend Eileen now,' he says. Patsy is well known as a storyteller at home and abroad.

ROSEMARY QUINN: Mother, teacher, wife, painter, poet, short story writer. Living in Buncrana, County Donegal on the shore of Lough Swilly. 'My greatest joy in life is the company of my seven grandchildren who keep me young by laughing with me at the absurdities of life'.

MICK RANSFORD: A regular contributor to radio, Mick has just finished his debut collection of short stories. He has been published in the *Sunday Tribune*, *Cúirt*, *Comhar*, *West47*, *Poetry Ireland* and in various US magazines. He won the Galway Now short story competition, and was short-listed for a P. J. O'Connor Award and a Hennessy Emerging Fiction Award.

MARK ROPER: Mark Roper's collections include *The Hen Ark* (1990), which won the Aldeburgh Prize for best first collection; *Catching The Light* (1997); a chapbook, *The Home Fire* (1998) and *Whereabouts* (2005). He was editor of Poetry Ireland for 1999. *Even So: New & Selected Poems* was published in Autumn 2008.

GABRIEL ROSENSTOCK: Poet, haikuist, playwright and novelist, author/translator of over 100 books. Among his titles are *A Treasury of Irish Love, Rogha Dánta/Selected Poems*; two anthologies of sacred poetry, *Guthanna Beannaithe an Domhain 1* & *2* and his musings on haiku, *Haiku Enlightenment* and *Haiku, the Gentle Art of Disappearing*.

NUALA ROTHERY: Nuala Rothery is a counselling psychologist and group leader, now retired. Her main interests have been in literature, personal development, mountain walking and yoga. She has a husband, two sons, a daughter and three beautiful grand-children, all living in the southern hemisphere.

NOLLAIG ROWAN: Nollaig Rowan won first prize in the Dromineer Literary Festival poetry competition 2008, and has been shortlisted for the Fish International Short Story Prize. She lives in Dublin but escapes frequently to an island off the south-west coast.

DAVID ROWELL: Rowell has been a prize-winner in the Swift Satire Competition, the Goldsmith Festival Poetry Competition, the Amergin Poetry Competition, the Golden Pen Poetry Competition and the Francis Ledwidge Poetry Competition. He was chosen by Poetry Ireland to read in their *Introductions* series and has broadcast pieces on *Sunday Miscellany* as well as *Lyric Notes*.

CATHERINE RYAN: Catherine Ryan's passion for opera began in her early teens in London, where Callas, Gobbi and Vickers proved far more alluring than the Beatles. Now, with the miracle of DVDs, she travels the operatic stages of the world from her sitting room.

JOAN RYAN: Joan Ryan was born and raised in West Cork, and now lives in County Louth. She holds a Ph.D from the Department of Modern English, Trinity College, Dublin. She works in Adult Education and is involved in writers' groups both as a facilitator and practitioner.

MARTIN RYAN: Martin Ryan is a scriptwriter and biographer. His *William Francis: A Life 1838–1910* is published by The Lilliput Press. His radio work includes portraits of Robert Louis Stevenson and Franz Liszt.

BARBARA SCULLY: Barbara describes herself as a homemaker, freelance writer, spiritual pilgrim and occasional Reiki therapist. She tries to write every day and is an enthusiastic blogger (*www.serenityspace-barbara.blogspot.com*). Barbara is married to Paul Sherwood and they have three daughters, four cats and a dog all living under one roof in South Dublin.

BERNARD SHARE: Bernard Share is a writer and former editor of *CARA* magazine for Aer Lingus and *Books Ireland*. His new novel, *Transit*, has recently been published, together with a reprint of *Inish*, which Spike Milligan said was the funniest novel he had ever read.

TOM SIGAFOOS: Tom Sigafoos moved to Donegal from the US in 2003. He writes pantomimes, mystery party scripts, and tourism articles about the personalities and events of Northwest Ireland. His detective novel, *Code Blue*, is available through *Amazon.com*.

DERMOT SOMERS: Dermot Somers is a writer and broadcaster.

RICHARD STEVENS: After a lifetime of travelling all over the world, Richard Stevens decided to see the States by Greyhound bus. His writing for *The Quiet Quarter* introduced us to some of the people he met along the way – their music and their lives. Richard is writing a novel and a collection of short stories.

KATE THOMPSON: Kate Thompson is the bestselling author of eleven novels which have been widely translated. Her twelfth, *The O'Hara Affair*, will be published by HarperCollins in 2010. Her grandfather was the model for the art master in Muriel Spark's famous novel *The Prime of Miss Jean Brodie*.

CARL TIGHE: Born in Birmingham, he has published the fiction collections *Rejoice and Other Stories* and *Pax: Variations* and the novels *Burning Worm*, *KsssS: A Tale of Sex, Money and Alien Invasion* and *Druids Hill*. His non-fiction includes *The Politics of Literature*, *Gdansk* and *Writing and Responsibility*. He teaches Creative Writing at the University of Derby.

JOHN TROLAN: John was born in Dublin in 1960 and educated at Ballymun comprehensive and Kings College, London. He is the author of two novels, *Slow Punctures* and *Any Other Time*, and is currently Programme Director for a UK charity, The Nelson Trust.

PAOLO TULLIO: Paolo Tullio is a restaurant reviewer, writer, actor and broadcaster, whose credits include the television series and book *North of Naples, South of Rome*, and *Mushroom Man*, a novel set on the Internet. He has had parts in *The Butcher Boy*, *The General* and *The Tailor of Panama*. Paolo is a resident critic on the RTÉ television series *The Restaurant*.

WILLIAM WALL: William Wall is the author of four novels, two collections of poetry and, most recently, a book of short fiction entitled *No Paradiso*. He is a full time writer and lives in Cork City.

THOMAS F. WALSH: Born in Headford, County Galway, he is the compiler of the highly successful series *Favourite Poems We Learned in School*, published by Mercier Press, as well as the author of an autobiography, *Once in a Green Summer* and a collection of short stories entitled *In Silent Moments*. He now lives in Westport, County Mayo with his wife, Nuala.

NOREEN WALSHE: Formerly a teacher of languages and music, Noreen trained at NCAD, Dublin and NSCAD in Nova Scotia, Canada, and has been a professional artist since 1992. The image on the front cover is from her original watercolour *Fairy Tree –Tara*. See more of Noreen's work at *www.noreenwalshe.com*

DICK WARNER: A writer, broadcaster, environmentalist and former RTÉ radio producer, he is best known for his television documentaries on environmental subjects such as *Spirit of Trees*, *Waterways*, *Ironing the Land*, and *Voyage*. He is the author of a number of books and is a regular contributor to the *Irish Examiner* and several magazines.

DOLORES WHELAN: Dolores Whelan has studied the Celtic tradition for over 20 years. As an educator and spiritual teacher, she offers learning opportunities that weave this wisdom together with modern psychology and scientific insights. She is the author of *Ever Ancient Ever New: Celtic Spirituality in the 21st Century*. She lives in Ravensdale, Dundalk.

MARY P. WILKINSON: Mary won the Listowel Writers' Week Originals Competition on two occasions. Her writing has appeared in publications including the *Irish Times*, *Books Ireland*, *Crannog*, *West 47*, *The Dublin Quarterly Literary Review* and *A Living Word Anthology*. She is currently working on a book of reflective vignettes.

MÁIRÍDE WOODS: Máiríde Woods lives in North Dublin and writes short stories and poetry as well as radio pieces. Her first collection of poetry, *The Lost Roundness of the World* was published by Astrolabe in 2006.

VINCENT WOODS: Poet, playwright and broadcaster, born County Leitrim. He worked as a radio journalist and presented RTÉ news programmes including *Morning Ireland* and arts programmes including *Rattlebag* and *The Arts Show*. He currently presents *Arts Tonight* on RTÉ Radio 1. He has won several awards for his work and is a member of Aosdána.

ENDA WYLEY: Enda Wyley has published four books of poetry with Dedalus Press, the most recent of which is *To Wake To This* (2009). Her books for children include *The Silver Notebook* (2007) and *I Won't Go to China* (2009). She has won several awards for her work and lives in Dublin.

GRACE WYNNE-JONES: Grace Wynne-Jones is the author of four highly intimate soulful novels that have received widespread praise for their humour and insights into human nature. Their main themes are the search for true love and ful-filment in a complicated world. Sample chapters are available on *www.gracewynnejones.com*.